— a —

NIGHT

twice as

LONG

NIGHT twice as LONG

ANDREW SIMONET

FARRAR STRAUS GIROUX · NEW YORK

Farrar Straus Giroux Books for Young Readers
An imprint of Macmillan Children's Publishing Group, LLC
120 Broadway, New York, NY 10271

10 9 8 7 6 5 4 3 2 1

Fiercereads.com

Library of Congress Cataloging-in-Publication Data
Names: Simonet, Andrew, author.
Title: A night twice as long / Andrew Simonet.
Description: First edition. | New York : Farrar Straus Giroux, 2021. |
    Audience: Ages 12–18. | Audience: Grades 10–12. | Summary: Three weeks
    into the blackout, sixteen-year-old Alex and her best friend Anthony trek to the
    next town looking for answers, but end up breaking Alex's autistic brother out
    of the school he was placed in by Child Protective Services.
Identifiers: LCCN 2020023457 | ISBN 9780374309329 (hardcover)
Subjects: CYAC: Brothers and sisters—Fiction. | Autism—Fiction. |
    Friendship—Ficton. | Electric power failures—Fiction.
Classification: LCC PZ7.1.S565 Ni 2021 | DDC [Fic]—dc23
LC record available at https://lccn.loc.gov/2020023457

Our books may be purchased in bulk for promotional, educational, or business
use. Please contact your local bookseller or the Macmillan Corporate and
Premium Sales Department at (800) 221-7945 ext. 5442 or by email at
MacmillanSpecialMarkets@macmillan.com

for my brother

all the while

believe me

I prayed our night would last

twice as long

—Sappho

a
NIGHT
twice as
LONG

CHAPTER ONE

The lights went out.

I shaved my head.

Now I'm going to find the truth.

⸻

Those were Anthony's words: "Want to find out the truth?"

I didn't know how bottomless that question would turn out
to be.

"What truth?" I say through our tattered screen door. My
hair, still intact and bushy at this point, droops over my eyes.

"About the blackout." The lights—and everything—have
been out for three weeks.

"Which is?"

"I don't know, that's the point. That's why you should come

with me tomorrow." The white stripes of Anthony's soft plaid shirt glow in the twilight. The blackout makes washing clothes astonishingly difficult, but he looks clean. He could use a trim, though. He had tight braids at the beginning of the year, then a fade, and now his curls are getting puffy.

"Where?" I say.

A neighbor drags an enormous tree limb up the street, firewood from the creek, the branches scraping across both empty lanes.

"To the VFW in Bethany." Anthony presses the doorbell. "Why doesn't this work? I was looking forward to 'Twinkle, Twinkle.'"

Music is getting scarce. "You mean 'Baa, Baa, Black Sheep.'"

"'Twinkle' is the original."

"We took the batteries out for a flashlight." That was a while ago. That flashlight's definitely dead now.

The neighbor hauls the branch toward a bonfire circle on his lawn, white plastic chairs around a fire pit. Some people are more social in the blackout, hosting cookouts, chatting you up. Some aren't, like the couple up the street who pulled the shades and chained their Doberman to the porch.

"How are you getting to Bethany?" I say.

"*We* are walking."

"That's far."

"We're young. And there's no rain in the forecast."

"There's no forecast."

"Says the negative girl. Positive boy says: 'Not a single weath-erman is calling for rain tomorrow.'"

"Yeah. I don't, um . . ." There's a distracting swollen spot where I bit my cheek yesterday. I rub it with my tongue and think of how to say no.

Headlights sweep the budding leaves of our front yard tree. Driving's a privilege now that most gas is reserved for emer-gency vehicles and hospital generators. Anthony's grandma says there's a black market, people paying thirty or forty dollars a gallon. It must have been like this when cars were first invented. You see someone drive by and think: Who's that lucky person?

"I don't think I can go." That's the right way to say it: passive, vague.

"Mm." He nods six times. "I figured."

"I just think it's . . ."

Anthony waits for me to finish. The neighbor pulls a blue tarp over the tree limb, tucking his firewood in for the night.

"Sorry," I say.

"No, I'm sure you've got"—he giggles—"stuff to do."

"What? I do. I can't spend a whole day walking to Bethany."

"Plus you'd have to actually go outside."

"What are you saying?"

"Look at you. You're huddled behind a screen door."

"I'm not huddled. This keeps the bugs out."

"Except where it's ripped."

"Fine." I step outside. Huh. I do feel a little exposed out here.

The crickets are screeching. With less human noise—you don't hear many cars or lawn mowers or planes—nature's getting louder.

"I'm just saying you don't go out much," he says.

"I go out every day."

"To get water?"

"Yeah. Sometimes twice."

"Mm."

Anthony gets you to say things that make him look right. He's brilliant at asking innocent, matter-of-fact questions, and, normally, it cracks me up. But now I'm on the receiving end.

"Don't act like I'm some kind of a shut-in." See? He got me to say it.

"Of course not." He grins.

"What?"

"You're kind of a shut-in."

"Am not."

"Are too."

"Shut up."

"You shut up."

"There's a blackout, Anthony."

"So you'd rather sit in the dark and stare at the walls?"

This is not a new argument. For the past year, ever since they took my little brother away, I've been a homebody. Anthony comes around to check on me and tries to get me to do things. To be honest, no one but Anthony comes around anymore.

Other friends tried at first, especially Margo, who kept inviting me to her family's board game nights. I never went, and honestly, I was relieved when she stopped asking.

Anthony didn't stop. And I should be grateful. I am grateful. But this conversation always annoys me. What do you call the difference between what you should feel and what you do feel? Life?

"No, I read books. And I . . ." I'm about to say I do jigsaw puzzles, but that does sound like a shut-in. "It's better than walking to Bethany so some know-it-all can explain the blackout."

Someone's playing the recorder badly. *Three blind mice, three blind—screeeeech.* Start again.

"You mean my mom," Anthony says.

"What?"

"So my mom can explain the blackout."

"Your mom's in the Pacific Ocean."

"Exactly. So she'll know if the blackout was, you know, a bomb or a solar flare or somebody stuck a spoon in an outlet."

"She'll know this how?"

"The military knows stuff, right? National security. Plus she's far away, so if she's somewhere not affected by the blackout . . ." He shrugs, but with an edge. Something about that *if.*

"And why Bethany?"

"So we can talk to her."

"Do the phones work there?"

"No, there's some guys, veterans with a shortwave radio.

Apparently, they can talk to different branches of the service and put you in touch with family members who are deployed."

"Huh. And your mom has a radio?"

"Her ship does. I assume."

This is a shaky plan. I can't tell if Anthony believes it.

"You're just gonna ring her up?"

"I don't know. All I know is Matt Martinovich says I should go to Bethany and tell my mom I'm okay." Matt is an overly enthusiastic freshman with a sister in the air force. He talks smack about the navy as a way of bonding with Anthony.

I hear the thud and splash of someone pouring out jugs of water, filling a kiddie-pool reservoir. Water stopped last week. They say the water tower got drained and there's no power to pump it full. We fill jugs, bathtubs, and basins by hand. One thing the blackout taught me: Water is much heavier than you'd think.

"*Are* you okay?" I say. "You seem worried."

"I'm good. It's just . . ." He shrugs and looks around, then picks something out of his eye.

"Oh my god, you're so scared."

"No, I'm fine, I just—I'll be psyched to talk to her."

Of course. He usually talks to his mom every day when she's deployed. Now, it's been three weeks. When the blackout started, Anthony agonized about how anxious his mom must be. *I gotta let her know we're okay.* This is different. He's worried about *her*.

"She's on this destroyer, right, big navy ship. Should be safe," he says. "But then I start thinking: What if the power goes out on board? Is that even possible? Do ships get blackouts?"

Next door, a flashlight beam sweeps coldly around an upstairs room. Normally at dusk, the homes in our neighborhood glow cozily. The blackout reversed that: Our dark bulky houses crouch in the bright twilight.

"Are you asking me?" I say. "I have no idea."

"Me neither. You do start to picture it, though."

You. When Anthony talks about his feelings, he switches to second person. Whenever our conversations get deep, I am the one having his most profound experiences. "*You wonder if people actually like you.*" Or: "*You get scared you're gonna turn out like your dad.*"

"You picture this huge dark boat," he says now, "drifting in the middle of the ocean, water leaking in."

I whimper, an involuntary moan of sympathy. God, what an image to have of your mother.

"I get that twitch, you know, when you want to look it up, blackouts at sea. And you reach for your phone."

It's true. The first week, we took out our phones constantly, held them overhead, turned around, searched for a signal. Now, it's a reflex, hands reaching for empty pockets. We touch our hips and our butts, two quick pats front and back, like we're worried our pelvises might disappear.

Anthony stares at a windowsill spider. "I'm sure she's fine, but—"

"I'll come."

Anthony needs me.

"Really?"

Always strong, always helpful Anthony needs me.

I'm in, goddammit.

"Of course."

"Wow. Amazing."

"Don't be so shocked," I say.

He acts like I'm a recluse who would never leave the house. I am not. I'm a recluse who will definitely leave the house if her friend needs something.

"I'm not shocked. I'm pleased." His shoulders drop, and he smiles, showing his endearing crooked tooth. I'm very fond of that tooth. "We'll go early, seven A.M. Six forty-five Alexandra Unstandard Time."

In the blackout, my mom keeps time with an old digital watch that, according to Anthony, is fifteen minutes slow. Without electricity, being fifteen minutes off rarely matters. No school, no TV, no schedule. We're all unstandard now.

"We'll walk there, do the thing, and walk back. Home before dinner. Simple," he says, and then immediately contradicts himself. "It'll be an adventure."

Yes, Anthony.

It will.

When the lights went out three weeks ago, my mom and I were at the pharmacy. The manager shouted, "Shoppers, please wait outside until our computers come back on." Wonder if anyone's still waiting.

Everything stopped. Electricity, internet, phones, radio. Cars mostly work, but gas pumps mostly don't, or they got pumped dry, so the roads are getting empty. And it's not just here. Far as we can tell, it's everywhere. If it was just our town or county, or state even, there'd be utility workers, trucks of supplies, and TV cameras by now, right?

The first couple days were fun. Eat up the food before it spoils, light candles, play a card game. A neighbor with a generator projected cartoons on the side of her house. Anthony made brownies on his barbecue, sweet and smoky. People stopped staring at their phones. That's still a revelation. Take away our devices, and we're just flesh and bones, blinking at one another in the bright silence.

Then it got hard. Flashlights ran out of batteries. Our neighbor with the generator stopped sharing. We cooked gummy spaghetti over a sputtering, damp fire.

We wondered about the cause, of course, but the real gap, the missing piece, was the end date. How long should we prepare to endure? We arranged ourselves for six hours of darkness, then a day, then several days, and now weeks. Each new timeline feels like a loss, a new crisis.

And the stories started. Friends, neighbors, people at church—everybody passed on explanations, claiming a reliable source. It was solar flares. A cyberattack. A nuclear test. A nuclear attack. A rogue computer virus. An electromagnetic pulse weapon, followed by: *"Yeah, that really exists."* Those are, amazingly, the reasonable explanations. Then there are the magical ones. God is punishing us. Aliens are invading. Mother Earth is fed up. People proclaim Armageddons they fear and Armageddons they want. You can't check any of it, of course. You can't even look up *electromagnetic pulse* unless you have a printed encyclopedia. If Anthony's veterans know something, even a little something, it'll be worth a day of walking.

Three weeks in, computer viruses and solar flares seem to be the top contenders. Some people claim they've heard government announcements. I haven't. Houses in Elysburg got flyers from the police department—again, supposedly—saying it was solar storms, and we'd all have power in three days. That was two weeks ago. People got excited and let their guard down, feasting on stored food, burning the last of their gasoline on silly drives.

The deacon at our church said there was official news on an AM station, but all we could find on our car radio was a blowhard yammering about *"who's really behind this."*

People also say shortwave radios can talk to people on the other side of the planet, which seems unlikely. It gives me that twitch where I want to fact-check it.

A computer virus seems plausible. It feels right: sudden, widespread, and hard to fix, especially if there's no power. It also means we'd have a culprit. *Whoever did this, tell you what, we're gonna make em pay.* Harder to get revenge if the sun caused it.

There are constant and conflicting rumors about when the lights will come back. Later today. Two weeks. Six months minimum. Never.

I'm gonna tell you right now: The lights do come back. Not today, but on day twenty-nine.

Phew. Good to know.

But on this day, day twenty-one, we don't know that. We're floating and a little dazed. Imagine weeks of confusion and pain-in-the-ass struggle to live without power. Imagine all your news is cut off, replaced by your neighbor quoting scripture: *The book of Matthew specifically explains the blackout, Alexandra, here in chapter twenty-four.*

Imagine a blank, muddled future. It's not a catastrophe, but it is rickety. Always, there's this background question: Am I the right amount of worried about this?

That's a question I ask a lot, and not just about the blackout. You don't want to panic unnecessarily. But then there's the risk that when the tsunami hits, you're digging a sandcastle. Or you're getting cake.

See what I did? *You.*

More than anything, it's the silence. On normal days, we swim in a torrent of stories and information and chatter; we're wired into the nonstop blahblahblah. That cut out all at once, and it's jarring, like when there's not another stair and you stumble forward. We're storyless, infoless. We have hours to fill every day, time we'd normally spend transmitting and receiving the countless messages and images that narrate our days.

Everybody's a bit edgy. It's not a free-for-all—though my mom heard people looted, or "liberated," the dollar store in Youngsville—but it is strange.

We're in a state, that's what you need to know. I care less about the blackout and more about what the blackout did to me and to other people. I care about possibilities.

And here on day twenty-one, there's a lot of possibilities.

You wouldn't know that from looking at my mom.

"Hey, Ma, Anthony wants me to go do something tomorrow."

"That's nice." She's in her overstuffed armchair, nested into the blankets and pillows. It's a burrow, a part of her body. If she stood up, it would stick to her. The coffee table is stacked with her supplies: books, word searches, a beverage, and piles of papers about my autistic brother's situation. He was removed from our house last year, and one good thing about the blackout is Mom's organizing the files, building our case to get Georgie back.

"We're gonna leave early, like seven o'clock," I say.

"What are you doing?" She's working on a crossword, glasses on, leaning toward the not-bright window.

"We're sending a message to his mom."

"Interesting. How?" She still hasn't looked up.

"There's a veterans' group with a special radio."

"Hmm, sounds fishy. Make sure he doesn't pay for it. Where is this?"

This is what I have to sneak by her. "Not too far. I think it was . . . Bethany, maybe."

She looks up. "Bethany? How are you getting there?"

"I guess he's planning on walking."

"Honey, that's almost ten miles away, you can't walk." She reaches for her glass, which is blurry with lip smudges and fingerprints. We each have one glass we reuse and wash once a day. No dirtying unnecessary dishes. "What if something happens?"

"Nothing's gonna happen," I say, the wrongest of wrong pronouncements.

"You could get hurt. You could get stuck."

"We'll be fine, Mom."

"What if the veterans thing is a scam?"

"Anthony's not stupid."

"I'm not saying he's stupid. I'm saying without a grown-up, you're vulnerable." She takes a big sip. Bright-yellow crystals sludge the bottom of her glass. She's been drinking the hardened lemonade powder we found in the back of a cabinet. Treats are getting scarce. She ate through our candy and cough drops the first week.

I sit on Georgie's old rocking chair. Most of the specially designed and expensive things for autistic kids didn't do much for him, but he loved rocking on this.

Loves, I mean.

"Then come," I say, rocking a little. It does feel nice. "You're a grown-up. Come with us."

"Alex, I can't spend an entire day walking to Bethany and back."

God, that's exactly what I said. "Why not?"

"I have things to do."

Anthony's right. It does sound ridiculous when members of my household talk about how busy we are. "Mom, you're doing a crossword in the dark."

"I don't do crosswords all day."

"Right, you also nap. And stare at the floor."

"Alex, what I do with my day is not the issue. I'm not comfortable with you walking three towns over to hang out with some adults I've never met."

"We're not hanging out. There's—"

"We are in a blackout. I can't look these people up and see if they're legitimate. And I can't reach you if there's a problem."

"Anthony needs my help."

"Maybe his grandma could drive him."

"You know she doesn't have gas."

"Alex, I can't be worrying all day that you might not make it home. Until the lights come back on, I need you to stay close."

She can't lose me. Can't lose another child.

"Anthony's going," I say.

"Well, you are not."

"His face, Mom, when I said I'd go, you should have seen him, he was so relieved."

"If you want to do something with Anthony, invite him over. We could . . ." She waves at the many exciting activities our house offers.

I stop rocking and look around at the half-completed projects that clutter the living room. A stack of magazines tumbles into a box of dishes we were definitely getting rid of. A trash bag bulges with junk for the thrift store. Or maybe trash. Our house was never that tidy—a special needs kid makes that hard—but now it's downright chaotic. "God, he's right."

"I'm sorry?"

"We're shut-ins, Mom. We don't leave the house."

"Sweetie, there's a blackout."

"Before the blackout. We hide in here."

"If the power was on, things would be different."

"Right, then you'd be doing a crossword on your phone, and I'd be . . ."

I see it. I'd be in my room, door closed, rereading a fantasy novel, hoping no one comes looking for me. God, I am a recluse. I'm a pasty old lady crouching behind the curtains, terrified someone might knock.

Gotta get out.

"Are you okay?" my mom says as I climb the stairs.

"No!" I shout back and then, weirdly, laugh. This old lady's starting to crack up.

I shut my door. Here it is, my lair.

The plastic bin by my bed is heaped with clothes, some clean, some dirty. My bunk beds were donated to Georgie by someone who clearly didn't know him, cause they're much too dangerous for him. Next to it, my reread stack teeters, the books I can lose myself in that have no surprises. Surprises are mostly bad.

My windowsill has a pillow for my butt and a chain of faded circles from my water glasses, the Olympic rings breaking apart. This is my reading spot, looking down on the yard and our out-of-gas minivan. That was also donated, by someone who definitely does know Georgie, cause minivans are his preferred—in some ways only—vehicle. Good luck getting Georgie into a regular car.

I wipe my hand along the cool white paint of the sill. I should get a sponge and clean it. But for that, I need water. Which means a walk to the creek. No, thanks.

I do go out every day, though. Twice!

I laugh. The phrase I hear in my head is: *Neighbors sometimes saw her in the upstairs window.*

Change it. Open it.

The window's stuck. I bang the frame and heave it up three inches. A humid breeze floods in, the smell of a wood fire. I hoist the window all the way open. Flakes of paint and a dead fly flurry down to the sill. The screen is torn, from when Georgie, giggling wildly, shoved his cowboy hat through in a hide-the-hat game we were playing. That was, what, a year and a half ago? Might be the last time this window was open.

I lift the screen and lean out. The warm evening, two cooking fires across the street, our next-door neighbor singing. Weird how close the world is. Those few inches, just poke your head out and you're part of it. Doesn't feel close when you're inside. *You.*

I should put a chair out here on the tiny porch roof and read, a real eccentric old lady.

A neighbor kid walks his German shepherd up the street. He's a middle schooler, comes around twice a year selling candy for his teams. What's his name? Darryl? Dallas?

Stay out here, Alex. Don't hide.

The dog shuffles along the road, cause there are no sidewalks in my neighborhood. I wait for the kid to look up, so I can— what? Say hi. Be neighborly.

He's close, and now I feel like I'm spying. I wave.

He's right in front of the house.

"*Hem.*" I clear my throat. "Hey." I'm still waving. The parade queen on a float.

The boy looks around and behind him, but not up. He hustles off. Was I not loud enough? Should I say something else? No, too awkward. I keep waving in case he looks back.

Oh crap. There's a girl on a bike staring at me. She watched the whole thing. We lock eyes, my arm still swaying uselessly.

What does a well-adjusted sixteen-year-old girl do in this moment?

I duck back inside, behind the plaid curtains.

The shut-in takes cover.

CHAPTER TWO

I wake at dawn, tangled in a heap of blankets, hugging my pillow. My open window is letting in chilly air and a riot of birdcalls. How's a recluse supposed to sleep?

I'm dreading telling Anthony I can't come. I should have done it last night.

I'll bring him snacks for his journey. I think we still have granola bars.

I shut the window and flip the light switch.

Nope. Day twenty-two.

My mom taught me this trick to figure out if you're dreaming: Try to change the lighting. Turn a light on or off in a dream, and nothing happens. Our unconscious doesn't know about electricity, because it's too recent. Once, I dreamt of a flood, watching from my window as a car floated by, a bewildered kid staring out from the back seat. I pulled the chain on my desk lamp. She was right. Nothing.

I creep along the green hallway carpet, past my mom's room. Silence. Past my brother's room. Dangit. My mom's twitchy breathing. She's whimpering, maybe half-asleep, in Georgie's bed. Again.

Jesus, Mom, we talked about this. Georgie's bed doesn't help you sleep. It doesn't help anything.

My breakfast waits on the kitchen counter: two packets of instant oatmeal, not cooked but soaked in water overnight. It's a gloopy room-temperature treat. Cinnamon & Spice tastes pretty much like Maple & Brown Sugar, gritty and sickly sweet. I'm not hungry.

In the bathroom, the window by the toilet glows gray blue with the first light. I'm getting better at moving around in the dark and near dark. We all are. We moan about the blackout—the inconvenience, the stress—but mostly, we adjust. It's wild how quickly your animal senses come back. From our yard, I can hear a door close two blocks away.

On the shelf with the hairbrushes and deodorant, our phones are optimistically, pointlessly plugged in. It's my mom's old rule: When you brush your teeth before bed, you're done with your phone. For now, we're really done with them.

I think of all the messages and stories and pictures that flowed from that cracked dark screen the minute I turned it on in the morning. Every day for the last three weeks, we've asked: When is that coming back?

This morning, I think: Maybe it's not.

Maybe none of it's coming back.

Maybe these veterans will say it's time to bury our phones, time to move on.

Georgie's bed, five feet above my head, creaks and clunks as my mom rolls over.

Maybe the blackout wiped everything clean. Maybe the treadmill we all trudge on, our heads down, has stopped.

In the mirror, I'm a silhouette, a gray outline, my frizzed-out hair making me vague and approximate. My mom coughs out a string of sobs, high-pitched and whiny, like giggles. Our floors are thin, and her whimpers, so soggy and immediate, could be mine. It's karaoke weeping. My reflection is sobbing. I am the one stranded and stricken.

I bring a hand to my mouth. No, I'm not sobbing. I'm not collapsed in my little brother's bed. I am standing.

I pull my hair back, and my bangs droop forward. I've hidden under this mud-brown tangle for months, letting it grow. It's the untended hedge of a deserted house. It's the frayed screen door Anthony knocks on, trying to coax me outside.

Sweet Anthony, the one person who still shows up, he needs me today. He said so.

All right, shut-in. Time to tear the screen door off. Time to chop the damn hedges down.

I look for scissors. Clippers would be best, but, with the power out, scissors will have to do.

Wait. Georgie's clippers are rechargeable.

Bottom shelf, behind the cough medicine and the broken hair dryer. I thumb the ridged switch to ON. That hard snap as the clippers start, then the soothing hum. The first electricity I've touched in days.

Upstairs, my mom blows her nose, the bleat of a party horn.

As dawn turns the white bathroom tiles gold, I run the clippers front to back, like I used to for Georgie, the pitch falling as my thick hair clogs the blades. Heavy coils tumble silently. I knock the clippers clean on the counter, building a nest of me in the sink, a soft mound of what I've been carrying.

The first rays of sun show my true outline. This is where I begin. This is my edge, my boundary. I look like my brother: My ears stick out, my nose is big, and my eyes droop.

I pull off my shirt, itchy with hair, and see my round belly and my pale scalp, my thick arms and my scrawny boobs. I am uncovered.

I've been hiding for a year. I take my hair off and I'm visible.

I silently thank Georgie for the clippers.

Georgie. He hates haircuts. You can't use scissors, cause he might flinch or grab them. And you can't take him to the barber. Mom tried.

"You don't owe me anything, lady, just get your kid out of here!" the barber yelled after Georgie smashed a jar of disinfectant on the floor, bright aqua swallowing clumps of brown hair. Georgie's half-shaved head bobbed down the sidewalk, arms in the air, celebrating his escape.

So we got clippers. His haircuts last ninety seconds: Put the number one guard on, the shortest, run it front to back. It made him look mean, punchy, like a military kid, his normal I-smell-something cringe turned into a scowl.

I could use a second pass now, but the charge ran out. I'm uneven, patchy. Stubble, not hair.

All right, Anthony, let's go find some truth.

———————————

"What's that scar?" is Anthony's second question this morning, after: "Do that yourself?"

"Kid threw a rock at me."

I'm on Anthony's unpainted porch, watching him feed the puppies. I thought we'd have a big moment of "Hey! You're coming," but, of course, Anthony assumed I was coming. No high fives for my bravery or for disobeying my mom.

"Damn. When?" He pulls a squirmy fur ball out of the pile and drops it by a separate bowl.

"Second-grade recess," I say. There's an inch of pink scar tissue above my hairline, a wound no one's seen. I've never seen it till today.

"Bit late for stitches then."

I lean on the splintery railing. I'm wearing my blue hoodie with the fuzzy lining, my green army shorts, my backpack, and my mom's old hiking shoes. Ready for a trek. "How do I look?"

Anthony matters. His opinion matters.

He scans me up and down. I scan him back. The inner cavity of his ear shines like it's wet.

"Like a cocky twelve-year-old boy," he says.

Nice.

Is there a word for this, for what Anthony and I are to each other? I was eleven when I met him. We were elementary school kids, little guys. Then he turned into a young man whose T-shirts hang on muscular shoulders. A young man whose deadpan sarcasm flips into a twinkly grin when I crack the right joke. And I turned into a young woman who finds all of that appealing. But our friendship was formed from simpler things. Board games, bikes, homework, hot chocolate.

It's fine.

If you have one person in your life, you can't kiss him. Cause who would you tell about it?

"Make sure Pepper eats." His grandma—so young, could she really be?—steps outside. Her pale belly parts her tight shirt and pants, dark wiry hairs trailing down from her navel. "And take that bag when you go, see if you can find kibbles. Hell of a time to have puppies, huh?" She looks at me now, no hello, just inserts me into the conversation.

Tiny crunching noises from the dogs. The buzz of a green fly orbiting their butts.

"How they doin?" I say.

"Fine. What do they know? Soon as the lights come back, I'll get good money for em. Feeding them's gonna kill us, though. It's like having two families."

We talk about *"the lights coming back"* as if that's what we're missing. Lights are the least of it. We could live without lights, do stuff in the daytime, build fires at night. We lost our story. We lost our agreement. Or the illusion of agreement.

"Is that Alex?" Anthony's little sister, May, peeks through the screen, tongue poking out of her Kool Aid–smeared mouth.

Anthony calls his home "diverse." His grandma looks white, paler than me, May looks pretty Black, and Anthony looks, well, like Anthony. Tight curly hair, bronze skin, dark-green eyes. He has a Black mom and a white dad, and he gets endless questions from people of all races. *What are you? What's your background?* Before moving to Little Falls, Anthony lived in what he calls a *"regular Black neighborhood."* And while our little town has a lot more Black people than most towns around here, the trio of Anthony, May, and Gram can still confuse people. One lady thought May was Anthony's daughter.

"Yes, May, she got herself a haircut, now go finish your breakfast." His grandma doesn't ask about my hair, immediately accepts it, relays it as fact. She never judges, never pins assumptions on you. That must be where Anthony gets it.

Through the screen door, I see the couch covered with a plaid sheet where Anthony and I used to watch the shows I couldn't see at home. Georgie fixates on TV, so it's strictly rationed at our house. Was.

"If you do talk to your mom, Anthony, tell her we miss her and we're doing fine. Don't get her worrying." His grandma sighs. "I don't know, what do you think, Alex?"

"About what?"

"Talking to someone halfway across the world. Think it's real?"

"I'm hopeful," I say.

Since when am I the optimistic can-do person? Since I saw that fear in Anthony's eyes.

"Anything else?" Anthony says, folding the dog food bag into his backpack.

His grandma shakes her head. "News."

What everybody wants.

There's endless "news," explanations of what happened and what's coming, everybody filling the void with paranoia and wishes. The less people know, the more they proclaim. The thirst for a story line, any story line, turns opinions into rumors and rumors into facts. The strangest explanation is more comforting than no explanation.

Not for me.

I don't want news. I don't want a Story.

I step off the porch, smell the moist ground warming in the May sun.

I want to stay wide open.

———◆———

"Glad someone's keeping track," I say.

Anthony's neighbor has a piece of plywood counting up the blackout:

NO POWER DAY #~~1 2 3 4 5 6 7 8 9 10 11 12 13 14 15 16 17 18 19 20 21~~ 22

NATIONAL DISGRACE

NO LEADERSHIP

TRUST IN OUR LORD!

Across the street, a cardboard sign yells in all caps:

WILL TRADE FIREWOOD FOR TOBACCO

The blackout is an empty box. Put whatever you want in it. One person wants a savior, another wants a smoke.

"We should make a sign," Anthony says.

"'*Puppies for Sale Cheap*'?"

"'*Need a Ride to Bethany.*'"

"Yeah, why aren't we hitchhiking?"

"Gram wouldn't let me. And your mom would freak."

"She's already freaking," I say.

"About us going to Bethany?"

I nod.

"But she's okay with it?"

"Uh. Well."

A big lady huffs by on a too-small bicycle, her lumpy knees winging out to the side. There are more bikers now and more parents, like this one, riding their kids' bikes. Anthony gives a half wave, says hello. People acknowledge one another more since the blackout, but this woman doesn't. Maybe she's out of breath.

I wish my bike worked. That's the problem with the blackout. I need to get my bike fixed because our car's out of gas. But is the bike store open? And how would I get there? Plus, I don't have cash. Ugh.

"You did tell your mom," Anthony says.

"Of course. And she said: 'No way.'"

"But you convinced her?"

"In my head."

"What about her head?"

"Mm, not so much."

We cut through the Marinos' yard, over to Route 12. Mr. Marino doesn't mind, but his little dog yaps frantically at the window.

"Great, she's gonna yell at my grandma," Anthony says. "I should walk you home right now."

"Pretend I never mentioned it."

"Mentioned what?"

"Exactly. I'm not gonna tell you till much later, when things get crazy."

"When's that?"

"I'm guessing sundown."

"When we're home?" he says.

"Mm. Not what I'm picturing."

"What are you picturing?"

"Mayhem. Shenanigans."

"Chicanery?"

"Mm-hmm. Maybe some hornswaggling." That's an Anthony favorite, a pirate word that means swindle or con. One could say he hornswaggled me into this trip, though soon enough, I'll hornswaggle him right back.

We cut through rows of blossoming apple trees at Kelleher's Orchards, past the long, stinky cow barns at Highview Farm, to a quiet stretch of Church Street along the creek, the smell of cold water over rocks. Little Falls is little. Our Main Street has a Mobil station specializing in tractor repair, the Four Corners deli, and the sporadically open Downtown—*Downtown!*—Collectibles Shop. Someone built a housing development here in the 1960s, a circle of boxy two-story homes. Whatever was supposed to happen next didn't, or didn't yet, since everyone says the suburbs are heading our way. For now, Little Falls is still a faded farm town with a ring of houses dangling off: "the Loop," where Anthony and I both live. Walk ten minutes from my house, and you're in farms or forest—you're alone. Drive ten minutes, and you're in the grid of shopping centers and developments, the sprawl Little Fallers fear, though we spend all our time and money there.

Georgie stays in one of those sprawling towns. Stays, not lives. He lives with us.

Another sign, this one at DeGroot's Dairy:

BLACKOUT SALE!
RAW MILK $8/GALLON
OR TRADE FOR CANNED GOODS, FUEL, BATTERIES, ETC.
MOTHER NATURE'S HEALTHIEST DRINK!

Right. Cows keep giving milk, and they can't refrigerate it, so they're selling it raw. And I guess at room temperature. Sounds icky. A smaller sign by the barn warns:

SIGNED WAIVER REQUIRED FOR PURCHASE.

"You're not really worried, are you?" Anthony says. "We're gonna be fine. We'll just walk there, talk to the veterans, and then just walk back."

One thing this day will gloriously prove: There is no *just*.

When people start saying "we'll just," get nervous. You're in for a ride.

I didn't know that.

I didn't know there would be fire and water and invisible buildings and naked people. We were *just walking to Bethany.*

"I'm in, Anthony. I already told you."

"Great. I just feel like . . ."

"I know how you feel."

"Mm, I doubt that."

"I do. I know all the Anthony layers."

"All of them?"

"Heck yeah."

"Let's hear it."

"One." I count on my fingers. "I, Anthony Golden, feel grateful that Alex is here." Golden is his middle name, so marvelous, so fitting. He keeps it a secret. I only know because May told me.

"True."

"Two. I feel scared about my mom in a way I don't fully understand."

"Uh, okay. Sure."

"Three. I don't want to admit that, cause it sounds weak."

"Except I did just admit it."

"Only when I pointed it out. Should I keep going?"

"I don't think so."

"Four. Underneath that, I actually do want people to worry about me."

"I do?" he says.

"Especially Alex. She should worry about me, cause I'm not as strong as she thinks."

"Okay, five. I wish you'd stop."

"Yup. And six. Underneath all of that, I feel like I'm broken and I don't know why."

"Whoa."

"Six is a gimme. Everybody feels that. I assume."

We cross over a culvert, a big metal tube that pipes the stream under the road. Water striders hover near the outlet, waiting for insects.

"Too much?" I say.

"Way too much."

"Accurate, though."

"Well, you're right that I'm worried about my mom. I mean . . ." He looks straight up. I can see his nose hairs. "Let's just say I'd walk a lot farther than Bethany to talk to her."

"Let's do it. All the way to the Pacific."

"We'll need more granola bars. And a change of socks. And wow, okay, are they naked?"

On the corner, a man and woman are lying back on recliners. Not lawn chairs, living room chairs, brown corduroy with cup holders.

Told you there'd be nudity.

"Damn." Anthony turns away. "That's a lot of white flesh."

Their one-story brick house has metal awnings over the windows and a fraying brown tarp on half the roof, an interrupted project. Pink packages of shingles droop across the roofline, waiting for a roofer, crumbling in the weather.

In the yard, the two of them are settled in. They have a plastic bin for an end table, water, bug repellant, books, and sunscreen.

"Let's keep moving," Anthony says.

"Hold on. I have to ask."

"No, you don't," he says, but he follows me across the road.

I stop on the gravel where the couple's grass begins. Anthony stands behind me, facing the woods in protest.

"Morning," the naked woman says. Her breasts flatten sideways, her dark, bumpy nipples sliding off her torso.

"Hi," I say. Now that I'm close, I want to flee. *Don't, Alex. Stay.*

The man shifts, smiles. His hairy belly rolls out over his crotch.

"I was wondering . . ." I'm staring. The woman's black pubic hair spreads up her thighs, which are cracked like sunbaked sand. Yesterday, I was a homebody; today, I talk to naked strangers.

"We're free to do this," the man says. "We're not harming anyone."

Behind me, Anthony huffs.

"Yeah," I say. "I'm just curious: Is this new? Did you do this before the blackout?"

"Oh, sure!" She levers her recliner up, thighs creasing like folded dough, breasts rolling down toward her belly button. "We've done it at the beach and around the house, but never, you know, like this." She sips from a blue plastic cup.

She doesn't have normal tan lines. She is unified, one steady color from crotch to armpit, and it's striking. There's always that ghost bikini, especially for us pale people, that highlights our privates. Her breasts aren't circled; her crotch isn't in quotes. She is whole.

"All bets are off, right?" she says. "Everything's a mess, nothing works. This is the least we deserve."

Those words will stick with me. *All bets are off.* I'll use that argument a lot in the next twenty-four hours, convincing myself and others to make trouble. Thanks, nude woman.

She pushes the recliner back, open to the sky. The dirty soles of her feet frame her dark groin.

"Is it . . . ?" I close my eyes to focus on my question and not their captivating nudity. "Is it as good as you hoped?"

"So good." The man stands up, folds his muscled arms over a round belly. Anthony grabs my hand and pulls me back a step. "I gotta say, sharing this here in our community, talking to people like you, explaining the lifestyle, it's incredible."

"Not everyone's friendly," the woman says.

Anthony is pulling harder, and I have to lean forward to counterbalance. Makes it seem like I want to jump on them.

"Sure, we get the jerks driving by with their comments." The man shakes his head, and his retreating penis, shriveled and shy, shakes, too. "Not everyone's as polite as you, son."

Son! Told you I look like my brother.

"Do you know"—he's in interview mode, a veteran nudist sharing his expertise—"I wake up every morning thinking about coming out here. This is what we've been waiting for. It's perfect."

Anthony squeezes my hand, and I squeeze back, a silent laugh. There's an odd tingle here, these naked people and Anthony's warm grip, something lewd in front of me and something affectionate behind. It's inappropriate and delightful.

"Perfect," I repeat. All these bodies. What do they even want? What are they for? "Sitting out here . . . natural, is that what you call it?"

"Or 'nude,'" the man says.

"I say 'nekkid.'" She cackles. Her breasts ripple like a pool with a rock thrown in.

The man chuckles, too. "Oh, Joanne'll sass ya." His belly jiggles and rolls.

"I'm a big girl," she says. "People see me out here, they ain't calling me natural. They say: 'Jeezus, that woman's nekkid.'" Now I'm laughing. "Butt nekkid."

She's looking right at me, and we are cracking up, crying.

Three humans, one clothed, giggle together in the stark sunshine. I turn to Anthony, who's looking down at his shoes, but even he has a smile tugging his lips.

"Whoo. God. You two." The man wipes his eyes and catches his breath. "I will say this, son. I was never comfortable with myself, not for a minute, till I got comfortable in my own skin. I mean, look."

I look. A yellowing scar runs up from his hip and disappears into the rolls of his stomach.

"If I could go back to when I was your age and have this feeling? This comfort in who I am?" He shakes his head. "I wish I'd known earlier."

"All right, John, have a seat." She rolls her head toward me and squints. "He's a bit of a salesman for the lifestyle."

"I'm not selling the lifestyle. The lifestyle doesn't matter. What matters is . . ." He puts his arms out to the side, his face to the sky.

We are quiet. Through his gray chest hair, freckles—or maybe sunspots—rise and fall with his breaths. Sunlight glints off Joanne's water and throws a trembling circle onto his torso where ribs meet belly. It's a healing beam, a window into this pulsing, fuzzy human animal.

He coughs, a clenching in his groin that pulls at his throat and chin. His coughs turn to a wheeze, and he doubles over.

"Honey, have some water." Joanne holds up the cup.

He waves a hand, the top of his balding head bobbing up

and down as he hacks. "I'm all right," he grunts, then pops up with a forced smile. Stray coughs flutter his lips.

Anthony tugs me toward the street, his grip tightening. Maybe we'll walk all the way to Bethany holding hands. Not the worst idea.

"I'm really glad to meet you." I bow my head and, strangely, back away, like I'm leaving royalty. "And I'm glad you're out here."

"Thank you, son. You should try it!" he says. "Don't ever let em shame you." He raises the cup to his lips and coughs as he takes a sip, water spraying his face.

She laughs, passing him a towel as I turn away.

All these crotches and butts and bellies, hiding behind curtains, behind clothing, waiting for chances. Waiting to be seen.

I want a body like theirs, one that takes up space and does what it wants.

Where do I get one?

CHAPTER THREE

"So much to talk about," Anthony says. "Lotta firsts."

When May got poison ivy, a bee sting, and kicked in the head at a classmate's birthday, Anthony's grandma carried her into the house saying: "Big day today. Lotta firsts."

We step out of the road to let a manure spreader pass. The stink engulfs us, grassy and ripe.

"I agree," I say. "We've never held hands before. Your hand is so soft."

"I was holding your hand so you wouldn't get too close."

"To their pubes."

"Please. I'm trying to forget it."

My clothes feel ridiculous now. Not ridiculous, contrived. Who put all this fabric on me? And why is Anthony wearing those scratchy pants?

"Those people have always been here," I say.

"Not in recliners with their junk out."

A yellow butterfly flits out of the grass and orbits us hurriedly, a jerking sketch of the space between us.

"So they're out in the open," I say. "That's not a huge change."

"Except it is." He swats a bug on his neck, and his fingers leave a mark.

We cross Five Mile Creek in silence. A squirrel skitters up a pine tree, the bark like crocodile skin. It's colder down here, like early spring. I look through the metal grate at the rushing water and the Day-Glo green algae waving in the current. One thing the blackout showed is how little I understand the world. When the water stopped, I assumed we'd drink out of the creek. My mom explained that, because of all the farms, there's bacteria in the creek, "pig poop," as she put it. We'd have to boil it, without a stove, over an open fire. I remembered all the times I drank from that creek as a kid. It didn't taste like pig poop. I also didn't know you can flush a toilet with a bucket of water. It's all gravity, no electricity needed. Incredible.

"Did you like looking at those naked people?" Anthony says, kicking a pine cone down the road.

"I was interested."

"In what?"

"Anthony, I spent the last year hiding in my house. So, yeah, when people who are ashamed or embarrassed come out and do the thing they want—even a silly thing—I want to know about it."

I kick the pine cone, and it skids into the gully.

"Maybe you should get a recliner," he says.

"What do you think this is?" I point to my scalp.

"Oh, right. Your head's nude."

"Yup, I'm exposed."

"Like a naked grandpa."

"Seriously. I feel raw. It's different."

"All right then, good for you." He rubs my stubble. Nice. People don't do that to girls with long hair. "And I'm worried about you."

The shadow of a hawk, maybe a turkey vulture, slips soundlessly across the road. If we were field mice, we'd run.

"Anthony, the time to worry about me was months ago. I was a mess. Not today. Today, I'm on my feet."

A silver sedan passes us, a thumping song overloading the car speakers and vibrating the front grille. Music mostly went away when everyone ran out of charge. The blackout quieted the incessant background hum of refrigerators, airplanes, and phones and replaced it with birds and wind and, sometimes, a silence so deep my ears tingle. Our neighbor sings hymns on her porch in the evenings, and, every time, it's monumental, holy, the return of music to a silent world.

"I did," Anthony says.

The car is gone. Silence.

"What?"

"Worry about you. Months ago."

Yes, you did, Anthony.

You sweet boy.

⸻

No one's ever gotten Georgie right except Anthony.

We were Sunday school exiles together at Saint Benedict's, a converted Grange hall with an unconvincing cross on top. Church was my mom's idea—Dad went occasionally—and, as it turned out, a real lifesaver. After my parents split when I was in eighth grade, people at Saint Benedict's hooked my mom up with food, rides, furniture, and a job. They were crazy generous.

That came later. One hot Sunday in the summer before sixth grade, my job was taking squirmy Georgie to Sunday school. He never stayed, so, as usual, I hung with him in the parking lot, and in the play area with its patchy grass and broken swings.

Georgie was nine and rambunctious. I was eleven, and so was Anthony, who sat on the curb behind a massive pickup in his ironed button-down shirt, clip-on bow tie, and creased black pants.

Three Sundays in a row, Anthony lingered in the parking lot, out of sight of the church, while Georgie and I roamed, finding twigs, struggling on the heavy seesaw, and singing nonsense songs. One time, Anthony had a book; another time he scratched curving lines into the gravel with his shiny loafers.

On the third Sunday, Georgie sat down near him, so I had

to start a conversation. I asked what he was doing in the parking lot.

"It's a religious war," he said.

"You're fighting?"

"I'm in the middle. My mom thinks church is superstition. My grandma says if I grow up without God, I'll end up on the wrong path."

"What do you think?"

"Doesn't matter what I think. I let Gram bring me here when my mom's away. But I skip Sunday school."

"Cause why?"

"To stand up for my mom."

Later, he told me about the disputes between his Black mom and white grandma, how church was an easy symbol to fight over. Later still, when he trusted me, he mentioned the nasty Sunday school boys—white boys, I assumed, cause it's a pretty white congregation—who teased him about his clothes till he walked out.

"Your mom's away a lot, huh?" I said.

"She's in the navy. Duty calls."

And that's when he met my brother—stood near my brother, really, cause you don't meet Georgie like you meet other people. And Anthony said: "Wow. I've never seen a person like that."

Georgie pumped his elbows back and forth, wiggly air punches.

"Right?" I said.

I didn't say: thank you. Thank you for not talking about how special he is. *He's so sweet.* No, he isn't, not always. He's brilliant and hilarious, and he's like anybody: He has lovely sides and crappy sides. He broke a plate on a three-year-old girl's hand. He bent a windshield wiper back cause he didn't recognize the car my mom borrowed. I think that's why anyway. You don't always know. We comfort ourselves with explanations. *Little kids make him anxious.* Or: *Rooms without doors scare him.*

"God, what's it like?" Anthony said.

"Being his sister?"

"Being him. Must be so different. Can you imagine?"

Man, I try. Always. I put myself in Georgie's body, in his eyes and fingers and brain. I imagine being him so I can calm him, soothe him, and avoid the meltdowns, the fits and fists.

But mostly: *Wow, Anthony.* Nobody's ever real when they first encounter Georgie. Some people are repulsed. That's easy to handle. Screw them. Screw Normies thinking everybody's neurotypical. No one's neurotypical. I know a girl who counts stairs, needs them to end at eleven. She'll jump three steps at a time to make the math work. No special ed for her, though.

The pitiers are harder, frowning and nodding:

Must be so hard for your family.

Is there a cure?

Gosh, you're an angel to be such a loving sister.

No, I'm not an angel. And I'm not loving all the time.

But no one wants to know that. You can't be pissed at your disabled brother. You're not allowed to wish he was easier, not allowed to scream at him when he ruins family dinner for the fourth night in a row. He doesn't mean it. He has no idea. Everyone in the world does cruel things, mean things, but disabled kids are always doing their best.

Bull. If I'm gonna treat him like a real person, I'm gonna call out when he's an ass. That's what siblings do.

He wouldn't let this lady into the supermarket. He kept leaning forward and back, triggering the sensor and flapping his hands when the door whooshed open.

"Sorry," I said.

"Don't apologize." She waited pertly behind her cart. "He's having fun."

"No, he's being a dick. He knows you're waiting."

"That's a horrible thing to say about someone like that."

Like that. One of those.

Why can't I treat him like one of us, like a person? You wouldn't let me block the door, so don't let him.

It all leads to the same place: I'm selfish. I'm a jerk. I'm upstaging the real star of the family, the Sign of Our Goodness. A disabled kid puts you 100 percent in the Deserving category. Fundraisers, coin cans at the checkout, free admission, prayer circles. Whatever you need.

Until you screw up. Then you are truly, utterly Undeserving.

"Mind if I stick with you guys?" Anthony asked, squinting back toward the church.

"It's not much fun," I said.

"It's good to have more heretics out here. Plus, if I'm helping with your brother, they won't scream at me for skipping Sunday school."

Disabled siblings can be so useful.

Later—again, once he trusted me—Anthony told me he liked me: "You were the one interesting kid at that white people's church." Anthony has layers. He'll give you a totally believable explanation and then, days or months later, a different one.

We spent an hour a week together that summer, wandering after Georgie, talking and, even better, not talking. Georgie's energy makes silence tolerable; you don't have to fill every quiet second. It's part of how I got close to Anthony. How often do you meet someone by spending long stretches of time in comfortable silence?

One week, his mom came back—I assumed—and I didn't see him at church anymore.

When I got on the bus for the first day of sixth grade, a voice from the back called out, "Heretic!"

Anthony and his three-year-old sister, May, were now living full-time at his grandma's. His mom took an overseas deployment and was gone for long stretches. Anthony was in my class and in my neighborhood. He was easygoing and funny, friendly with a lot of kids, not especially tight with anyone. We talked on the bus more than we did at school, where he had Black friends and white friends, mostly boys except for me and Beth, an older girl who knew his grandma and called him Tony. I call him Tony to annoy him.

His arrival into our house was simple and immediate. He walked in and instantly belonged. The first day, he blew up a whole bag of balloons for Georgie (I usually did only two or three), which turned into hours of Georgie bliss. The next day, he sat down in front of Georgie's Disney movie as if he'd been invited over specifically to watch. There was no transition, no getting-to-know-you phase. Maybe we'd done that silently in the church parking lot. He was like a cousin you've known since birth, fitting easily and unremarkably into whatever was happening.

Two months later, I was reading on the porch, a book about a boy who's in a lot of trouble and meets a girl from far away.

"Read it to me," Anthony said.

I flipped back to the beginning, and he said, "No, just start where you are."

"Don't you want to know the story?"

"I'll figure it out."

And he did. I started midparagraph with no explanation. Anthony asked occasional questions: *Where is his mother? Why does she have a fake name?* Over three days, I read him the last half of the book.

Anthony and I started in the middle and figured it out.

In eighth grade, after my parents split, he started dropping by my house, bringing "extra" muffins or chili or tuna salad.

One time he brought a bag of hot dog rolls, and I thought: This kid is darn nice, but who brings buns and no hot dogs?

It took me a while to figure out that his grandma, a regular at our church, knew about our needy family and was sending food over.

It took me even longer to figure out that Anthony was using the donated food as an excuse to come by. To be my friend.

It also helped that Anthony's house become a destination for me and, more importantly, for Georgie, who was generously and matter-of-factly welcomed.

MAY: Who's that boy?

GRANDMA: His name is Georgie. He's Alex's sister. He goes to church with us.

MAY: What's wrong with him?

GRANDMA: He doesn't act like everybody else, but neither do you, sweetie. Now give him some of your grapes.

"Stop right there!"

We stop. It's quiet except for a bird that sounds like: *Real, real, real!*

We're off the road. Anthony insists he knows shortcuts, including dubious ones like this arduous walk over hilly fields.

Half a girl appears up ahead, just her torso and face visible above the grass.

Real, real, real!

"Get down," someone says.

"Did she say that?" Anthony says.

The girl waves a gloved hand and smiles. Mixed messages. We walk toward her.

"Get down!" The voice is angrier. Half a little boy appears next to the girl. He is holding a shovel across his body like a rifle.

"Gabe, relax," the girl says.

Turns out they're standing in a waist-deep hole, big as a bed, and surrounded by shovels, a wheelbarrow, and piles of dirt and rocks. Behind them, knee-high hay slopes up toward a barn and a graying play set—swings, slide, and a frayed rope ladder.

"Freeze!" The boy is out of the hole. His red bandanna is dark with sweat, his white T-shirt smeared with dirt. "Are there grown-ups with you?"

"No, we're—"

"'Cause if there's grown-ups, we have to go back to the house." The boy aims his shovel at us. *"Pyew! Pyew!"*

"Easy, soldier," the girl says. She's tall and solid, maybe an athlete, with a round face and dark eye makeup that makes her gaze intense. She climbs out, black hair sticking to her damp forehead. "What are you all doing?"

She drops a football-sized rock onto a pile that looks bigger than the hole. The soil around here is like that. We got azalea bushes donated—a disabled kid attracts all kinds of charity, including things that are in no way relevant—and they died by the front steps cause my mom couldn't face digging up our rocky yard.

Anthony says, "We're heading over—"

"Don't talk to them," Gabe growls to the girl.

Silence. *Real, real, real!*

"Can I explain where we're going?" Anthony says.

"No," Gabe says. "We have to work."

Bugs buzzing in the warm sun. The mineral stink of earth beneath the topsoil.

"What are you working on?" Anthony says.

"We can't tell you," Gabe says.

"Oh. Well—"

"We can't even talk to you."

"Jesus, Gabe," the girl says.

"I'm telling Mom!" Gabe scrambles up the hill with his shovel, a mini marine leading an assault.

"Sorry about that," she says. "He's a little excited. Thinks this is all a movie."

"A movie about a large hole," Anthony says.

"Yup." She eyes Anthony. Probably thinks he's cute. "What do you think it is?" She peels off her work gloves.

"A swimming pool?" Anthony says. "Or, you're burying a giant coffin."

Anthony's fine-looking, more charming than hunky. He's a bit skinny, his ears stick out, and his hair goes poofy when it grows. If I met him on the street, I wouldn't stare. Like this girl is staring.

"It's a hide," she says, glancing over to include me, but going right back to Anthony.

I have two reactions at moments like this. I'm a tiny bit jealous: *Who's this girl checking Anthony out?* And I get a fond, affectionate feeling: *Aw, my little buddy is flirting. How sweet.*

I might be making that second part up.

"A what?" Anthony says.

"A place to hide stuff. In case of . . . you know."

It is a concealed spot, tucked into the slope of the field. If no one was standing in it, you'd never notice. I look down in the hole. A worm falls out of the dark topsoil and flops around.

"Actually, I don't know," Anthony says.

"Invasion."

"Who's invading?" he says.

She shrugs. "My mom says most invasions, you just have to be safe for a couple days until things stabilize."

Again, that question: Am I the right amount of worried about this? No one in my house is talking about invasions.

"But it's really just to give my brother something to do," she continues. "My mom's sick of having him home, so she said: 'Dig a hole big enough to hide in.' I've been helping for an hour, and I'm like: 'I can't believe he's been digging for two straight days.'"

This is exactly the kind of crap people say in the blackout: *Well, we're sort of preparing for a war, but really, we're just killing time.* Were we always like this, half catastrophe and half boredom?

"You're gonna hide in there?" Anthony says.

"Not really. I guess if we had to, yeah." She wipes something out of her eye and blinks quickly. "Are you going into town?"

"We're headed to Bethany."

"Great. Could I come with you? I'm sposed to go to school, but I'm not allowed to walk alone."

"I think schools are closed," Anthony says.

"Not Harrison. It only closed for three days." She wipes her hands, holds one out. "I'm Kimmy, by the way."

"Hi, Kimmy. I'm Anthony, this is Alex."

Wait. Harrison.

"Please get me out of here," she says. "I'm sweaty and bored, and it's not even ten o'clock."

"Georgie's at Harrison," I say. "My brother. Is it really open?"

"They're down here!" Gabe yells, sprinting down the hill, now with a cardboard sword tucked into his belt. "Mom! Come on!"

Gabe and Kimmy's mom, wiping her wet hands on her jeans, hustles down the hill.

<hr/>

My mom must be worried by now.

After I shaved my head, I left her a note:

I'm going with Anthony.

I'll get home as soon as I can.

I'll be safe.

I'll bring back news, that will help. If these veterans or Anthony's mother know something, I can pass it on to my mom, and maybe she won't punish me. Or she'll punish me less.

She's hard to predict these days. She's relaxed about some things—we watched a stunning number of movies before the blackout, something we couldn't do when Georgie was in the house—but anxious and rigid about others.

We are a dwindling family. We were four till my dad left three years ago. I was in eighth grade, and it was a massive shock. When you have a brother like Georgie, it's tough to see your parents clearly. Do most parents trade off constantly, tagging in to take care of the kids and disappearing whenever possible? Are most parents drained and hollow-eyed by dinnertime? Are Mom and Dad having a hard time, or is it just hard to raise a kid with a disability?

So we were three, down a man. And now we're two, just me and Mom. I get why she might be thinking: Who's next?

Life with Georgie was a constant low-level crisis. There was warmth and ridiculous fun, for sure, but nothing could be regular or planned or on time. Everything adjusted to his energies, his fickle reactions. A game or hat or cracker thrilled him one day, outraged him the next. We chased his moods, treasuring his laughter and fearing his temper, staggering toward an imagined stability.

It was never easy. But when they took him away, we fell.

Our days crumbled and collapsed. My mom missed meals, cooked at midnight. I was out of school for a week, which sounds fun, but sitting at home was agony. The stillness, the silence broken by tears, stomps, or, once, my mom throwing advice books out a window she didn't bother to open. Shards of glass stayed on the dirt for months, alongside moldering copies of *Raising a Special Needs Child* and *School Smarts: Advocating for Your Autistic Child's Education.*

The worst thing about life without Georgie is how often I'd wished for it. Without him, my mom and I could take road trips, get good at cooking, and—this was really specific—read in a hammock. A hammock is too much like a swing, something Georgie fixates on and therefore we could never have. We had a tire swing out back when we moved here. The second night, Georgie was on it at 4:00 A.M., hanging on for dear life, barking out his joy.

In reality, life without him is hollow and weepy. My mom's heavy feet on the way to the bathroom. She turns on the tub faucet to cover her crying, thick sheets of water slapping porcelain, flowing down through our home, into a bottomless river, the heaving underground ocean of our grief.

"Tell those boys to leave," Gabe says, shovel raised.

Hilarious. Being taken for a boy is jarring but freeing. I don't have to be the girl who hid in her house. Or any girl.

"Can I help you?" Their mom smiles, a tape measure dangling off her belt.

Well, yeah. We need kibbles, a ride, a generator, and a way to talk to Anthony's mom. No, even better: We need to bring his mom home.

"They're going to school," Kimmy says. Not true. "They can take me."

"Oh, you go to Harrison?"

"No," I say. I watch Kimmy, behind her mom, nodding and cranking a finger in the air. "I mean, yeah, my brother goes there." Kimmy nods and gives me a thumbs-up.

"And so you're . . ."

Kimmy, eyes wide and nodding.

"I have to go see him. At school," I lie.

"Well, it's late. By the time you walk there, it'll—"

"Come on, Mom. I've been waiting all morning," Kimmy says.

"I understand. But we have things to do here. And, no offense . . ." She puts her palms up. She has calluses at the base of each finger, an arc of yellow bumps. "I don't know these boys."

Anthony has already started back to the road. Normally, I'd walk away, too.

"I'm not spending the whole day digging this stupid hide," Kimmy says.

"Shh! Don't say what it is!" Gabe says.

Today, I don't walk away. I move toward the mom, toward the heat.

"I'm not a boy," I say. I take her hand. She has acne scars on her cheeks, a tangle of short hair ringed with sweat. "I'm Alexandra. I'm going to see my brother, Georgie. He's disabled, and I'm worried about him."

Double thumbs-up from Kimmy.

"Oh." The mom squeezes my hand, her bony arm dangling from a hunched shoulder. "Gosh. I hope he's all right."

Anthony and I have an ongoing competition: What gets you more perks and sympathy, a mom in the military or a disabled brother? Score one for me. Disability is the Story Everyone Can Get Behind. Even right-wingers who blame the poor for being poor and the uneducated for being uneducated don't blame disabled kids for anything. They are guiltless and, therefore, the perfect objects of charity. Shriners, McDonald House, Harley riders, NASCAR, everybody rains love and money on disabled children. We get free car repairs from Frank Urness, who was famous for his PUT OUR PEOPLE FIRST signs. I told my mom we shouldn't go to Frank cause he's kind of a bigot. She said, "*Well, this is his way of making up for that.*"

I've done my part for Kimmy. She keeps arguing her case as I nod goodbye and follow Anthony down to the road.

A motorcycle roars past with two orange five-gallon jugs roped to the back. The blackout makes gas mileage a major topic of conversation. Everyone covets motorcycles and small cars.

"Tell you what," Anthony says. "If there is an invasion, I'm getting behind that Gabe kid. Dude's a warrior."

We walk.

I try to picture our route. Will we go past Harrison High? Could we see if Georgie's there? I need a map. I don't pat my pockets for my phone, but I'm tempted to.

The motorcycle pulls in at Gordy's Service Center, which used to be a gas station but is now a parking lot for junked cars. A bunch of guys stand around the old pumps. One guy's running a hose down into the tanks. He's flat on the concrete, arm shoulder-deep in the hole, tongue squeezed between his teeth.

I run my hand over my stubble. Stiff corduroy, it snaps back to its grain, but it's soft. I've got a new feature, a new texture. Somebody might want to touch this, right? Run their fingers or maybe their cheek over the downy nap. It could be flirtatious, a new rite of passage between first and second base: *I fondled her fuzz.*

"Your head okay?" Anthony says.

"Yeah, I love how it feels. Here." I put his hand on my scalp.

"Different."

So different.

I move my head, and it's only my head, no possum-sized tail flipping around half a second later. I'm tight, compact. When I turn to look at something, I just look. There's nothing bouncing or second-guessing me. There's no bushy halo, no wispy hesitation, no *Or maybe not.* When I nod, I nod. Period. My long hair was an ellipsis at the end of every thought, a shrug at the end of every sentence.

I am no longer plural; I am singular.

And there's no pushing bangs out of my face or, as I used to, into my face. No tucking behind my ear, no pulling back into a ponytail. No barrettes, elastics, or brushes. Hell, no shampoo, I assume. This must be what getting contact lenses feels like, or that laser surgery where you see perfectly afterward. A lifetime of tiny, tedious chores is instantly gone.

Why didn't I do this sooner? Why didn't I leave the house sooner?

"Wait up!" Kimmy runs up the road, clutching her backpack.

"Huh," Anthony says.

She arrives panting, cheeks red. "Nice work. You convinced her." Is she going to hug me? "And sorry my mom thought you were a boy."

No hug. Too soon. I touch her bicep, a cool layer of sweat over warm muscle.

"I knew you were a girl. Obviously." She roots through her backpack, pulls out water. "Man, I'm glad y'all showed up. I was gonna be stuck in that hole."

"And you'd rather be in school?" Anthony says.

"Oh, I'm not going to school. I'm going swimming in the quarry." She offers water. We drink. "You guys should come."

<hr />

Georgie can't swim.

Georgie loves water.

Georgie went in Long Lake and stayed under until the lady with the turquoise jewelry pulled him out.

The police report said he was submerged "less than ten minutes." The doctor estimated three to four.

Later, I watched the sunflower clock in our kitchen, the red second hand gliding past gold petals. Twenty seconds, twenty-five. My dear little Georgie panicking in eight feet of water. One minute is agony, a catastrophe. Three is unthinkable.

For those three minutes—that's the most I will allow it to be—I stood in line for cake. I could see the swim beach, but not the dock where Georgie left his sandy sneakers, his shirt, and his shorts with a half-eaten hot dog in the pocket. That sweet, sweet boy knew not to get his clothes wet.

A woman was shouting, running down the hill to a clump of people by the water. Somebody was hurt.

Not Georgie. He was in the sandbox, waiting for cake.

Someone yelling: "Call 911."

Georgie was fine. I was sure of it.

Let me just lay eyes on him.

I asked a girl in a mermaid bathing suit to save my spot in line, as if that mattered. Can you imagine? The last nice thought I had was: I can't lose my spot, because Georgie might temper if he doesn't get cake.

Remember when that was what I worried about? An autistic tantrum, sand kicked across the playground, Georgie grabbing some other kid's dessert. I remember that me. I glimpse her in the morning, in that soft moment as the sea of sleep recedes. I wake up as the old me: *Hey, it's sunny, my blanket's all tangled, I'm—*

Oh god.

And the weight descends.

"Mind saving my spot?"

The girl in the mermaid bathing suit nodded. I remember thinking: *That's not what you mean. You mean: "No, I don't mind."* She was staring at the emergency down the hill.

I just needed to lay eyes on Georgie.

A fit guy, all jangling keys and arm muscles, almost knocked me over as he streaked down toward the concussion or broken collarbone or heart attack. His energy infected me, and I started running. Georgie wasn't in the sandbox, wasn't on the swings.

Something I learned about playgrounds and parks: You feel like you can see everything, but you can't. There are tons of hidden spots, behind the slide or that pine tree or those three people. I'd learned to move sideways. Georgie would appear when I shifted my angle.

I ran along the playground edge. The more I didn't see him, the more I was running to Mom, standing behind the Saint Benedict's table, selling fundraiser balloons.

"Mom! Do you have Georgie?"

She shook her head.

And that was it. That was the moment I woke up on the heavy, brutal planet I now inhabit.

I flew down the hill, bare feet slapping the dry ground. "Geez!" a kid yelled as I crashed through the rainbow bubbles he was blowing.

I got low and pushed through the legs of the watchers.

Why is Georgie wet? Why is he naked? Everyone can see his penis, his first pubic hair like a high school mustache.

"He's alive."

What? Of course he's alive. It's Georgie. I'm getting him cake.

Vomit on his shoulder, someone giving mouth-to-mouth, his chest convulsing.

My mom crashing through the crowd, screaming.

And I knew. I knew the whole story.

I left Georgie. He got in the lake, alone, and the lake closed over him. He swallowed the green water, gagged, thrashed his arms and legs, his underwater screams scattering the glassy fish. The lady with the turquoise jewelry dragged him to shore, his underpants pulled off along the stony bottom and later recovered by the police, put in a Ziploc bag like evidence.

My mom hurled herself on top of Georgie, knocking the mouth-to-mouth woman back. Everyone yelling at once. They pulled my mom off, held her as she fought to get on Georgie, to cover her strange, magical son with her body, her anguish.

And then she crumpled, fell to the ground, the indifferent, heavy soil that watches your heart break, patient and ruthless, and waits to swallow your skeleton. Or your child's.

The ambulance, the hospital, the fluorescent corridor.

Tender bodies collapse, lose their breath in lakes, and there's nothing you can do, you can't take it back because this world is merciless, this world makes you pay endlessly for one mistake, one three-minute mistake.

Police questions under the waiting room TV. Why? If someone is struck by lightning, you don't take statements from eyewitnesses.

That's when I learned that the worst possible thing could get worse. My brother nearly drowns, what could be worse than that?

Being blamed for it.

CHAPTER FOUR

"You kids should be in school." A woman holds out a handwritten flyer, a crayon drawing of a church and three smiling stick figures. No computers really brings out the arts and crafts.

ALL DAY SCHOOL, TWO MEALS INCLUDING ONE HOT!

READING, WRITING, MATH, AND COMMUNITY IN CHRIST.

NEWCOMERS WELCOME!

COVENANT BAPTIST CHURCH, 2449 ROUTE 17 BYPASS,

BEHIND RENT-A-CENTER

We're on a "quick detour" through the town of Jordan. Kimmy's going to trade eggs for coffee beans, or try to, one reason her mom let her leave.

Jordan isn't huge, but it dwarfs our town, with its two banks, pharmacy, supermarket, and pizzeria. Today, all three blocks are bustling, people walking in the street, occasional cars, some bikes, several wheelbarrows, and one horse. I haven't seen this many people since before the blackout.

"Come to Covenant for a week, and you get a hundred-dollar credit at our church store," Church Lady continues. Her mouth of big whitened teeth slopes right down to her chest, no chin at all.

Kimmy pulls me away. "Not interested."

"We have a generator!" the woman yells after us, and then turns to accost someone else.

"Careful with the religious people," Kimmy says. "They think the blackout is a sign."

The IGA parking lot is half flea market and half encampment. Pickup trucks with the back gate down, cars with open trunks, pop-up canopies in empty parking spaces. Outside the supermarket's front door, a woman picks through pallets of dried-up plants: dead pansies, tomatoes, and sunflowers. A panel truck offers to take trash (where?) for six dollars a bag. People have very different energies. Some are chatty and gossipy, like it's a street fair. Others have their heads down, going about their serious business. A few watch too intently, cowboys before the barroom fight. Guns sit conspicuously in holsters.

"Where did all this come from?" Anthony says.

"The firefighters started a clinic," Kimmy says. "Then other people showed up. Apparently, we're one of the better towns for doing business." She leads us past a grinning banjo player whose "tips" include a Canadian one-dollar coin, a pack of crackers, and a depressing number of pennies. "Here, I gotta check the Board."

Outside the volunteer fire department, burly guys stand around in rubber boots, and a long line leads to a nurse station with a privacy screen. A carefully painted sign instructs:

PRIMARY CARE 10 A.M.–3 P.M. DAILY. FOR SERIOUS HEALTH PROBLEMS ~~GO TO SIMONTON HEALTH CENTER~~ UPDATE: CLOSED. GO TO HARFORD COUNTY HOSPITAL, EMERGENCIES ONLY. DOCTORS, NURSES, AND CERTIFIED NURSING ASSISTANTS: PLEASE SEE CAPT. DARNOLD TO VOLUNTEER.

I pass a mom and a crying toddler at the back of the line. A firefighter bends down and offers his yellow helmet, almost as big as the girl, who promptly screams louder.

I catch my face reflected in the square window of the firehouse garage. Who is that? My features are blocky and out of proportion, like you shaved an alien and revealed its strange organs: air duct, food hole, light sensors. My ears are enormous, my cheeks puffy. I look like a kid you don't mess with.

It's astonishing how quickly and completely I changed. If you have long hair, it's important to know: You can be a different person in the time it takes to toast bread. I'm not saying you should—and maybe I'm not a great argument for it—I'm just saying you can.

"Stop staring at the bald chick. It's not polite." Anthony's face appears over my shoulder. He doesn't look like an alien.

And it's endearing when he hides his smile like this, his eyes beaming and mouth flat.

"Do I look ridiculous?" I say.

"How you want me to answer that?"

"What are my choices?"

"Honest, comforting, or in-joke."

"I'll take all three."

"Yes, Alex, you do look pretty unusual. No, Alex, your beauty has nothing to do with your hair." He leads me around the corner.

"And what's in-joke?" I say.

"Now we have a three-way contest. Who gets more sympathy: disabled kid, military kid, or cancer kid?"

"Cancer kid obviously."

"We should raise money."

"Knit her a hat."

"Will trade granola bars for wig."

The Board is on the side of the firehouse, a wall with notes sorted into columns. Some have been up long enough to fade in the sun.

URGENT NEEDS is mostly health care. Antiseizure pills. Advice about discontinuing chemotherapy. A veterinarian for a sick horse.

REQUESTS & OFFERS is less dire, but still full of hurt.

REQUEST: RIDE TO KANSAS CITY (OR ANYWHERE CLOSE) FOR A STUDENT SEPARATED FROM HER FAMILY.

NEED JUNIOR TAMPONS FOR A GIRL WHO GOT HER FIRST MENSES. HELP OUT A SINGLE DAD!

OUT OF COOKING WOOD. NEED TO BORROW OR RENT CHAINSAW.

And people offer to trade things no one needs for things everyone needs.

BLACKOUT ANXIETY AND DEPRESSION ARE REAL! CERTIFIED LIFE COACH OFFERS COUNSELING IN EXCHANGE FOR FUEL OR PRECIOUS METALS.

WHO NEEDS THE INTERNET? I WILL READ ALOUD TO YOU AND YOUR CHILDREN FROM MY EXTENSIVE COLLECTION OF STORYBOOKS. TRADE FOR CANNED GOODS OR CIGARETTES.

MESSAGES is a lot of reassurance and a few calamities.

ANYONE IN THE DELVECCHIO FAMILY: WE HAVE RUFUS AT HARWICH KENNELS. PICK UP SOON, PLEASE.

KENNY SMALLWOOD AKA KEN JUNIOR AKA SMALLZ (OR ANYONE WHO HAS SEEN HIM) PLEASE LEAVE A NOTE HERE TELLING US YOU'RE OK. YOUR PARENTS ARE VERY WORRIED.

This one is in pencil, shaky and desperate. No electricity means lots of handwriting, and it tells you more than the words.

"I should do one," Anthony says.

"About what?"

He laughs. "Seriously? About my mom."

"Nobody here is gonna find your mom. She's on the other side of the world."

"Thanks for the positivity." He takes an oversized index card from a stack and tests a dried-up marker.

"I do feel positive. I'm sure she's okay, Anthony."

"What makes you sure?"

"She's in the navy. She'll be safe."

"Because no one ever gets hurt in the military."

"It's a blackout, not a war."

"How do you know? I've heard people say the only thing that could cause a blackout this big is an attack."

"Yeah, but other . . . stuff hasn't happened." It's tricky, no? How do you prove that you're not in a war? "We aren't being invaded or bombed."

"*We* aren't. Maybe my mom is. If there's a war, she's in the middle of it."

"You're getting paranoid, like that Gabe kid."

He waits for a turn with the roll of masking tape.

"Can we be friends about something, Al?" That's a phrase from his mom. *Can we be friends about something, guys? No crackers in the living room.* He rips a piece of tape with his teeth. "I won't minimize your problems." He tapes his card high up and steps back. "And you don't minimize mine."

I follow his eyes as he scans the wall, his message in the sea of messages, a mosaic of need.

"Wow," I say. "You just posted on the internet. The blackout internet." An URGENT NEEDS card detaches from the wall and flutters to the ground.

The messages are not only on the Board. People carry signs or tape them to telephone poles:

NEED DIAPERS, SIZE 4.

WILL DO CARPENTRY, FARM WORK, CONSTRUCTION.

CHRISTIAN READING GROUP ON THE GREEN AT NOON: WHAT IS GOD'S MESSAGE?

And two neatly painted signs with no names or explanations:

WHY IS THIS HAPPENING?

and

WHAT'S NEXT?

They're square and carefully hung, anonymous speech bubbles voicing our private thoughts.

Yeah, what is next?

In the parking lot, everyone is swapping, bartering, and acquiring. We miss shopping. When that went away, folks got twitchy. A lot of stores opened after the blackout, but the problem was money. People spent their cash quickly, credit cards didn't work, and banks closed. There was stuff to buy, but not much to buy it with.

On day seven, I bought toilet paper and wooden matches from the Four Corners Deli with coins we dug out of the car. NO SCRATCH-OFF SALES OR PAYOUTS said a scribbled sign over the lottery machine. Who buys lottery tickets in the dark? The owner used a flashlight, a pocket calculator, and a notebook to record my purchases. "No sales tax today, hon," she said. "If they can't keep the lights on, they don't deserve our money."

They is blackout shorthand for whoever you resent. Everybody shakes their heads at how incompetent *they* are. "They put satellites in outer space, but they can't keep my lights on," our neighbor Lisa whined. That one hung me up, cause both of those seem impossibly difficult. Launch a rocket? Deliver electricity to millions of homes? I'm amazed they do it at all.

"Hi there, are you a resident of Jordan Township?" says a man with a plastic clipboard and a hat that says LOCAL.

People are usually blurry and general to me. *Little kids* over here. *Bunch of grown-ups* over there. Today, everyone's particular. Everybody, every *body*, glows. I stare at the pointy red hairs sprouting out of this man's neck, the way his puffy eyes circle you without seeing you cause he's nervous, he likes being alone.

"Who's asking?" Kimmy says.

"I'm with the Jordan Citizens' Committee. We are overseeing public safety and behavior during the crisis, and we're gathering signatures of support. Would you like to read our statement of principles?"

"Sure, I'll take one."

His puffy eyes stare down at his hands. "We only have one. It takes a long time to write it out." He offers the clipboard, which trembles.

Kimmy laughs. "You want to rule the town, but you can only make one copy? Not a good look."

"We aren't ruling the town, ma'am. We're coming together to push back against the chaos and the drugs."

I step aside as a young kid lurches by with a wheelbarrow of firewood.

"Pretty sure there were drugs here before," Kimmy says.

"It's different." His voice drops to a whisper. "There's a guy back there selling opium seeds. In *Jordan*. And god knows what else." He looks back and forth, reading us. "Is that the Jordan you want?"

"I'm not sure I want to live in your Jordan, either, sir," Kimmy says. "Who appointed you the boss?"

I shade my eyes. My last three weeks have been mostly in dim interiors, my house with its tiny windows surrounded by shade trees. This midday sun is shocking.

"I-I'm not the boss," he stammers. "We are simply hoping—"

"Can I ask something?" I say.

"Certainly." He turns to me, happy to be out of the debate with Kimmy, but he still doesn't make eye contact.

"What"—I put my hand over his on the clipboard—"is scaring you?"

"I'm not scared." He looks at my hand. "I'm . . . confident we can keep Jordan safe. But this is an opening. Either good people step up, or bad people will."

"Or, I don't know, maybe both?" Kimmy says. "Like life. Like everything."

"Then you need to decide which side you're on," he says.

"Not yours, I'm pretty sure," Kimmy says.

"That's up to you. But when we get three hundred signatures, we're going live. And, trust me, you'll want to be on our side then."

"Says the good person." Anthony, facing away, has been listening.

"I'm sorry?" Clipboard says.

"That sounded like a villain line."

"Are you even from here?"

"Whoa. Jesus. Okay." Anthony shakes his head. "I get it."

"Well, are you?"

"No, I couldn't be, cause Black people aren't allowed in Jordan."

"That's not what I'm saying."

"It's exactly what you're saying."

"Anyone can live in Jordan provided they"—he circles his free hand in the air, coaxing out his confused words—"live here."

"Excellent point. That kind of insight makes me want to support your Citizens' Klan."

"Citizens' Committee."

A firework screams into the sky, bursting white. It's daylight, so it's mostly smoke, but the sound is jarring, too loud. The firework is a reset. We all turn back to Clipboard and stare. What now?

He lifts a finger and looks only at me. His blue eyes are watery, two oysters drooping off his forehead. "We are not. Losing control. Of this town." He strides away, stiff-legged, to harass someone else.

This guy makes me glad there's no internet. In a different disaster—a war or a drought, say—a little tyrant like him could build a real following online. Thankfully, the blackout has him huffing around with a clipboard and pen, a wannabe scoutmaster.

"What an idiot," Kimmy says.

"Worse than an idiot," Anthony says.

"Well, you were a little harsh," Kimmy says.

"I'm sorry?"

"He wasn't saying: 'Do you live here, nonwhite person?'"

"Uh, he definitely was."

"No, he asked us the same question," Kimmy says, leading us through the parking lot. "Right, Alex?"

A dirt bike zips along the sidewalk, engine snarling, pedestrians hopping out of the way. The volunteer firefighters watch but do nothing.

"Well, no. He said to Anthony: Are you even *from* here? That's different," I say.

"That's one word," she says.

"Kimmy, when he asked if you live here, he was hoping for a yes," I say. "When he asked Anthony, he was definitely hoping for no."

Another firework screams into the sky and explodes into a flower of gray smoke. Then another.

"They emptied out Phantom Fireworks," Kimmy says. "Every night's the Fourth of July. It gets so dark, you know, it's the most beautiful thing." She pulls a half egg carton out of her bag. "Anyway, I just think that guy was an asshole to all of us, not just Anthony."

"Look," I say, and take a deep breath. "I'm generally pretty ignorant about this stuff, as Anthony often points out."

"I do not," he says.

"I spend a lot of time with Anthony and, you know, a lot of time not with Anthony. He gets treated differently. All the time. And when I'm with him, I get treated differently. And I'm a white girl."

"Not anymore," Anthony says, grinning. "Now you're a white guy."

Kimmy needs examples, so I tell her about the clerk who tailed us at the pharmacy. And the thrift store where Anthony had to check his backpack but I was free to walk around with mine. And the time our creepy neighbor Vic was checking me out. That's what I thought anyway. Anthony said Vic was pissed that a white girl was walking with a Black boy. *"Does Vic look at you like that when you're by yourself?"* Anthony said. No, Anthony, he doesn't.

"Well, yeah, that does sound crappy," Kimmy says, and shrugs. "I mean, I'm not—"

"See? Perfect example," Anthony says. "Black guy says he's singled out, and you're like: 'Nah, didn't happen.' White girl says it, and you believe her." He socks Kimmy on the shoulder. "I did appreciate '*Not a good look*,' though. That was funny as hell."

Wait. I know that shoulder punch. That's what Anthony does with me. He calls out my bull, and then reassures me that, hey, it's okay, we're still cool.

Jesus. What else does Anthony do that I don't notice?

⊶≡⊷

"There's a guy back here with dog food, supposedly," Anthony says, pointing across the parking lot.

Kimmy's off trading her eggs. I follow Anthony past some desperate tag sales. Books, silverware, and clothes seem superfluous, but a toaster, at this moment, is truly ridiculous. Then the real sales, the stuff you need—flashlights, canned food, toilet paper—but the prices are ridiculous. Twenty dollars for two candles.

Anthony stops at a blanket spread with first-aid kits, folding knives, and energy bars. A sign taped to a solar panel reads: CHARGE YOUR DEVICES, $8/ONE HOUR, $12/TWO HOURS. Three phones are plugged in. Why are people spending their scarce money to charge phones that don't work?

I don't miss my phone.

After Georgie's accident, my phone sat under the back seat of our car. I couldn't read another message, another person shrieking: *What happened?*

Two weeks later, my mom brought it in and left it by the charger in the bathroom. I saw it every day and didn't plug it in. Know why I finally turned it on? To play a game while I pooped. A stupid time-wasting game. I sat on the toilet and plugged the phone in. It started chirping. Message. Message. Message.

oh god, where's georgie?

Georgie ok?

Are you OK?

Oh god I heard about G, where are you?

Call me.

I watched them scroll by, frantic questions from those hellish hours when people from my school, my church, and my neighborhood all wondered: Did Georgie survive?

Is he gonna make it?

Someone told me your brother's in an ambulance. Where are you?

please tell me is everyone alright alex? you're scaring me.

Because he could have died.

Are you at the hospital?

Is your brother still unconscious?

If the woman with the turquoise jewelry didn't see him, or saw him ten minutes later, he'd be gone.

I slid onto the floor and sobbed.

Hope everybody's fine!

Let us know if we can do anything. Praying for you, Alex.

I dry-heaved, then wretched, spitting sour yellow phlegm into the toilet I'd meant to poop in.

Chirp, chirp, chirp.

Eighty-three chirps.

Eighty-three messages I will never answer.

<hr>

Anthony is having a ludicrous conversation with the kibbles guy.

"The era of the pet is over, son. If it don't give milk, meat, or eggs, destroy it and eat it." The man has glasses on a chain, thin gray hair, a tucked-in white polo shirt, and a pistol holstered on his khakis. A friendly hardware store manager with a sidearm. "What do you think this is—a blackout?" He picks up a sandwich and bites it. Bread's hard to find. He could probably get ten dollars for that sandwich.

"Is that a trick question? It's definitely a blackout." Anthony's enjoying this.

"This is a reckoning. Here." He puts on reading glasses and pulls out a white binder: BLACK SKY: THE RECKONING.

Anthony flips through the binder. CURRENCY COLLAPSE AND THE RISE OF PRECIOUS METALS is followed by PILE OF CRAP: THE SEWAGE CRISIS IN HIGH-DENSITY SETTLEMENTS. "Just to be clear, kibbles is a no?"

"Why do you think the power went out?" the guy says. He takes a huge bite, crumbs falling on his khakis.

I miss bread.

"Well, some people with special radios say the government's telling everyone it was solar flares."

It's true. People with shortwave radios and generators say there's announcements that "massive solar storms" knocked out the power grid. No one I know has heard it.

"And who do you think broadcast that?" The guy looks at us over his glasses, a jaded teacher tutoring thick-headed kids.

"It was a government broadcast, so, I dunno, the government?" Anthony says.

"Exactly."

"Oh. Right." Anthony's deadpan is spot-on. Am I the only person who finds that attractive? Good.

"And if I wanna measure solar flares," the guy says, "I need telescopes and special detectors, right? All of that stopped working as soon as the blackout hit, so who exactly was measuring these flares?"

"Well, that's—"

"Who has the most to lose here?" His questions are speeding up.

"Other than my puppies?"

"You know what the Nazis told people walking to the gas chambers?"

"Okay, that feels like a swerve."

"They said: 'Don't worry, these are showers. Delousing stations. No need to panic.'"

A woman in khakis, a powder-blue sweatshirt, and bright-white sneakers steps out of the truck. Cheerful co-owner of the hardware store, also armed.

"Hey, Annie, I got two kids here hoping this quote-unquote 'blackout' ends tomorrow." This will prove to be, of course, not far off. "What should I tell em?"

"Mornin." Annie unwraps a sandwich. Damn, these people are bread millionaires. "Here's what I say to young people: That first phase of your life, everything before now, that's over."

Right. I'd love that, actually. Wipe it clean.

"This is a new time, and you need to reset. I don't think we're ever going back to the way things were," she says.

"Yes," I say. This shut-in is ready for a reset.

"That means being prepared. Here, I have a little something for you." She digs through a plastic bin as I hover.

Their truck has a green-and-blue bumper sticker: MY GRAND-SON IS A STAR AT STARWOOD ELEMENTARY.

She hands me a Ziploc. "In here, you've got matches, bandages, water purification tablets, and a whistle."

"Thanks," I say. "How old's your grandson?"

"Eleven. And we have two granddaughters, twelve and fifteen." The crucifix on her necklace gets caught on the bin handle, and she delicately unhooks it. "They're far away, unfortunately. Virginia."

"But they know to come here," the man calls from his folding chair.

"Well, I don't know how they would, Ron," Annie says. "Where are they gonna get gas?"

"I told him to keep a reserve."

"Well, he didn't."

Ron turns to look at her. "Did he tell you that?"

"You know he didn't."

"Then he's a damn fool, and he deserves whatever comes to him."

"Ron, please." Her mouth strains into a smile. She says quietly to me, "The grandkids don't deserve it."

"They don't deserve a goddamn idiot for a father either, but they got one," Ron says.

"My gosh, Ron. How can you say that?" Her face tightens into a mask of worry, the supple clay turned dry and crumbly. "They can't make it through this alone—I don't care how prepped they are. And why should they? We all need other people. Everybody needs . . ." She pauses.

What? What does everybody need?

"Everybody," she says.

CHAPTER FIVE

"That was scary," Anthony says. We're heading back toward the firefighters, looking for Kimmy.

"They seemed nice," I say.

"No, The Reckoning. Turns out, after we eat our dogs, there's gonna be food riots and then water riots."

We step aside for a man in overalls pulling a kid's wagon with canned beans, a five-gallon jug of water, and a stack of magazines. Party in a cart.

"I liked what she said, though," I say. "It's a new beginning. We can't go back to the old messed-up world."

I open my backpack to put the day kit in. My now-frivolous-seeming supplies include a notebook, markers, a deck of cards, and my brother's harmonica. That actually is—or was—an emergency item, the fallback to get Georgie's attention when he wouldn't listen. Maybe I should join the banjo player and earn some pennies.

"Can I at least have a working refrigerator?" Anthony says.

"That's her point. Don't think about what's missing, think about what's possible now."

We pass folding chairs under a canopy, with a sign saying *Blackout Sobriety Meeting*. The double meaning is a joke, right?

"And she's right. We shouldn't all be in our separate little houses," I say.

"Says the shut-in."

"Seriously. We should come together more."

"I love that you meet those survivalists and go: 'Man, we should all just live together in harmony.' I'm pretty sure that's not what they meant."

"It's what she meant. Everybody needs everybody."

"That's easy to say when you're carrying a pistol."

"Come on, if we wanted to, our families could live together."

"Alex, I can barely get you to leave your bedroom. Are you seriously claiming you want to share a house with my crazy family?"

"You don't understand me."

"Kinda think I do."

"No, you have no idea."

"Actually, I'm pretty sure I know you better than anyone does."

"Okay, then: Why am I stuck in my room?"

"Uh. Cause you don't wanna go outside?"

"No. I desperately want to go out."

"Oh. All right. I give up. Why?"

"I don't know."

"Wait, that was an actual question?"

"Yup."

"So you were right about six," Anthony says.

"Six what?"

"Six. Underneath it all, you feel like you're broken and you don't know why."

The previously screaming toddler walks by with her mom, grinning and trailing chunks of crumb cake.

"It would be hilarious," Anthony says. "'*Did you hear? Anthony and Alex live together.*' People are already curious."

"What do you mean?"

"'*Oh, you two are together all the time. What's going on?*'"

"People ask you that? What do you say?"

"I tell em the truth," he says. "I say I'm having your baby."

"Bet that calms them down."

"Come on, remember Harvest Day?" It's a fair and music festival every September. "We sat way up in the bleachers, eating corndogs and listening to that surprisingly good country band."

"Can't believe you liked them," I say.

"Shockingly, people see that and assume we're a couple."

"Who's even noticing us?"

"A white girl with a Black guy? I'm gonna say: most people."

"I must be embarrassing for you."

"Absolutely not," he says. "You're my favorite person, outside my family."

"Watch out, pretty soon I might be inside your family."

"It does affect things, though."

"Cause I'm blocking the ladies."

"Hundreds."

"Well, don't worry, you're not keeping me from other people. No one's interested."

"Mm, you might be surprised. People ask."

"About me? Who?"

"Swore I wouldn't tell."

"But I'm your favorite person outside your family."

"Good point. Okay, but you didn't hear it from me."

"You are the only person I talk to, though," I say.

"Marla Santoro asked about you, quote, *'for someone else.'* Pretty sure she likes you." Wow. "And Greg What's-His-Face. The Evangelical kid."

"Greg Dooley?"

"Yeah, he wanted to invite you to a cookout."

"Oh my god. Greg. His church donated a stove to us, and he just hung around. I remember thinking: 'Thanks for the stove. Why are you still here?'"

Kimmy is at the Board, her fingers pinning the quivering papers against the weathered bricks.

"Yeah, you are pretty clueless," Anthony says.

"Cause I don't know Greg Dooley likes me?"

Anthony checks his card on the MESSAGES wall. "You don't know a lot of things." He wanders down the Board, looking at other notes.

I read Anthony's card, which is right above a purple poster with a birthday message.

ANTHONY SAYLOR SEEKS INFORMATION ABOUT HIS MOTHER, LT. FIRST CLASS ELEANOR SAYLOR, USN, DEPLOYED ON USS HIGGINS, PART OF THE USS NIMITZ CARRIER STRIKE GROUP 11 IN THE PACIFIC. ANY INFORMATION ON HER, HER SHIP, OR THE NIMITZ MUCH APPRECIATED!

The exclamation point is heartbreaking.

And he checked it. He put it up twenty minutes ago, and he went back to see if anyone answered.

My god, Anthony.

I *was* right about six.

<hr />

We follow a dirt road to a path winding up into the woods, a shortcut to Bethany, Kimmy promises.

"I can't believe you and my brother go to the same school," I say.

"Yeah, what grade is he?" Kimmy says. She hops smoothly across a fallen tree trunk.

I lumber up and over. "Ninth, officially, but he's an IE kid." Individualized education. "Special needs."

"Oh, rad," she says.

I appreciate when people are nice about disability. "*Rad*" is a perfectly decent response.

"His name's George Waters. Or Georgie," I say. She shakes her head. "Short hair. He waves his hands over his head a lot." That detail sometimes jogs people's memory.

"Oh, wait, the music dude?"

"Maybe."

"I'm in choir, and, you know, nobody really likes our concerts, but there's this one kid, he's just way into it, waves his arms like this." She does a darn good Georgie imitation.

"That's him!"

"He's fabulous. He pumps us up, makes us sing out."

Georgie is known. By a Normie. It's beautiful and a little sad.

I know nothing about Georgie's life at Harrison. How is that possible? How does Kimmy know more than I do?

"I'm curious how you even have school in the blackout," Anthony says.

"It's chaotic," Kimmy says. "The school closed at first, because of fire laws."

"Same at our school," he says.

Our district mails out "enrichment assignments," but they aren't graded. People in our town assume that, at a certain point, our district's gonna say: *Screw it. We're opening the schools.*

Fire laws don't matter. But how long do you wait? How bad does it have to get before you say *screw it?* That's the blackout question.

Maybe that's the life question. My life question.

"Then they set up classes in the gym with all the doors open." Kimmy waves her hand to clear the spider strands crossing the trail. "But the fire marshal said it was still dangerous, so we had these endless fire drills. My Spanish teacher gave up and started having class outside. I haven't been this week, so I don't know what's happening now."

I step around a nest of broken bottles, foil labels molting off the green glass.

Screw it.

"Kimmy, I want to go to Harrison," I say.

"Yeah, it's not a bad school. Lotta cool people."

"No, I want to go now. I want to see if my brother's there. Is it far?"

"Fifteen minutes. I could take you."

If Georgie's that close, I need to see him.

"We should probably keep going to Bethany," Anthony says.

"It's fifteen minutes," I say.

"You're the one who said we'll be running around lost at sundown."

"I also said I'm fine with that." I need to see Georgie. I need him to see me shaved, out, badass.

"Georgie seems like a big variable to add to this trip." Anthony senses he's being hornswaggled.

Tough.

"Maybe he's not even there," I say. "And if he is, we'll give him a hug, and I'll get him to make a drawing for my mom. That'll calm her down when we stagger home in the dark."

We're climbing now, rocks jutting out of a steep slope, forking paths abandoned when they got worn too smooth.

"Why don't we visit him at his foster family tomorrow? I'll go with you," Anthony says.

"They're not his foster family."

"Oh, right, his, um . . . ," Anthony says.

"Outplacement for special needs. It's different. Happens all the time." I can call them his fosters, but no one else can.

"Ohh, I see how it is," Anthony says. "You don't wanna go to their house. That's why you wanna visit him at school."

"Shut up."

"You don't wanna deal with those people."

"Shut *up*."

"Because I'm right."

"Because you're a jerk."

"And I'm right."

"Of course you're right. Jerk."

"Damn. You two are like twins," Kimmy says. "You finish each other's sentences."

"No," Anthony starts, "we—"

"Don't," I say.

Kimmy laughs. "It's eerie."

My relationship with Georgie's emergency host family is complex. I resent them in a completely unjustified and completely passionate way. But when I visit them, I have to act grateful and compliant. Plus they have an autistic son, Mason, who's way "higher-functioning" than Georgie, a fact they attribute to their brilliant parenting. *We taught Mason how to do his dishes. Maybe Mason can help Georgie pick out clothes and get dressed.*

So, yes, I'd much rather visit Georgie at school, meet his teachers and classmates. I was close with all of Georgie's teachers at his old charter school for learning differences. There was Ms. Stephanie, who got the kids to shake and jump whenever the room got out of control. And Mr. Tim, who was so beautifully slow, never rushing or pushing. I watched him spend ten minutes once with Georgie setting up five plates for a birthday party.

I miss them. Losing Georgie meant I lost touch with all of that, the wild, gorgeous energy of those classrooms.

Those rooms! That universe!

There is another world that's parallel to the Normie world. It's the Nation of Difference, a secret country inside our country. Once you step inside the Nation, you see it everywhere. That van of adults at the rest stop. The elderly woman walking her middle-aged son around the park. The school bus that waits for five minutes in front of a house.

Mostly, the world of difference hides. Normies don't want to look at bodies that aren't straight and symmetrical or hear voices that moan or bark. They don't like seeing teenagers who wear diapers, adults who drool. The Nation of Difference spends a stupid amount of effort on this: Don't upset the Normies.

The park by our old house was next to a school for kids with cerebral palsy. A tall row of hedges kept the CP kids' playground out of view. And that hedge? It was inside the school fence. The Normies didn't have to wall it off; the school did it for them.

The Nation of Difference has babies and old folks and everything in between. And the Nation has parents, so many parents, heartbroken ones, grateful ones, but always, goddamn *always* humbled. Think you got everything figured out? Think your money or your hard work or your god can handle any situation? Raise a baby with a traumatic brain injury and you'll get over yourself real quick.

The Nation of Difference has subcultures, leaders, fights, rivalries, and hierarchies. There are radsters and activists, people with Down syndrome who demand to make their own decisions, manage their own care, get married. You meet extraordinary Normies, too. There is this one unbelievable trait I've only seen in the Nation: People are genuinely comfortable with whatever another human being is like. Plenty of folks talk about acceptance and getting along with people different from you, but it's usually a narrow range. We should accept people who are exactly like us except they speak a different language or follow a different religion. But what about a three-hundred-pound woman who cackles and hugs everyone she meets? Or that young woman with the torqued spine, her chin twisting left as she gurgles? Leigh, one of Georgie's occupational therapists, came with us to the state fair. And when that exact young woman came by in a wheelchair, drooling and moaning, Leigh knelt down, got quiet, smiled, and . . . stayed. She didn't need it to go a certain way, didn't need to prove she was a good Normie. No pity, no fear. Leigh was present.

Nothing happened for a long time.

"She doesn't speak," the girl's mom said apologetically.

Leigh nodded but didn't look away from the girl. Finally, the girl's clenched hand wobbled toward a big-eyed stuffed monkey in her lap.

"I like the monkey," Leigh said.

Then another epic silence. And the girl started laughing, a loud, wheezing giggle, the kind of sound that freaks out most Normies.

Leigh stayed.

Who can do that? People who live in the Nation of Difference. People like Leigh made me realize every adult I'd ever met was (a) impatient, (b) judgmental, and (c) anxious as hell. I wasn't like her. I was mortified when Georgie lay down in the middle of a store. I was terrified he might temper in the doctor's office.

But after spending time in the Nation, it all started to seem arbitrary. Why not listen to the same song forty times in a row?

Why is it "normal" to listen to forty different songs? Looking someone in the eye and shaking their hand is one way to greet a person. But so is moving to the farthest corner of the room and tilting your head back and forth. "*Weird means feared*," Leigh used to say. We call a thing weird when it brings up something we're scared of.

The Nation is the real world. Normies live in a gated cognitive community, mowing their lawns and acting like everything's fine. But late at night, even us Normies panic that someone might find out what we're really like, how strange we are, and how much effort it takes to keep up appearances.

The radical truth of the Nation is: We are all strange. And we are all going to be okay.

You're not like everybody else. But neither is everybody else.

"My god." Anthony, way ahead, stops at the crest of a hill.

"Wow." Kimmy sounds surprised, too.

I jog to catch up, huffing up the muddy slope. And I see them. All of them.

Class after class of Harrison High students sit outside in perfect rows. Room boundaries are painted on the grass like football field lines. Hallways, offices, everything is perfectly aligned and gridded, as if a tornado carried away the walls and left behind the school blueprint, the map.

"Man, they moved everybody outside. Good thing it's a nice day," Kimmy says.

A few bodies move through the grid, turning pretend corners down pretend hallways. Off to the right, students run lazy laps around a real track.

"It's beautiful," I say.

"From over here," Kimmy says. "I had a couple classes outside last week, and the sun was brutal."

A golf cart zips by the actual school building, a stack of folding chairs rattling on the back.

We're mesmerized. The classes aren't full, maybe fifteen or twenty kids in each, but they are orderly, ranks of soldiers, a seated marching band.

A whistle blows. We turn, and so do many of the students, and watch the gym teacher wave the runners over.

Silence.

A breeze troubles the pale leaves above our heads and blows papers and wrappers across the grass, which, in contrast to the orderly classrooms, is trashed like a field after a music festival.

Someone hammers a bell twice, and the students burst into motion.

"Whoa," Anthony whispers.

It's an ant farm. Kids pick up backpacks and file out through door-sized breaks in the lines. They mostly stay in bounds, though some hustle around the edges, pop through "walls." And they all talk at once. It's a gentle roar, like an ocean, piercing high notes of laughter over throaty yells.

We watch the bodies course through the hallway arteries, finding new rooms, new chairs. The bell rings twice; students scurry into seats.

Silence again.

"I could watch this all day," Anthony says.

Teachers pass out papers, write on whiteboards.

"We got work to do," I say. "Come on."

"I can't go any closer." Kimmy says. "Might get grabbed." She reaches into her bag. "Hey, if phones ever come back, you guys should call me." She says "you guys" but hands the slip of paper, where she has already written her number, to Anthony. How bout that?

Don't say anything, Alex. Don't block the hundreds of ladies.

"Let us know when you finish digging that pool," Anthony says.

"Definitely." Kimmy turns to me. "Say hi to that fabulous brother of yours."

"If they let me see him," I say.

"Why wouldn't they?"

Right. I assume everybody knows my family's story. That's one reason I stay home. It's refreshing to remember that not everyone's judging me all the time. I bet if I started telling it, though, Kimmy would go: *Oh yeah, I heard about that.* Best to keep it vague.

"Long story," I say.

Let Kimmy imagine something. I guarantee you it won't be as bad as the truth.

⋘━━━━⋙

When Georgie was dragged out of Long Lake a year ago, we became Undeserving. The worst. The family who neglected and harmed their disabled boy.

People were nice to my face, mostly—"I'm so sorry to hear about your brother. Is he going to be okay?"—but they shifted.

The charity went away, and it was more than I realized. Our neighbors and community and church weren't just helping Georgie; some of those gift cards turned into clothes for me and Mom or paid my phone bill when money was tight. My bedroom set was donated by J&R Home Furnishings for my brother's room. It never seemed strange that I had it until Georgie was gone.

Maybe we were the worst. Did we use him to get more stuff, nicer stuff? Were we the beggars pushing our crippled child out front?

My mom's jobs were mostly charity, too. Secretary in the church office, after-school coordinator at a Christian school, and arcade supervisor at the community college. Jobs she could show up for or not, jobs that always paid her full hours even when she spent half her time at Georgie's doctor's appointments, Georgie's speech therapy, or just Georgie's rough week.

The jobs went away. Maybe Mom quit, maybe they fired her. All I know is she was home all the time.

We unraveled. We became ragged, unstructured. Mom slept. She cried. She talked about money problems, how we'd have to move, how nobody understood our situation.

But maybe they did. Maybe they understood us in the creepy, outraged way you understand someone who hustles you. They were ashamed of us, and for us. They looked away because we reminded them of a tragedy, and because we reminded them of how they'd tried, how they'd done their part, and, hey, if that family can't even keep an eye on the kid . . .

Much as I used to resent people's pity, I sure miss it.

Mrs. Cleary, our neighbor, used to drop off homemade jam and have her guy rake our leaves. Now she hustles away when she sees me.

I hate how much that matters to me.

Anthony and I stumble-run down the steep hill. A wall of blue-and-white porta-potties comes into view in the school parking lot. There are cars in the lot, not many, and a jumble of bicycles. An art class sits cross-legged on real bleachers, sketch boards in their laps, squinting at their wall-less school.

Closer now, I can make out individuals. A hulking kid spins a pen around his thick hand. A girl in an army jacket and shimmery skirt chews her pinkie and stares at someone in a different class. The wind blows kids' hair across their faces; they push it away and go back to reading and writing intently. Some notice as we walk past the real building toward the pretend building. A teacher carrying a trash can hustles by.

"Thanks for doing this," I say.

"Thanks for doing this whole trip."

"I'll make it quick."

He nods. "No, you won't."

"Dammit, how do you know everything?"

"Twins."

"We are eerie," I say.

"Not as eerie as this."

Up close, it's a labyrinth, a corn maze without corn. As we walk by, rows of chairs line up straight and then swing, like crops in a field. We pass the "cafeteria," a meager buffet of rolls, chips, and fruit, ready for the lunch bell. We enter the imaginary building.

"Did you feel that?" I say.

"What?" Anthony says.

"We're inside now. It's different."

A tense lady runs up, freckles, hair tight around her head, wearing a blue blazer over a green dress. "Stop right there," she shout-whispers. "Visitors must use the front door."

Don't piss off the staff, Alex. Make nice, and see if Georgie's here.

"Sorry," I say, and we turn back toward the real building, the one with a door.

"No, the *new* front door." She points across the grass, the gold buttons on her blazer cuffs catching the sun. "Between the flags. You need to go outside and walk around."

"Outside," Anthony repeats.

"Yes, do you realize where you're standing?"

"Um. Outside," Anthony says.

"In the supply room." She points at a line on the grass, the crumbly white powder of a baseball foul line.

"Where are the supplies?" Uh-oh. Anthony's doing that thing where he asks innocent questions.

"The supplies are in the physical building. Obviously."

Physical building. Great phrase. This is the *mental building*, the *emotional building*.

"But you have a supply room out here?" he says.

"We keep everything as it was, where it was. Otherwise, people get lost and go to the wrong class."

I'm enjoying Anthony's routine, but it's not going to help us see Georgie. "Great," I say. "We should go that way?"

"No, you need to walk around."

"Around where?" I'm genuinely confused.

"You wouldn't walk through a wall at the physical school, would you?"

"If I could, yeah," Anthony says.

A napkin blows by, the flimsy kind you get in pizzerias, and she pins it under her black ankle boot. "I will ask you, as visitors, to please respect our agreements."

Anthony nods slowly. He's not done. "You mean the chalk lines."

"Our community agreements."

"Pretty sure it's chalk."

"Why are you here?" She turns to me.

"I'm here for my brother," I say. "I'm Alex."

"Hello, Alex. I'm Ms. Wapner, the vice principal. I'll walk you to the office, but please keep your voices down." She doesn't ask Anthony's name. Just saying.

We pass classrooms, inches away from students working. I hear the fluttery tap and scratch of pencil on paper.

I need Ms. Wapner on my side if I want to see Georgie. If he's even here. "This is amazing," I whisper.

"Mm-hmm." She nods, hustling along a hall of worn-down grass. She smells good, like flowers and spice. Most of us don't. Bathing in cold water and washing clothes by hand are too darn hard.

"How do you get the kids to be so good?"

"They're incredible, aren't they?" she whispers. "We had to teach them not to talk through walls or socialize across classrooms. Now they don't even see the other classes. Isn't that magic?" Not true. Lots of kids are catching my eye as we hustle past. "Look." She points at a large rectangle with THE PATIO scrawled in plump orange graffiti letters on the grass. "The seniors re-created their hangout space. They come here during free periods and lunch and do exactly what they did at the old

Patio." Two kids reading books look up at us. "Carry on." She leads us away and whispers, "They completely get it."

We pass a water cooler surrounded by paper cups and mud. Our shoes slurp in the wet grass, the smell of soil and springtime.

"What are they doing in class? It's so quiet."

"Practice exams for our statewide assessments. We're very fortunate that we had them on hand. No computers needed, just a pencil, and everyone has to be silent. It's perfect, right?"

We cross a dotted line. MAIN OFFICE ENTER HERE is painted on the grass, clover, and unopened dandelions, sprayed ghostly white. Three adults and two kids cluster by the front desk, next to an easel with a whiteboard:

THURSDAY MAY 15

SCHOOL IS OPEN

REMEMBER YOUR SUNSCREEN!

IN THE EVENT OF RAIN, STUDENTS WILL MOVE TO THE

GYMNASIUM (9TH AND 10TH GRADE) AND CAFETERIA

(11TH AND 12TH GRADE)

TODAY'S LUNCH: BUILD-YOUR-OWN SANDWICHES, FRUIT, AND

COOKIES (DONATED BY THE JAYCEES)

WE APPRECIATE YOUR PATIENCE AS WE WORK

TOGETHER THROUGH THIS EMERGENCY!

"Shauna, this young man is here to pick up his brother."

That's not what I meant. I'm just here to see him. But okay.

"Uh, girl, actually," I say.

"Sorry, he's picking up his sister."

"No, I'm a girl. I'm here for my brother."

"So sorry."

"It's fine." It really is. I only correct her because we are in Official World, and I don't want to mess this up.

"Be with you in a moment," says Shauna, a lady with a pink blouse and gray blazer. All these blazers. Her silver glasses are perched on either a wig or some intensely permed hair.

A breeze ruffles the papers, all of them weighed down by rocks or books. Right, that's why there's trash in the field. The wind grabs anything that's not pinned down.

"Wait, are we picking up Georgie?" Anthony says.

"No, she misunderstood me."

"Phew." He looks around. "This is wild."

"Which part?"

"Everyone's pretending we're in an office, and it's working. I'm starting to believe it."

It is surreal. Two potted palms sit on the grass by the main desk, houseplants that escaped to the wild.

"Scuse me." Anthony waves at another woman. "Can I make a call?" He points at the black telephone on the desk, a grid of buttons and extensions.

"Sorry, that doesn't work." The woman smiles.

"Right, of course. Duh." Anthony shrugs at a kid who's watching him. "Who was I gonna call anyway? So stupid."

"Are you authorized to pick up your brother?" Shauna opens a filing cabinet and drops her glasses to her nose.

"Uh, yeah. I think so."

"What's his name?"

"George Waters."

"Waters, Waters." She flips through the files.

"Can I ask: Do you move all this inside at night?" Anthony says.

"Oh, gosh no. We cover it with plastic. Things do tend to be a little wet in the morning with all the dew. Here we go. Waters. And your name?"

"Alexandra Waters."

"I don't see you listed." Her nostril has a bump of flesh hanging down, a runny-nose stalactite.

The vice principal is back. "Shauna, did anyone come about the trash?"

"Not yet, no." Shauna pulls out the WATERS, GEORGE file and opens it on the desk. "Now, some of our paper files are not as complete as the digital records, but I don't see an authorization for George Waters' sister."

"Did you say George Waters?" the vice principal says.

"Yes," Shauna says. "This is George's sister, and—"

"You're his sister?"

I nod.

"Biological sister?"

I nod.

"We cannot release him to you."

"Oh," says Shauna. "Is there—"

"I'm family," I say.

The vice principal takes a deep breath and opens Georgie's file. I wait. She taps a silver nail on the desk. Behind us, a porta-potty door thuds closed.

"I'm sorry. George is picked up by his caretakers. That is the only way he leaves our school."

"Oh, *that* George?" Shauna says, lighting up. "What a dear, always makes me laugh. You know, he loves the outdoor classroom, thinks it's a hoot."

"I don't need to pick him up. I just want to see him," I say.

The vice principal shuts the folder. "That's not an option, Miss Waters."

A golf cart speeds across the parking lot, the low electric hum getting fainter.

"Can't I just visit him for a minute? In his class?" Dammit.

I shouldn't have gone along with it when she said I was picking him up. I asked for too much.

Then she says it. "The school was notified by Child Protective Services that the Boyers have custody of Georgie."

Other people stop talking and stare.

"I am allowed to see him," I say. Which is true. CPS wants us to visit Georgie as much as possible. Before the blackout, I was at the Boyers' house twice a week, sometimes more.

"During school hours, Georgie is our responsibility, and we cannot hand him over to—"

"Don't call him that."

"I'm sorry?"

"Don't call him Georgie."

"We cannot let George Waters leave school with someone who is not only unauthorized but also . . . specifically . . ." Her hands loop in the air: *You know what I mean.*

Everyone's watching.

"Specifically what?" I say.

I'm panting, my nostrils flaring and pinched like a horse's.

"Say it," I whisper. Or maybe I just think it.

Say it, goddammit.

After Georgie's accident last May, my mom spent six nights in the hospital with him. She doesn't think she did. In her mind, she tucked me in, went to stay with Georgie, then came home at sunrise to make me breakfast. That happened once, and she was so exhausted she slept the whole next day.

I figured out food and went back to school eventually. Nothing new. I knew how to cook, clean up, and get myself to bed, because life with Georgie meant everybody was a grown-up.

But I wasn't prepared for Arleen. Chatty, big-eyed Arleen, with her ID badge on a gold necklace and her black cardigan down to her knees.

She came on a sunny Friday afternoon, her frosted blond hair bouncing as she nodded her way into the house. I let Arleen and her coworker in.

Arleen from Child Protective Services.

"We're here to make sure your brother will be safe and smiling once he leaves the hospital."

Here's the problem: I was used to making our situation seem hard, making people feel good about paying our gas bill or fixing the porch steps. *"It's not easy,"* I'd say. *"But with God's help and this amazing community, we make it work."*

I was used to talking about our needs and our problems because pitiers want sob stories. Arleen's questions ambushed me. While my mom was interviewed at the kitchen table by the other woman, I took Arleen through the house—actually she led me—her eyes scanning each room before landing back on me with a smile. Her charm bracelet jangled as she wrote on her clear plastic clipboard. She tossed offhand questions while she took pictures of Georgie's broken dresser and his door with no doorknob.

"Do you think Georgie would do better with more people around, trained people?"

"God, yes. That would make a huge difference."

"Are you ever solely in charge of Georgie?"

"All the time."

"That must be hard."

"I'm used to it."

"You probably don't have any training in dealing with special needs children."

"I figured it out. You learn fast. Trial and error."

"Does Georgie ever get hurt?"

"He has tempers sometimes."

"So he has gotten hurt?"

"He put his hand through the kitchen window once. Right there. You can still see the broken glass."

"Did you take him to the emergency room?"

"I bandaged him up. He was fine."

"Your mother wasn't home? That must have been a lot for you to handle."

Her frowning nod looked like the sympathy that usually turns into donations and offers of assistance.

Why didn't I figure it out? She wasn't there to help; she was there to condemn. The photos she took weren't of our needs; they were of our sins.

Three days later, my mom stormed upstairs, panting. "What did you tell them? What did you say?"

The letter laid out all the risks to Georgie's well-being if he remained "in his present home with his mother and sister."

It described the accident at Long Lake, of course, the primary sign that Georgie was too much for us, too free to roam, too unprotected. But there were other incidents, things Arleen had coaxed out of me, quotes from a "family member," damning assessments of the state of our house.

"You lost Georgie! You gave him away!" my mom wailed, the letter crushed in her fist.

These are two sentences I will never forget. They sing in my head.

You lost *Geor*gie.

You *gave* him a*way.*

The refrain collapses to a rhythm, an endless accusing loop.

Da-duh *da*-duh.

Duh-*da* duh-duh-*da.*

And then Arleen's trick question, and the one word I'll regret forever. I still flush every time I remember it.

"Sounds like it's a lot for you to be responsible for your brother after school." Arleen frowns and nods in Georgie's room, clipboard clutched to her chest. "Would it be better if other people helped with that? What if you could be in charge of your brother when it was a good time for you, but not all the time? Would that be better for everybody?"

I pictured babysitters at the house, playing with Georgie, clearing the sink of dishes, while I did homework or read a book.

"Yes. Definitely."

At the bottom of Arleen's letter: *Subject's sister confirmed she is unable to adequately care for the Subject, and that outplacement would benefit the entire family.*

"Why didn't you tell me?!" Mom shouted. "Why didn't you say you want Georgie out of the house?!"

Because I don't. I never said that. I never *meant* that.

My mom fought and talked to lawyers. She tried to get my dad to petition for custody, but he was mostly out of state and unable or unwilling to step up. In the end, she signed, agreeing to the "set of facts" that made "immediate outplacement in the Subject's best interest."

And we fell.

I came home from school, and Georgie wasn't there. I didn't have to fix him Triscuits with cherry jam. We didn't battle over watching his Disney movie for the nine hundredth time.

Is this better for me, Arleen?

No.

That's the word I want to go back and throw at her. I am cartoon tantrum, a quivering NO flying out of my mouth, knocking over chairs and blowing Arleen's curly hair straight.

No, Arleen.

It's much, much worse.

⸻

"I'm sorry?" Ms. Wapner blinks at me.

"Say. It." I spit the words.

She clears her throat and reads from the file. "The Waters family has been ruled unfit to provide George Waters with proper care, appropriate supervision, or a stable, safe home environment."

Shauna leans away like I'm contagious.

"You have no idea," I say.

"These are not my words. I am simply—"

"You have no idea!"

"Alex, come on." Anthony steps between me and Ms. Wapner, facing me, head down.

"You don't know my family!" I shout.

"Miss, that tone of voice is not permitted inside our school—"

"We're not in a school." I push past Anthony.

The vice principal walks around the desk, right up in my face. She's tall, and her breath smells like fruit gum. "You are on district property, and I am asking you to leave. Do you need to be escorted out?"

"Where's my brother?!" This isn't me. I don't yell at adults. I do now.

She grips my shoulder and guides me firmly toward the invisible door. "I understand you're upset, Miss Waters, but I cannot help you."

Even as I struggle, I notice the double dimples around her mouth, quotation marks that deepen when she speaks.

"I want my brother." I shove her away. I will go right through this woman to get to Georgie.

"Okay, Al, let's go." Anthony grabs my wrist—apparently, I'm reaching toward the vice principal—and pivots me away.

"This behavior"—she points a manicured finger at me but talks to Shauna—"is exactly why we are charged with protecting Georgie."

I stumble as Anthony herds me out.

"Don't call him Georgie!" I yell. Anthony has me halfway to the parking lot. "Get off," I growl, and spin away.

I'm leaving, but not politely. I stomp through a wall, across a pretend hallway, through a pretend science class. "There's no school here!" I yell to everyone and no one.

"Scuse us. Sorry, just passing through." Anthony trails behind me, apologizing.

"You're sitting in a field!"

Anthony catches up and whispers, "Gosh, you're right, this *is* a field. I didn't notice till you mentioned it."

"Goddamn her!" I'm not whispering. "She could have been nice about it. She could have—"

"Hey!" a teacher barks. "Do not walk through my room." She puts a hand up to block me.

I swat her hand away. "Don't touch me!"

She recoils, hides behind two students. One giggles, the other stares, her open mouth showing colored braces, aqua on top and pink on the bottom.

I run out through the cafeteria and the supply room. Now we'll trudge on to Bethany, miles of humiliation, hours to stew over what the vice principal said. *Unfit.* And the way they all looked at me.

They don't know, goddammit.

I want a bullhorn. I want to shout this school to a standstill. I want to tell Georgie and the world I'm here.

Anything for a microphone. Or a drum.

Or a harmonica.

I dig through my backpack. The day kit has spilled, and underneath Band-Aids and water purification tablets, I find it.

It's dented on the high end where Georgie bit it.

I raise it to my lips.

Blow-blow-suck. The stupid non-song I play for Georgie.

Blow-blow-suck. He would wave his arms and jump, an arched-back, frozen leap, half ecstasy and half worry.

Blow-blow-suck. Louder. I scan the crowd.

Blow-blow-suck. I run sideways, cause that's how you find Georgie. Is that him? No, just a kid staring.

Blow-blow-suck. There he is! Hands in the air, Georgie tilts his head, trying to locate the sound.

Blow-blow-suck. Georgie walks through a wall. He knocks into a desk. *Blow-blow-suck.* Georgie's running. One of his IE teachers takes off after him, but Georgie is fast. Gloriously, troublingly, can't-catch-me fast.

Blow-blow-suck.

Kids stare as Georgie smashes through wall after wall, cinder blocks turned to powder, windows shattering. The cafeteria crumbles, the gymnasium collapses. He thumps across the baseball field, kicking up infield dirt, while I *blow-blow-suck*, his heavy footed, lurching stride somehow always accelerating. His teacher yells and falls farther behind.

I'm running too, leading Georgie up over the hill.

My sweaty brother howls and waves his arms as he runs past me, past the harmonica, down the hill.

Picture the cartoon trail of dust as he streams through woods, across farms, over the horizon.

Run, Georgie.

Get out.

CHAPTER SIX

I went back to school a week after the accident and was hit by a confusing wave of attention. A poster-sized card in my Literature class shouted: *Welcome back, Alexandra!* As if I'd gone on a trip.

Breathless questions in the minutes before class: "Ohmygod, Alex, did your brother wake up?"

Then the story got around. Arleen, the investigation, Child Protective Services. Georgie didn't come home; he went to stay with the Boyers. There was an article in the goddamn *Valley Sun*, our weekly so-called newspaper that's mostly photos of softball teams and stories about zoning meetings: REPORT CLEARS PARK STAFF IN NEAR DROWNING. The gist was: Don't blame the staff, blame the family. "Family members supervising the disabled victim were momentarily distracted, allowing the child to enter the lake unseen."

The hugs and cards went away. And I went away. I skipped lunch to work in the library, slipped into every class as the bell rang and left the second it ended. Within a week, I was invisible.

People appreciated it, I think. It was all too confusing, no one knew what to say or what to feel. People had rallied around Georgie, partly because my mom's a shrewd operator, but mostly because people care. They saw a disabled kid with a single mom, and they stepped up, and that's beautiful. As much as I moan about the BS people put on disability, a lot of folks in Little Falls showed up.

Then the kid gets hurt, nearly dies.

Then the family gets blamed for it.

It's jarring. People want to rise up and protect Georgie, but from what? His mom and sister? Jesus. I'd hate to be my friend in that moment. How do you even begin to sort through it?

So I think I can speak for all of us when I say: Alex needed to disappear. And I did. Everybody let me, and everybody felt better for it.

I had a non-optional session with the counselor, Mr. Gonsalves. Kids pronounced his name *Gonzalez* and tried speaking Spanish to him, which, being Brazilian, he didn't. He coached a cycling team, something no one here knew was a sport, and they did insanely long rides, fifty miles, seventy miles. He was known for talking tough kids off the ledge, back into class, and sometimes onto a bike.

He orbited school events, drifting through the cafeteria, hovering at dismissal, his round face looking a little lost but somehow always finding this boy or that girl and sharing a whispered exchange. He was good with bad kids. I guess now I qualified.

"Miss Alexandra. I'm glad to see you." He waved me onto a chunky, indestructible blue couch and wheeled his office chair over, its seat and back the bouncy fabric of a trampoline. "I've been thinking about you."

He offered a bowl of dried fruit. I passed. He chewed on an apricot, the tendons in his throat stretching his dark-blue turtleneck.

"It must be hard coming back to school and the old routine."

"It's good. Being at home's no fun." This place wasn't much better: plants that don't need light, boxes of tissues, carpeting like maroon TV static. Bike trophies lined the windowsill, lots of shiny crouched cyclists, and one made of actual pedals and gears, like you could ride it out of here.

"How's your mother?"

Jesus. I squinted my eyes closed. "How do you think?" You really need me to say out loud how horrid it all is?

He took my question at face value, a nice move, probably part of his training. "I would guess she is anxious. Can't sleep. Racked with guilt. And frightened about the future."

"About right," I said.

Behind his head, a poster promised WHAT YOU SAY IN HERE

STAYS IN HERE. Less reassuring, underneath, in much smaller type, it said UNLESS and listed the reasons your confidentiality could be broken.

He picked out a dried cherry. "My father passed away when I was fourteen, Alexandra. One of the hardest parts was how devastated my mother was. She completely fell apart."

"Sorry to hear that."

"I got through, in part because other family members and friends stepped up. But it made me sympathetic to young people whose parents can't parent."

He chewed. I was supposed to answer.

"I already did a lot of stuff for myself," I said. "Georgie took up most of my mom's time." That didn't come out right. It sounded like I was agreeing with him.

"So nothing's changed," he said.

I shrugged.

"And you don't want to be here."

I nodded.

"You wish I'd shut up and let you leave."

"Yup." That sounded rude, so I added, "I'm missing Biology, and we have a test."

"Mm. It's not that you're uncomfortable talking about this."

"Talking about what?"

He stopped chewing. "Your brother."

"What do you want to know about my brother?"

"Anything."

"Maybe you should ask him."

"What would he tell me?"

Jesus. "If he could talk, which he can't, I bet he'd say: 'This conversation with Mr. Gonsalves is a trap.'"

"A trap?"

"Whatever I say, you're gonna ask another question."

"And how does that make you feel?" He paused. "I'm kidding. You don't have to answer that. Or any questions." He rooted in the bowl and pulled out something the size and color of a cat turd. "Do know that it's perfectly normal to feel grief, anger, and shock after an experience like this."

What about guilt, shame, self-hatred? Did no one tell him what happened? I didn't need counseling, I needed punishment. I should be suspended, locked up.

"Look," I said. "I know you want me to process everything and come to terms with it, but that's not gonna happen."

"You're right," he said.

"I am?"

"You can't process something like this. No one can." And then the sentence that haunts me. "All you have to do—all you ever have to do, Alexandra—is feel what you are feeling." He bit the cat turd in half.

Feel what you're feeling. Sounds obvious. Aren't we always doing that?

Those legs.

The high school is out of sight, and Georgie is still sprinting. His legs are magnificent, rippled with muscles, but pliable like a cat's. You can slide your thumb right to his thigh bone. No one talks about the advantages of being Georgie. How could legs so strong and supple be anything but a sign of grace? I wish I could sprint fast as a champion hurdler on muscles soft as bread dough.

He doesn't integrate his arms with his run. His hands go up by his ears, his torso freezes. He is a cartoon character, relaxed on top while his legs spin in a blur.

"Stop. Blowing. That harmonica." Anthony, far behind, is slowing down.

Another advantage Georgie has is not getting tired, or maybe not realizing he's tired. He can run without noticing it. On the other hand, if he gets sleepy, he'll lie down in the frozen food aisle and close his eyes. He fell asleep in a bowling alley once. And he has no shame, another advantage. *The* advantage. Imagine not caring what other people think. Don't bother. You can't.

Uh-oh. "Georgie, stop! Wait! No! Georgie!"

I sprint ahead and grab his shoulder just before he runs across a road. A small road with no traffic. Still. He lifts his hand in a gentle point. His soft gesture means a lot, though you might not know from looking at it.

The state requires a transcribed interview with Georgie every year, questions designed to prevent abuse of people with disabilities. It's noble and essential and, in Georgie's case, hilarious.

INTERVIEWER: Georgie, do you know where your money
    is kept? For example, in a bank or wallet.

[GEORGIE rubs his fingernails on the couch.]

INTERVIEWER: Georgie, do you know who makes financial
    decisions for you?

[GEORGIE nudges a magazine with the back of his hand.]

INTERVIEWER: Are you satisfied with the financial decisions
    made for you?

[GEORGIE pushes the magazine to the floor.]

I love these transcripts. They put Georgie and the Normie world on equal footing. And when I read one, I instinctively add my interpretation to each Georgie gesture, each microshift. *[Georgie scratches the couch because money, something people around him talk about constantly, holds no meaning for him.]*

"Hold on, Georgie," I say. Pant, pant.

Georgie is doing one of the most common gestures in his dialect: the lazy point, or, as Mom calls it, his Adam Hand. Michelangelo's Sistine Chapel has God reaching out to Adam. Adam extends his arm lazily, bent wrist, forefinger tilting slightly toward straight. It's partial, indicated. Georgie often points with an Adam Hand, a gestural mumble, lackadaisical but meaningful.

"Aanh." *[Georgie points an Adam Hand toward the harmonica.]*

"Let's wait." Pant, pant. "For Anthony."

"Aanh." *[Georgie cranks his elbows. This refers back to his running, the game of sprinting away and outracing everyone. Why stop? Why ever stop? One question Georgie poses that the world has never satisfactorily answered: Why stop doing a good thing? Why not sing that song a fourteenth time? Why not start the movie over from the beginning? And why won't my sister keep blowing that harmonica?]*

"Aanh." *[Georgie glances at my head, then lifts a hand toward it.]*

"Yes, I shaved my head. With your clippers."

"Big G!" Anthony is out of breath and bringing up the rear.

"Aanh." *[Adam Hand to the harmonica, not because he wants to talk about it, but to protect himself from Anthony's arrival. Change takes time for Georgie and is best absorbed by restating what's already happening.]*

"Yeah, we came to see you," Anthony says, correctly interpreting Georgie's gesture as a welcome.

"Aanh." *[Tiny Adam Hand. Georgie often does the absolute minimum. Once he gets you to say the thing he's interested in, he'll do smaller and smaller gestures to get you to repeat it. It works. I know what he means.]*

"I played my harmonica."

"Aanh."

"Yeah, we all ran really fast."

[Elbow pump and seal bark, Georgie's highest form of approval.]

"Aanh."

This is conversation with Georgie. He says his one word—
"aanh"—points, and sometimes makes a sign language shape.
A slight rise in his arm is him putting his hand to his mouth. A
tiny turn inward is him touching his chest. He says, "Aanh," and
you say what you think he's talking about. Then he says, "Aanh"
again, and you continue the dialogue. Conversations with Georgie
are rhythmic, musical, call-and-response. You say whatever the
heck. He honks his approval. You say some more stuff.

I hear this rhythm in other conversations, Normie conversations. Listen to two guys talk about sports. Listen to anyone
talk to an elderly person or a kid. We think we're all having
scintillating, two-way conversations, complex back-and-forths.
Really, one person yammers and the other honks an occasional
"aanh."

*[Georgie unlooks at me. Not looking at someone is one of Georgie's
signals.]*

Anthony says, "What are you, twenty years old now? Nah,
fourteen, right?"

[Georgie looks right at Anthony. Silence. Everything stops.]

This is another part of Georgie's music, a moment I love,
one that Normies don't give you. It's a hold, an empty room, the
bottom of an exhale before the next breath. For me, it's where
Georgie's sorrow gets in. Like this moment: Georgie is fourteen.
Stop. Hold. My god. Where has time gone? So much changed
since his last birthday. So much. And what will happen to adult
Georgie? We grieve in the pause.

[Georgie bares his teeth in what looks a sneer but is really a smile.]
"Aanh." *[He half points at Anthony, half looks at me. It's the tentative movement of an old frail man, the bent limbs of a gnarled tree.]*

"You know who that is," I say.

Georgie's sweatshirt smells like chemical flowers, that spray you use when you can't clean your clothes.

"Aanh."

"That's right, I'm Aanh-thony. You almost said it, my man." Anthony puts a hand on Georgie's shoulder, not a hug, but a hug for Georgie. "How'd you get so fast? You're outrunning me."

[Silence while Georgie takes that in.]

He understands a lot of words, just doesn't say many. One time four years ago, Georgie was seemingly staring at his Disney movie, and my mom casually mentioned she was leaving early in the morning to visit her sister. The next day at 5:00 A.M., she found Georgie by the front door with his jacket on.

"Strong arms, too. You must be working out." Anthony learned to have these one-sided Georgie conversations by watching me do it. "You have school outside now, huh? That's crazy, school in a field."

"Aanh."

"It's Anthony. I walked all the way here to get you. I mean, not specifically to get you, but, hey, here we are."

In a house up the street, someone bangs a heavy backbeat on a drum kit, stops, then restarts.

"Aanh." *[Georgie grabs Anthony's hand.]*

"Excited to see you, too."

"Aanh." *[Georgie points at me.]*

"I don't know, Georgie, you have to ask him," I say.

Georgie's occupational therapist told my mom and me we were intervening too quickly. We should make Georgie interact with other people instead of speaking for him. "Allow Georgie to form direct relationships. Allow him to struggle with new people. Wanting to be understood is the impetus for learning."

"Aanh."

"Yeah, I walked from my house," Anthony says. "My house with May and Gram."

Georgie turns back to me.

"Uh, let's see," Anthony says. "I came to see you at your school. I came with Alex. We walked. No? Okay, don't tell me."

"I'm not gonna," I say.

"But you know, don't you?"

"It's so obvious."

"Oh, the kittens, right."

Georgie turns away, the counterintuitive sign that he's interested. He's a music nerd who presses PLAY on his favorite song and turns away from the speakers to savor it.

"It was the day after Halloween. The family in the pickup truck had a tiny kitten. And you held the kitten, and it sneezed right in your face, and we laughed."

[Georgie exults. His hands flap back and forth above his head, he grins

121

so hard his pink gums show, and he laugh-grunts on the inhale and exhale, like an accordion.]

It's contagious.

"The kitten kept sneezing, and we kept laughing. Yesssssss." Anthony likes to take credit for making Georgie laugh. The payoff, he calls it. "Come on, who made Georgie crack up?"

"With help," I say.

"You didn't help."

"I said it was obvious."

"That's the opposite of help. That's criticism."

The smell of a damp wood fire drifts over, the kind I've been building in our backyard. Heavy, wet smoke and no flame.

"Aanh."

"The pickup truck had a tiny kitten."

"Aanh."

"And the kitten sneezed in Georgie's face." Back to celebrating. "Yeah, that's right, Georgie. Ignore Alex. You and me are having a good time."

Georgie loves Anthony.

Anthony takes care of his little sister a lot because his grandma works and volunteers at church. I started bringing Georgie over, and we'd swap. Georgie followed Anthony around, the older brother he craved, the only man he saw regularly after my dad left. And May and I would huddle in her room, make potions in the kitchen, or act out stories for no one. I always said I got the better deal. Georgie's a handful, he craves repetition, he obsesses. May is a kid, a girl kid. Playing dress-up or hide-and-seek is knowable and linear. Anthony said it was easy to play with Georgie. He said his sister gets on his nerves, tries to boss him around. He said everybody struggles with their siblings.

And Anthony did get annoyed. He dragged Georgie inside once, said he'd been "asking for me," when really it was Anthony who was done. And he could be short with Georgie, manhandling him (which sometimes works) and yelling (which never does). Anthony and I argued so much about the yelling—"It's how I communicate," he, of course, yelled—we had to take a couple days off. That's the thing, everybody could take a day off from Georgie except Mom and me. And Georgie.

Most of the time, I think Georgie appreciated the blunt male confrontations Anthony provided, the boyness and the push-back. Anthony's house became Georgie's "other place," the destination, something I could promise when I needed him to get dressed or take his meds. When Anthony's family went to South Carolina for a wedding, I had to walk Georgie over there every day to show him no one was home. When they came back, Georgie was shocked, blown away, and celebrated for three solid minutes. I have to remember that. Things happen in Georgie's world forever or never. "*I'll see you twice a week,*" I told him when I visited him at the Boyers. Twice a week is a tough time frame for him. Twice a week means I'm never coming and then I'm here forever and then I'm never coming. It's the worst possible. I abandon him, return, abandon him.

Is this how divorced parents feel, torn by a kid who needs you every moment, the shredding guilt of constant goodbyes? Maybe that's why my dad doesn't visit.

Georgie, finished with the kitten story, starts walking in what I think is the right direction for Bethany.

"We should bring him back, right?" Anthony says.

"Back where?"

"To school."

"I just stole him from school. I can't go back there."

"I can do it. I'll tell them it was a mistake."

"We're not taking him back."

Across the street, a man pushes a wheelbarrow full of water. Half of it has sloshed out, judging from his soaked pants and shoes.

"Good to know. We're . . . what are we doing?" Anthony says.

"I don't know. Can we just relax for a bit? Oh geez, he's quick." I jog after Georgie, who's speed-walking across a parking lot.

"But we don't have . . ."

"What?" I say.

"Anything. A car, a phone, money. A plan."

"We have a plan. We're going to the VFW."

"All right. Just for the record, Georgie's school is freaking out right now. Pretty soon his fosters will freak out. Then, your mom will freak out."

"She's already freaking out cause I left." We pass a sign, plywood leaning against a tree, green paint spelling out STICK TOGETHER.

"Exactly."

"It's gonna be all right. I have a good feeling about this." I'm bluffing, but I think I sound convincing.

"Great. Yeah." A block away, a bottle rocket screeches into the air and pops. "Who needs money or a plan when you have a good feeling?"

⋇══════⋇

Having a disabled kid is, in a lot of ways, a story about money.

People talk about the lessons we learn, God's plan, the dignity of each person. But if you want to understand a disabled kid's life, ask about the money.

My dad did well financially, for a while anyway. He started a construction company with money from his father. He struggled at first, but then he got into solar panels early and built a business. He had a nice truck, employees, and a little warehouse full of shiny equipment. We certainly never got charity. If anything, my dad's company gave stuff, his MGW ENERGY SOLUTIONS logo on Little League jerseys and school fundraiser flyers.

There was a hard year when I was five. Dad got over his head in a community college project. Deadlines were blown, there were lawsuits and fourteen-hour days and huge losses for his company.

I saw it in his out-of-nowhere moments of panic. He had leased a used Toyota for my mom, a second vehicle, a real luxury, and it was time to trade it in, but the seat belt in back was messed up. He spent hours crawling around in there, yelling, "Twelve hundred dollars!" That was the deposit we wouldn't get back, which seemed, to my young brain, like a massive sum, our family fortune.

Georgie was three then, plump and goofy, everything a little brother should be, I thought. But Mom had seen many babies in her life, including me, and she sensed Georgie's differences. The story, maybe true, is that it took a specialist only ten minutes to give Georgie his first diagnosis: autism spectrum disorder. Over the years, that story was used by my father to show how different Georgie is, and by my mother to complain that the medical system was too quick to label him.

After the diagnosis, money became the top story. It drove what happened to Georgie and to my mom and dad. First came the tests, the hours watching waiting-room TVs while my parents talked to doctors. The pediatric offices had kids' shows, cartoons, animated movies. In the other waiting rooms, I'd watch daytime TV, girlfriends confronting cheating boyfriends, talk show hosts trying their hand at making meatballs. Whatever was on, I watched every second, even the ads, gobbling up images and stories so I didn't think about our story, the scans and the blood tests and the life-changing conversations these doctors must have weekly but my parents will have only once, only today. My mom would emerge weepy and shaky, my dad closed in on himself.

When they argued, it wasn't about Georgie's condition; it was about money. You can spend any amount of money on your disabled child. Literally. There's no limit. And why wouldn't you? I've seen wealthy people with round-the-clock care for their thirty-year-old daughter. There's not a minute she doesn't have a trained professional handling her needs. What does that cost a year?

If you could help little Georgie, if you could give him a shot at a life in the mainstream or near it, or even within sight of it, wouldn't you? What amount of money isn't worth spending?

Mom pushed for more expensive therapies. There was funding from the state, but keeping it required constant vigilance and an attorney. "With the money we pay that lawyer, we could have Georgie in full-time care," my dad grumbled. And Mom insisted on treatments the state didn't cover. She'd rail against the bureaucrats for not funding therapies that had no medical basis or track record.

When I was in fifth grade, Mom's desperation shifted. She wanted to help Georgie, but she also wanted to save her marriage. A higher-functioning Georgie might keep my dad around. She oversold Georgie's progress, neglected to mention his outbursts. One day on summer break, Mom and I slogged through a string of Georgie tempers. He broke a glass, scratched my face, and crapped his pants. But when Dad came home, Mom said: "We had a lovely day. Georgie helped Alexandra with the chores. He's having alone time in his room now. Maybe you should wait a bit before you go see him." Dad was more than happy to not interact with Georgie, who was sprawled in his now-trashed bedroom, stimming on a supposedly banned toddler toy that plays songs when you press the animals. My mom was surrendering, giving the junkie his fix so he'd stop raging. That, I could understand. There are battles that can't be won, agonies in Georgie that can't be answered. But the secrecy was new, and it changed the rhythm of our family. I was quietly enlisted in my mom's daily and desperate struggle to minimize Georgie's setbacks, emphasize his good moments, and convince Dad that Georgie was, all in all, a pretty easy disabled kid. I learned to give different reports to the "How's Georgie?" question. Mom got the messy truth, complete with bathroom mishaps, defiant rages, and Disney movie capitulations.

"I let him watch it again," I'd say.

"That's fine," my mom would say.

"Two and a half times."

"Oh gosh. Well, I'm sure he enjoyed it."

Dad got the highlights, and there were many. *We made seventeen drawings. Georgie chased geese around the cornfield. He's getting better at setting the table.* Dad had to hear that things were improving and

Georgie was turning a corner. When he saw things going badly, his mood blackened. "All that therapy, and Georgie's worse today than when he was three."

That wasn't fair. Three-year-olds are smaller, weaker, and less shrewd than eight-year-olds. Georgie wasn't worse; he was just better at imposing his will, better at making you feel his anxiety and confusion and anger.

I wonder if protecting my dad from all of that made it harder for him to stick around. If he really knew what we were struggling with, maybe he would have stayed and stepped up.

Maybe.

We lurched from one treatment to the next, each time convinced we'd found the answer. *We've gotten Georgie all wrong. His struggles all have to do with* _____. Sensory processing therapy, music therapy, cognitive therapy, auditory therapy, holding therapy. Every huckster and healer said they could help. Some of them may have believed it. They all knew to say the things my mom craved hearing:

"Your son is exceptional."

"We would love the opportunity to work with Georgie, because he is such a special child."

"I see a lot of kids in here, and I can tell you exactly what they will be like in twenty years. Georgie's different. His potential is unlimited."

Want money from a disabled kid's mom? Just say: "I see your child's potential." Because she sees it every day. Despite the children who back away at the playground. Despite relatives who stop inviting us for holidays. And despite her husband's growing desperation, his how-can-we-fix-Georgie hardening into how-can-we-even-live-with-this.

My mom doesn't see the noun of Georgie—disabled kid—but the verb. She sees a heroic soul battling relentless cognitive and sensory assaults, and battling the ostracism that results. I see it, too, a lot of the time.

Eventually, money became The Issue, the thing that pulled the rug out and drove my dad away. When I was in seventh grade, our house, built by my dad and owned free and clear, got mortgaged. The next year, with his business struggling again, the house was taken by the bank. We fled at the last minute, my mom convinced something would save us. We stuffed an MGW Energy Solutions panel truck with whatever fit, and abandoned the rest. We piled trash bags of clothes on top of coiled wire and strapped mattresses to the ladders on the roof. At our short-term rental, my dad sat in the truck, head on the steering wheel, while Mom set Georgie up watching his movie in the fluorescent-lit kitchen. I sat on the crumbly front steps, halfway, keeping a hand on each of my parents.

My dad started traveling a lot, taking gigs in other states, anything to keep money coming in. And then, in eighth grade, he left. At night. He'd just gotten back home after ten days away, and he didn't come to breakfast. Ever again.

He went far away, first to Arkansas, then Texas. There were

chipper phone calls at random intervals. He fooled me at first, made it sound like he was still in my life. Eventually, I got wise.

"Miss A, it's your dad!"

"Hi, Daddy! I miss you."

"Alexandra, it's your father."

"Where are you, Dad?"

"Hi, sweetie, it's me."
"Hey."
"Alex, it's your father. Alex?"

I handed the phone to Mom. "Hey, Mitchell, it's me. I don't think Alex wants to talk right now." Mom would yell at him about money, the support that he promised and that, after the divorce, he legally owed us.

But his company was bankrupt. When he walked out of our family, he was broke and flailing and under constant stress. Even more than that, he just couldn't do it anymore. He couldn't trudge another day through the slow-motion losing battle of raising Georgie.

Which makes him, to me, the worst. The worst person. Walk out on your family, you're an ass. Walk out on your disabled kid? You are garbage.

I'm allowed to say that, by the way; you aren't. You wanna take a shot at my dad, I'll tell you straight up: You have no idea. Come spend a month in our house, a week, one goddamn day, and then tell me you could make that your life.

You have no idea.

CHAPTER SEVEN

Anthony's mostly sure we're going the right way. I suggested we might want to be entirely sure, so he's asking directions from a guy with a Marine Corps flag on his porch.

Georgie and I sit by the side of the road. Georgie lies back on an elbow, smooshing the tall spring grass. He holds a tiny wildflower, white and yellow like a daisy, and spins the stalk between his fingers. The flower blurs to a white wheel and *pat-pat-pats* against his palm. He looks around at the trembling trees and the heat simmering off the pavement.

This is enough.

Take that, Normies.

Turn our phones off for a week and we twitch and tremble, aching for distraction. How many of us can sit back on a sunny afternoon?

I have a Three-Minute Test. I tell people who can't figure out how to be with Georgie: Sit with him for three minutes. Don't say anything or do anything, just sit there. I guarantee you'll find a connection. Don't make it happen; wait for it to happen. For most people, three minutes is the longest break they've ever taken from Doing Things, from the full-time job of being a Normie.

In sixth grade, my friend Margo sat for ten minutes. Georgie picked up a crystal and stared at the rainbows that twirled on the floor. Margo stared, too. Georgie laughed. Margo laughed. Soon, they were both on the floor, facing the ceiling, moving objects across their visual field. A sneaker, a pair of sunglasses.

Georgie makes a lot of Normies nervous. *What does this kid want from me?* It turns out he mostly wants one simple thing that people can't do. He wants you to be present and awake. *Be here, be with me.* Don't stabilize this moment or shove it into a familiar category.

It actually takes less effort than all the arm-waving desperation, all the clenched smiles and the do-you-want-this-no-okay-how-about-this-oh-I-think-he-wants-something-else. Georgie mostly doesn't want you to do stuff for him; he wants you to stop doing stuff. And that, it turns out, is the hardest thing.

I'm not even that good at it with Georgie. I can do it for a solid half hour with your brain-damaged cousin or heavily medicated uncle. But with Georgie, I tense up, because a lot of the time, I do need something from him. Get dressed, Georgie. Eat your lunch. Finish pooping. I can't lie back and bask in the glory

of a flying shoe. I'm on guard against his fixations. I'm anticipating broken rules, broken plates. I'm thinking ahead to dinner
or bedtime or the next transition. The people who are amazing
with Georgie—none of them are related to him—somehow stay
available and loose *and* keep things moving. They get him to the
dinner table without shutting him down.

The marine laughs and slaps Anthony on the back. The
military bonds Anthony to people quickly and deeply. Veterans
shake his hand and want to hear about his mom's deployments.
They ask if he'll follow his mom into the navy or choose a different branch, like those are the two options.

Georgie drops the flower and squints up at the bright clouds.
His jaw hangs down, the open-mouth breathing of a sleeper,
soaking up sun and breeze and birdsong.

It's not easy being Georgie. He has his torments, his daily
anguish. But some things he's right about, and this is one:

It is enough.

VFW Post 931 is a one-story white cinder-block building, freshly
painted, with a triple flagpole flying the US flag, a black POW-
MIA flag, and the post flag. We can see it from here—it's the
third building up Center Street—but Georgie won't make the
turn.

"Aanh." *[He points up River Road, straight ahead. His eyes are down, waiting for my answer with the impatience of a teacher, waiting for the correct answer, which is, obviously, "Let's keep going."]*

I forgot how determined he gets when he doesn't want to go a certain way. Walking here was bizarrely easy. Georgie was comfortable with, even anticipated, every turn.

"We are going to that white building so Anthony can talk to his mom."

"Mmh." *[A closed-mouth grunt. Georgie can't even be bothered to open his mouth. It's so obvious—to him—what's important that no enunciating is needed. His hand goes slightly up, maybe the beginning of a sign; maybe* home, please, Mom, brother, *or something else.]*

I take his sign for what I want it to mean, hoping to redirect him. "That's right, Anthony's mom. She calls you Gee-o."

"Aanh." *[He's insistent, doubling down, pointing up the street.]*

I drape my hand over his shoulder blade. I do this when I don't understand Georgie, when I need more information from his breathing, the texture of his muscles, his temperature and rhythm.

I look up River Road: three houses, a parked tractor trailer, and the sign for Holy Redeemer Baptist Ministry. Nothing that should matter to Georgie. Did I promise something? Did we mention a thing he loves and he assumed it was our destination?

"Right now, we are going to that white building to—"

"Aanh!" *[Georgie grabs my wrist and pivots his other hand up high. It's definitely a sign, maybe* hungry? *Maybe his fosters taught him new signs. Thanks for not telling us.]*

I can't miss this moment with Anthony. It's crucial. It's why I came, why I disobeyed my mom. "There is special snack at the white building." I'm bluffing. Worst case, he'll have a granola bar. "Later we can walk."

[His hand gestures haltingly toward his hair.]

It must be a sign. He's saying something, and I don't understand it. Is it because we don't live together? Or is it because—

Ugh. No. It can't be.

There are thoughts so dark, tar pits of shame so deep I have to tiptoe around them. If I'm not careful, I'll submerge and suffocate. This is one: *Did the lake change Georgie?*

He doesn't sing as much now, though he likes it when you sing. His balance on stairs seems funkier. His tempers are shaped differently, ending suddenly. He wanders off mid-fit, which sounds like an improvement, but it's unsettling. And now this confusing sign language and an urgency I can't interpret.

As Mom is quick to point out, it might all come from living with the fosters, away from his family. Massively disrupt an autistic kid's life, and, yeah, his behaviors will change.

After Long Lake, there were endless discussions of Georgie's "*cognitive baseline*." When a neurotypical person gets a brain injury, it's not hard to track the effects. Your short-term memory is shot. You can't balance on one foot. You can't feed yourself. But no one understood Georgie's brain before, so no one knows what those three minutes in Long Lake did.

My mom minimizes. "He never was good with utensils,"

she'll tell the neurologist. Or: "Getting dressed was always a struggle."

Privately, she says harsher, less speakable things. "It's not like his brain was pristine to begin with." And: "For chrissakes, they act like he was headed to law school. Who gives a damn if he's slow recognizing shapes? Didn't do him any good before." Maybe she thought we'd get in less trouble if Georgie was less damaged.

But that wasn't why we were in trouble. We were in trouble for those three minutes. For the unforgivable offense of standing in the dessert line while your autistic brother—who loves the water, who takes endless baths in the winter when the community pool is closed, who keeps his bloodshot eyes open underwater—carefully leaves his dry clothes on the dock and plunges in over his head.

Am I losing my Georgie fluency? Of all the punishments, all the repercussions, that would be unthinkable. Take him out of our house and blame me for it—fine. But, please god, don't break our connection, don't collapse this tiny, delicate tunnel we spent more than a decade digging toward each other.

[He looks me in the eye. He is conceding. It's an odd moment for the direct stare, a bit sudden, but it means he's done pleading his case.]

"That's right, first special snack, then second. Then we'll get going." I leave open where we're going afterward. He may forget.

[He bends his hand toward his forehead. He is marking the moment, warning me that, whatever this is, he'll come back to it.]

Georgie gallops after Anthony, or really, toward special

snack. It's a cheap move, promising food, a beginner move, and I'm a little ashamed.

Anthony waits in front of the VFW, our destination, the reason for our trip. It's a small, immaculate property, maintained with more attention than money. The lawn is perfectly cut, a rarity in the blackout, the parking lot freshly graveled. I get the feeling they do all the stuff my dad the builder—but nobody else—does: check the furnace twice a year, change the smoke alarm batteries, retar the roof seams.

"What's wrong?" Anthony says.

"I couldn't understand what Georgie was trying to tell me."

"That happens."

"Not to me."

"Uh, yeah it does. Georgie confusion is one of your favorite topics."

That's comforting. Maybe this is normal.

The VFW is not the scene I pictured. I imagined a crowd lined up outside, a huge antenna on the roof, a generator rumbling, people emerging from the doorway in tears. This was supposed to be the place of revelation, of communication and first contact.

I coax Georgie up the ramp and into the dim entryway, where photos in fake wood frames line the Wall of Honor, a mix of stern portraits in uniform and smiling later-in-life snapshots. A plastic wall clock says 1:53. The second hand is moving, which gives it some authority.

"Aanh." [*A full stop. Georgie doesn't like the narrow, dark hallway.*]

"It's okay. We're gonna talk to someone and have first snack."

"Aanh." [*Tiny dip of his chin. He is calling for the next part of the plan. We're back in sync.*]

"Then we'll have second snack. And then we'll walk."

Georgie needs a sequence. *Snack* is not enough to pull his attention away from fixations or anxieties. *First snack followed by second snack* does it. I make lines, not dots, progressions he can align with, a flow he can slip into.

Georgie lurches down the hall. This is still not the event I imagined. No hand-drawn sign with an arrow: RADIO THIS WAY.

We enter the main room, a wide dark-wood space with a drop ceiling, round tables pushed against the walls, and a green Formica bar. Double doors are open to the back, flooding a glaring parallelogram of light onto the brown carpet.

Anthony is talking to a short-haired white woman, whose clothes gleam in the dusky dimness.

"Pete Messer's place is right off Transfer Station Road," she says, waving at me and Georgie. "What's Pete's road called, Rodney?"

"*Hunh?*" comes a voice from outside.

"What's the name of Pete Messer's road?"

"*Hunh?*"

"Geez, get in here, someone has a question."

A bald Black man walks in, carrying a filing cabinet.

"This is Rodney. I'm Renata, by the way. What'd you say your name was?"

"Anthony. And that's my friend Alexandra."

"And this is my brother, George." I wave from behind Georgie's shoulder as he investigates a buffet steam table full of murky water. "He's disabled." That's my blanket sorry-for-whatever-happens-next announcement. It puts a cone of permission around Georgie and me. If Georgie starts yelling, or I start blowing a harmonica, *disabled* usually creates the necessary leeway.

"You're looking for Pete?" Rodney drops the filing cabinet underneath the VFW plaque, gold and red beams around an eagle.

[Georgie, tired of the steam table, wanders toward Anthony. He's getting to know the space, and soon he'll demand snack.]

"Someone told me there's a radio here that lets you talk to people in the military."

"There's somebody in the military you wanna talk to?"

"My mom."

"What branch?"

"Navy."

"Hooyah! A fellow squid."

"Aanh." *[Georgie gestures toward a gold-fringed flag in the corner.]*

I whisper, "It's a flag. Like the parade." Parades are Georgie's favorites. His unbelievable joy and instant understanding of them made me think parades aren't something people made up, they come from deep inside us. Parades are genetic. We brought Georgie to every one we could find.

"She's in a carrier group in the Pacific," Anthony says. "She's been gone a little over two months."

"Your father in the service, too?"

"My father's not in the picture."

"You have siblings?"

This interrogation is odd but encouraging. Maybe this is the screening process for the radio.

"A little sister."

"Mm-hmm." Rodney nods, frowns. "Thank you for your service, young man."

"Oh, I'm not in the service. I'm sixteen."

"Military families sacrifice a lot. Your mom's away, I know how hard that is. Our daughter used to hide my car keys when it was time for me to leave." He brings his feet together and stands tall. "So thank you." He and Renata give Anthony stiff, formal salutes.

And they stay there.

"Thanks," Anthony mumbles. "Thank you." At last, he does a salute, hand snapping to forehead, elbow sharply angled. It's clearly something he's practiced, though I've never seen it.

"Aanh."

"Shh," I whisper. I don't generally shush Georgie, but this moment deserves silence.

"God bless your family, son," Rodney says. "And God bless America."

"God bless America," Renata echoes.

I'm tearing up. Anthony's wiseass outsiderness, his smirking from the sidelines, is gone. He is saluting an older man proudly, with no eye roll. He's serious and manly, or trying to be. Maybe he *will* follow his mom into the navy.

"So you're trying to reach your mother."

"Yes, sir." That's a first. "Someone told me you all have a radio that can communicate with the military."

"Aanh." *[Georgie's hand rises toward his mouth, the sign for food. I pull him toward the tan barstools.]*

"Isn't this blackout crazy, Renata? People start talking and exaggerating, and pretty soon it's—what's that game called? Where you whisper in someone's ear."

Anthony is silent.

"Telephone," I say from the surprisingly comfy barstool where I'm unwrapping my last granola bar.

"We called it Whisper Down the Lane," Renata says. "Ever heard of that?"

Anthony shakes his head. "No, ma'am." So deferential.

"Point is," Rodney says, "somebody has a little radio hobby, and pretty soon people all over the county are saying: 'Hey, you can call up your relatives wherever they are.' I mean, talk about hearing what you want to hear, right?"

Anthony purses his lips and looks down.

Uh-oh.

"Aanh." *[Georgie starts the sign for food. He wants special snack, not this boring granola bar.]*

"Guy came in yesterday," Rodney says. "Said he heard we have a phone. Isn't that right, Renata? He said: 'Can I use your phone?' Like there'd be one working phone in the entire state. I mean, who are you even gonna call if you got one working phone? Are people even using their logic?"

"They sure aren't," Renata says.

"They never did before, why start now, right, Anthony?"

"Right." Anthony shakes his head.

Georgie gets up from his barstool and steps behind the bar, a quick and agile move. When he wants something, when he's focused, he glides straight to his destination.

"Sorry, son," Rodney says, "we don't have any magical phones."

"No, sir. Of course not."

"Georgie, no!" I shout-whisper, and hustle behind the bar. It smells of stale beer and bleach, and the floor is sticky.

"You go back to whoever promised this magical phone and—wait, know what you do? Get a banana and say"—Rodney holds his thumb and pinkie to his ear—"'Hey, I found that magical phone. It's for you!'" He chuckles, slaps Anthony on the shoulder. "Right?"

"Yeah," Anthony mumbles. "I'm sorry."

144

"Georgie!" He's got both arms deep in a bin of snacks. "Excuse me, um, I think my brother found your snacks back here." I'm warning them he might pilfer their food, but I'm also appealing for permission. Free treat for a disabled kid?

"Oh, help yourself," Renata says.

Yes. Temper averted. Now we can stay as long as necessary. Anthony can do what he needs, and we'll be enjoying honey-roasted peanuts, pepperoni sticks, and mini donut packs. And, look, those Handi-Snacks crackers with the cheese spread.

"Sorry if that's disappointing, son," Rodney says.

"It's fine."

"You could go talk to Pete," Rodney says. "He's a good man, a veteran, and he does have a serious radio rig up there. He talks to people in Canada and Ireland. Was it Ireland?"

"Yup. And France," Renata says.

"How'd you all get here, drive?" Rodney says.

"We walked," Anthony says.

I put a pepperoni stick on the bar for Georgie. I open a Handi-Snack for myself, take out the tiny plastic spreader, and smear fluorescent cheese product on a cracker. Good livin.

"Well, Pete's place is a good, I wanna say, seven miles from here," Rodney says. "Now, if you go, tell Pete you spoke with me, and maybe he can take your info down. That way, if he is talking to someone in the navy, he can ask about your mom's ship."

"It's okay," Anthony says.

[Georgie pushes the pepperoni away and points at my crackers.]

I'm a junk food bartender. I get another Handi-Snack from the bin. The bar wall is hung with newspaper clippings and a nonticking clock. Time is frozen.

"Problem is, your mom's out at sea—"

"It's fine," Anthony says.

When I turn back around, Georgie has his fingers deep in my cheese product, scooping the orange paste into his mouth. That's yours now, Georgie.

"If you tell Pete where she's based, he might—"

"It doesn't matter!" Anthony almost yells. "Sir. It's not gonna happen."

It's silent except for the crackling plastic as Georgie scrapes out the last bit of cheese.

"We can't go seven miles," Anthony says.

"Well, you came all this way," Rodney says.

"No, it's fine. I'm fine." Anthony looks around for us, ready to gather his people and get out.

Georgie points at the bin, a lipstick smudge of cheese on his mouth.

I grab another Handi-Snack and whisper, "This is second special snack. Last one." Georgie's slouched at the bar like an alcoholic. Is this how bartenders feel, pouring cocktails for drunks?

"What did you want to tell your mom?" Renata says.

The ceiling fan over Anthony's head turns in the breeze. It's ghostly, too slow.

"I want to make sure she's okay."

"Of course," she says quickly.

Anthony pokes at a ripple in the carpet with his toe. "People are talking about wars and terrorist attacks," he says. "You just wanna know what's happening. You wanna go home and tell your little sister: 'Hey, don't worry, Mom's safe.'"

Yes, you do.

Georgie grabs the pepperoni he rejected and eats it with a cracker. Technically, that's third snack, but I'm not stopping him.

"Well, to be honest, trying to reach your mom might not be worth your time at this point," Rodney says. "Places are already coming back on line. A lot of Texas, most of Arizona. It's only days, maybe a week, till we get power."

"Do you know what happened?" I say.

They turn toward me and cheese-covered Georgie.

"Oh, yeah. It was solar storms. Knocked out power in most of the hemisphere."

And there it is. Weeks of fantasy and dread and what-if resolved in a sentence. If Rodney's correct.

Solar storms.

I assumed knowing the reason would give the blackout meaning and depth, give it a sense of purpose. Hearing the cause, or, rather, what Rodney says is the cause, does change it, but not entirely. It's still the pain-in-the-ass, somewhat exciting mess that it was. It is, reassuringly and a bit disconcertingly, the same old blackout. To be honest, I'd rather know the end date than the cause.

"Yeah, no attacks, no computer virus. Just the good old-fashioned sun. You didn't know?"

"We heard that, but we heard other stuff, too," Anthony says.

"Yeah, the truth's never exciting enough for people, is it? They want all that action-movie nonsense. Well, it was solar storms. Fried a lot of transformers, thousands of em, that's why we're slow getting back. We didn't have nearly enough backups, especially the big ones. But there's some work-arounds, and they got a bunch of em from Europe and Asia, so things are starting to tip in our favor."

I have so many questions. "Are the—"

"Wait a week, son." He puts a fatherly hand on Anthony's shoulder. "Things should be up and running."

Anthony rubs his eyes.

Solar storms, nature, chance. If that is true, it's less frightening—no invading forces, no Reckoning, and no hiding in Kimmy's hole—but also colder. The universe swatted us down and might do it again.

Rodney from VFW Post 931 will turn out to be almost entirely right. I'd like to say I immediately believed him and let go of my fear and uncertainty, but I'm suspicious of all stories. And the blackout is strange. These three storyless weeks have contracted my universe. What's around me, what I can sense, that's what I know. The volume is turned up on my seeing and hearing and touching, and turned down on "information." When Rodney talks about Texas and Arizona, those states don't exist for my body. Until I can touch it and see it, it isn't happening. What *is* happening? Anthony's puppies piled around their dish. The nudist coughing. Kimmy's little brother charging up the hill. That's the News. That's my News. My body replaced the internet.

Here's what it feels like: My body is huge. Before, I was a tiny human, dwarfed by all the wires and systems. Today, I'm a giant, lumbering above the toy radio towers and telephone poles.

It's like taking Georgie from his school. At ground level, it seems reckless and disruptive. But when giant Alex walks up to that ant-sized school, she doesn't hear the teeny vice principal. Giant Alex looks down, finds her brother, and lifts him up and out.

I feel powerful, vast.

Maybe that's worrisome. Maybe giants break things.

<hr />

Leaving the VFW, Anthony is thrown, dazed, hands in his pockets. That's why, when we head out, we follow Georgie, relenting to his urgency. We don't have the energy yet to steer him homeward. We walk behind him in silence up River Road.

"You okay?" I say. Anthony nods. "You don't seem okay."

"That guy was like: 'We don't have a magical phone.' How could I be so stupid?"

"You were told you could talk to your mom."

"And I was so desperate to believe it I thought I could just, what, tune into her ship and chat with her?" A tear plops off Anthony's cheek onto his T-shirt.

Sweet boy.

He looks down. Really, he looks inside.

People say autistic kids are stuck in themselves. There are stories of autistics who "come out" and join the daylight world of Normie conversations and emotionally appropriate responses. One huckster who took my family's time and money had a "formerly autistic" son, a walking advertisement for the treatment, which, twenty years on, still has only one success.

It's that phrase, *coming out,* that gets me. *Coming out* implies that the rest of us are out, that we're always available and alert, dialed in to the agreed frequencies. But we're not. We all surface and dive.

I watch Anthony's mouth move, the half talk of a sleeper, maybe reliving the VFW conversation or maybe scolding himself. He shakes his head, a small but violent shudder, casting off whatever thought or feeling is coursing through him, and he glances around, maybe to see if I noticed.

I noticed, Anthony. I won't tell you I did, but I saw where you went, and it doesn't frighten me. It isn't awkward or disconcerting, and I don't have to joke about it: *Earth to Anthony.* I spend enough time with Georgie to know we all go inside, we all replenish and return. So why do we see Georgie as internal and Anthony as "out?" That hard line bothers me. It makes people—me included—miss Georgie's surfacing, his outstretched effort. And we miss Anthony's dives.

"I don't know. I just . . ." Anthony winds up and fails to kick an apple-sized rock, which spins off the side of his foot and nearly clips my leg. "Oo, sorry. I just . . . I wanna do something. I'm waiting around in the blackout, hoping things get better, hoping Mom's okay, hoping the puppies don't starve. I'm useless. And this whole trip is useless. I wanna"—his hand chops the air twice—"do something."

Here's something wild. Georgie, Mr. Submerged, knows when other people go inside themselves. Out of nowhere—wasn't he way ahead?—Georgie slides next to Anthony and plants a *love* on his shoulder. He holds his bony head there, hovering, not an embrace but a signal, full-body sign language. Then he slips away and stutter-steps down the road.

"Aw," I say. "Look who's listening."

"I know, I'm so pitiful, even Georgie's comforting me."

Georgie is far ahead. He delivered his love package successfully, and he's marching onward.

"Even?" I say.

"What?"

"You said '*even Georgie*.' Like he's not allowed to comfort you."

"No, I mean I should be helping Georgie. I should be helping you and May and Gram, and instead I'm fantasizing about a magical phone that'll let me talk to my mommy."

Ow. So harsh.

"There's nothing wrong with wanting to talk to your mother."

"When a sixteen-year-old boy is acting like a baby, there's something wrong."

That's what's going on.

"You're not a baby. You want your mother. That's normal. I do. We all do."

"You have your mother, Al. It's different. Try it with your dad."

"What?"

"Say this: 'I really need my daddy right now.'"

"Oh. No."

"'Where's my daddy? Why isn't my daddy here?' Say that."

"No, that's—"

"See?"

He's right. I wouldn't say that out loud. Or to myself.

But why not, goddammit?

Don't ever let em shame you.

All bets are off.

A woman is cutting her tall grass with a manual push mower. Her tank top is dark with sweat, but she's managing. See? We're gonna be fine.

"Hey." I stop Anthony and put my hand on his heart. "I think it's great that you want your mommy." I feel the girders of his ribs, the jellyfish of muscle. "I like you with your heart open. You should do it more."

"No I shouldn't." He stares at my hand. "If you start acting needy, it pushes people away."

"Not me."

"You say that."

"I mean it." I feel the thud of his heartbeat.

"Nobody means it," he says.

That's something, some piece of Anthony I need to remember and stay close to.

As we walk past, the woman slams her lawn mower down and shouts, "Impossible!"

Maybe we're not gonna be fine.

We leave the tiny town and enter farmland, plowed fields studded with forest. A collapsed house squats in the shade, its stone foundation overflowing with the walls that fell into it. A section of wood-shingle roof arcs impossibly, a mossy ski jump.

"Oo, look." I push through some thorny blackberry vines.

"Where are you going?"

"This is good. We'll take a b-r-e-a-k, and maybe we can t-u-r-n around. Come on, Georgie. Time for a drink."

"Ouch," Anthony grumbles, his arm caught on prickers. "This is not a good idea."

I scramble over a heap of foundation stones. Baby trees, maybe birches, crowd the doorless doorway, their leggy stems racing for the sunlight.

My dad used to stop at ruins like this, especially when he was building our house. We climbed debris piles and scaled leaning walls. He looked for old wood, timbers thicker than they make now, some from trees you can't find anymore. I searched for treasures: tin cans with old-fashioned labels, tiny bottles with elaborate etchings, and once, a toy metal station wagon rusted out like an actual abandoned car. I pictured the child who played with it, now older than my grandparents.

My dad would ask at nearby houses before taking anything. It seemed obvious to me no one wanted this stuff; it had been left to rot. He told me scavenging rights to burned or collapsed structures used to be sold around here, maybe still are. And neglect was not necessarily a sign of disinterest. The owners might be waiting for the right moment of need or opportunity.

"A collapsed home can make a new home even decades later if the materials are strong," he said.

Well.

Indeed.

In the house he built for us, out-of-time materials popped up unexpectedly, an ax-rounded beam in the kitchen ceiling, ancient moss-green boards framing a closet door, a diamond window in the bathroom, its glass wobbly with age.

When the bank mortgaged our house and later took it, these

all counted against its value. "Nonstandard building and finishing materials throughout," the appraisal said. Once again, the Normies misjudged our family, mistook our differences for deficiencies.

"Ridiculous," my father barked. "This place is twice as solid as those ticky-tacky boxes they put up in a week."

"It doesn't matter," my mom said. "We're getting the loan we need."

We'd pay it back, of course, there was no question. Nothing worse was coming over the horizon: That's what my parents told themselves. Each punishing wave was surely the last. It was impossible to imagine the storms to come.

"Doesn't look like anyone's home, Al," Anthony says, peering into a glassless window.

"We can move right in."

"Dibs on the second floor. Which is now the first floor."

"Georgie, come sit." The stone ledge of the foundation is sun-warmed and speckled with pale-green lichens, a bench for our b-r-e-a-k.

"Should I sit on the rusty nails or in that puddle full of broken glass?" Anthony says.

"Stop being a grump."

Georgie gulps from my water bottle, two streams trickling out of the corners of his mouth.

"Gentle, Georgie." I say this every time he drinks fast, to no effect.

"I'm a grump because I don't want tetanus?" Anthony plants himself higher on the wall. A mud-and-straw bird's nest, probably abandoned, cowers between the rocks.

"You're a grump because you're upset."

"I'm not upset."

"You know what Mr. Gonsalves says."

"The counselor? No idea."

"He says—"

"And, interestingly, I don't want to know."

"He says, 'The only thing you have to do is feel what you're feeling.'" A breeze sweeps through the house, pushing cold air out of the basement, the smell of minerals and damp, like a handful of pennies. "So what are you feeling?"

"Annoyed at your question."

"That's exactly what I said!"

"Twins."

"His next question was: 'Underneath that, what do you feel?'"

I told Mr. Gonsalves I felt frustrated and anxious. He said: "*Whenever you find yourself saying 'I'm anxious' or 'I'm frustrated,' just imagine my incredibly annoying voice asking: 'What are you trying not to feel right now?'*"

So much. Everything.

"Come on, Anthony, answer." A dragonfly hovers around Georgie, bright blue and vibrating, and zooms off before I can point it out.

"I don't know. I'm frustrated."

Mr. Gonsalves, I hear your incredibly annoying voice.

"And I'm embarrassed," Anthony says. "It's humiliating."

"What is?"

"I'm sitting in a fallen-down house with Georgie, who's miles from where he needs to be." The sun comes out and dapples us with forest light so rich and green it feels like my skin might photosynthesize. "And I just asked a nice veteran dude for a magical phone so I could call my mommy."

"You're being harsh."

"I'm being pathetic." He peers into a dark brick-lined hole, maybe a fireplace or coal chute.

"Jesus Christ, Anthony, you're a kid."

He tosses a chunk of plaster into the hole, and it hits something metal and echoey. "What does that mean?"

"You're a kid, you're sixteen. You do adult stuff sometimes cause your dad's gone and your mom can't always be there for you. But you're a kid, you're in high school. Give yourself a break. You're acting like a teenage grandpa."

"Well, isn't that funny."

"Teenage grandpa? Thanks."

Georgie quaffs my water again, and even more of it washes down his front.

"No, I could say all of that about you. Every word."

"No, it's different with me. I have . . ." I snort out a laugh. "Oh my god. You're right. I'm so obnoxious. I was about to say: 'I have responsibilities.'"

"See. You're a teenage grandma."

"Yuck. We really are twins."

"Elderly teenage twins."

"I like you better as a kid."

"I like *you* better as a kid."

"Then let's be kids," I say.

"Fine."

"Fine."

He clears his throat. "Yo, girl." He nods, a dumb smile on his face.

I laugh. "No, don't."

[Georgie pulls his shirt sideways. He wants it off, but it's too much work.]

"No, hold on." Anthony folds his arms. "Yo girl. You wanna go get a Fresca?"

"Aanh." *[Georgie stands and starts down the overgrown driveway that leads away from our collapsed house.]*

"Oh, we can't be kids. I forgot." I point at Georgie. "We're responsible."

We follow.

I hope this path leads back to the road. The muddy tire ruts are deep but not recent, and they're filled with rain, the bigger ones skimmed by water striders.

Our conversation is reminding me of a devastating thing my aunt Chrissy said.

"Anthony, do you feel like you get to be a kid, a regular kid?" I say.

"What's a regular kid?"

I tell him the story.

"Shame you don't get to be a kid," Aunt Chrissy said, watching me struggle to get Georgie's boots on. It was a snowy February morning, I was thirteen, and my cousins ran outside to build a snow fort. I had to get Georgie ready, and he's not great with footwear. He can't put it on himself unless it's slip-ons, and he goes all noodle-legs when I help, which is especially hard with boots.

"Push, Georgie, push."

His knees bent when I yanked his boots up. Yank, bend. Yank, bend.

"Can I help?" Aunt Chrissy said.

"No, I got it." I moved Georgie to the floor and sat on his thighs. I'd tell Mom he needed bigger boots. No, I shouldn't add that to her list. I'd just look at Saint Benedict's thrift next time we were there.

I was wrestling the second boot on when Chrissy said it. "It's a shame you don't get to be a kid. Doesn't seem fair."

I shrugged. Big deal.

But damn.

I wasn't embarrassed. I was *seen*. Someone called me out.

I thought about her words all day. When I cleaned snow

out of Georgie's gloves. When I sang "Frosty the Snowman" for the twentieth time. (Georgie got Christmas songs all year; in the winter, it felt less ridiculous). And when I tied Georgie's "napkin," actually a full-sized bath towel, around his neck at lunch.

That was a horrible seed to plant, Chrissy, an invasive weed that clogged my mind.

"*Doesn't seem fair?* What's that even mean?" Anthony says, stepping around a puddle that Georgie stomped right through, tracking a single footprint of orange mud behind him.

"She's saying kids should be kids, not have to look after somebody else."

"That." Anthony ducks a spiderweb. "Sounds like some white people talk."

"Whoa, what?"

"The idea there's some normal, comfy life you deserve, where you don't have to deal with all the crap? That's the kind of thing white people say. And I should know, cause I'm friends with several white people." He grins and socks me on the shoulder. Oh god, he's doing it. "Hell, I'm related to a bunch of white people." A bird squawks an alarm from the ground, and its comrades in the trees pick it up. "Come on, Al, you're twice the human being your cousins will ever be, cause you're in it. You're dealing with real life."

"What if I'm missing out? What if there's another life, another me?" A thornbush cane snags my ankle. I peel it back, and four pale-green thorns stick in my white sock next to four dots of blood.

"A bald one?" Anthony says.

Exactly.

The driveway doesn't lead back to the road. It peters out by a creek, and Georgie keeps trucking, his sneakers periodically sliding into the coffee-brown water. Repeated attempts at bribery, deception, and redirection do not turn him around. Anthony raises his voice, and I shut that down hard. No yelling today. Except me yelling at the vice principal, of course.

Anthony's worried about getting home, but, honestly, I'm not ready to head back. I'm not ready for the awkward questions and apologies. There's more for me today, I feel it.

Maybe it's Georgie. He's different, insistent. Normally, hours spent with Georgie are circular, stimming on a song or a game, over and over. Today, he's linear, pointy. Most afternoons, his legs drape heavy on the living room carpet, printing his bony hips and ankles into the rug. Today, his plasticky sweatpants swish on, the sound of purpose. Even if he's marching nowhere in particular, he marches on.

And maybe it's me. My hair is gone, and my shoulders and neck are out and urgent for something, stacked for a fight I can't yet see.

Let it come.

Whatever my body is meant to embrace or wrestle with, let it come.

And make it powerful. Make it worth this messed-up journey and messed-up year. Let it be weighty and drastic enough to catapult me out of my small, small world.

Please, for god's sake, don't let this day end with back-tracking. The point of all this can't be apologies and crappy consequences.

Sorry I took Georgie out of school.

Sorry I'm so reckless and irresponsible.

No. I'm reckless and visionary. Give me something momentous at the end. It doesn't have to be fun, but please god don't let it be ordinary.

CHAPTER EIGHT

I hustle to keep up as Georgie emerges from the woods behind an apartment complex. Civilization. Three stories of concrete balconies are crammed with overflow storage: plastic bins, baby strollers, and kids' bikes, covered with feathering plastic sheets.

Georgie marches past a dumpster surrounded by broken bedroom furniture and into the parking lot.

What?

No way.

I stop next to an abandoned horseshoe pit, the unmowed grass tickling my calves, and I stare at the white pickup truck.

"What is it?" Anthony says.

"What the hell?" That truck.

"Hold up, Georgie!" Anthony hustles after him.

The tailgate has a square dent from backing into a supermarket cart corral.

The fingerprint smudges on the back window, the gray bed liner.

"Al, what are you doing?" Anthony yells back once he catches up with Georgie.

The green lettering on the side: MGW ENERGY SOLUTIONS.

My dad's pickup.

"Stay right here, Georgie. One minute." Anthony jogs over to me.

I try the door. Locked.

"Al, what are—oh my god."

"It's my dad's truck." Georgie passed right by it, though I'm sure he'll remember it.

"Well, it's from his company, might not be his," Anthony says.

"No, it has the dent and the little plastic duck I wedged into the dashboard." I'm pressed to the driver's window, my breath fogging the cool glass.

"Maybe he sold it."

"No, he loves this truck." I hop up into the back and reach through the hand-sized opening in the bed liner. It's there, over the right wheel: a cough-drop tin stuck on with a magnet.

"What are you doing?"

"It's his truck. It's my family's truck."

"You don't know it's still his." Anthony steps onto the curb. "Georgie!"

I peel the clear tape off the tin, taking some of the blue-and-white SUCRETS letters with it, and slide the lid across, sticky with rust and tape goo. I pull out the battered key.

"Are you breaking into the truck?"

"No, I'm using a key."

"Maybe you should knock on a door and see whose truck it is."

"Which door?" The complex has dozens of apartments on three levels.

The lock is stiff, probably because the key is a copy. I wiggle it, then watch the old-fashioned knob rise out of the door. It's a no-frills truck, and Dad was wildly proud when he brought it home.

"They lettered it for free," he said. *"Look how nice the logo came out."*

He got it when I was eight. We took pictures of him next to the truck, fists in the air, while six-year-old Georgie picked at the tire. He'd been getting jobs for years, managing projects, but this was his moment. He drove around with his logo—his business—right there for everyone to see. His phone number was on there, too, and I remember thinking hundreds of people were going to start calling.

"Okay, you have now broken into someone's vehicle. Just gonna point that out. Georgie, no!" Anthony runs after him.

I climb into the driver's seat. It doesn't smell right. Perfume? No, one of those horrid air fresheners is clipped to the vent, a drooping wad of blue goo in a silver plastic cage. And barrettes by the stick shift, not mine or my mom's.

I open the glove compartment. Peppermints, hand wipes, a flashlight. Where's the registration? Where's my dad's name?

"Hey! What are you doing?"

Jesus. There's a girl by the driver's-side door, holding a dog on a leash.

"I was just looking for something. This is my, um, family's truck."

"No, it's not."

"Yeah, it is. I have a key."

"That's the spare key." She pulls the door all the way open, inviting me to leave. "You found the spare key and broke in."

"This is my dad's truck. MGW Energy. Mitchell's my dad."

"Mitch is your dad?"

Her dog sneezes, and a slurpy string of snot dangles from his nose.

"Yeah. You know him?"

"Of course."

"Does he live here?"

"He's . . ." She's deciding whether to answer. "He's my mom's boyfriend. He's gonna be my stepdad."

"What?"

Holy hell.

"And my mom drives this truck. Mitch has a bigger one."

"Wait, is he here?"

"No, he's in Texas, but he'll be back any day now." She pulls at her glittering gemstone earring. "He was here when the blackout happened, but he left. You know, solar power, everybody needs him." The dog yanks her arm, and she braces her legs to pull it back. "I'm Marisol."

I'm imploding. Nice to meet you.

"You must be Alexandra," she says. "Mitch told me about you."

"His name's Mitchell."

"Mitch is short for Mitchell."

"He was never called that before." I squeeze one hand tight on the steering wheel, which is stained dark with my dad's sweat. It's the closest I can get to him.

"Before what?"

"Before . . . three years ago." I shrug. It's not enough for her. "When he walked out on my mom." Is that what he did? He really walked out on Georgie. Something about Marisol makes me say it this way.

I climb out. Marisol has big teeth, light-brown skin, and black hair pulled back tight along her scalp. Her part is meticulous, each hair precisely allocated to a side and glued flat. Her dog aggressively sniffs my thighs.

"We're back." Anthony is dragging Georgie along. "I promised a puppy."

"George?" Marisol says.

What. No.

"Hey, George! Look, Crispy's here." The dog jumps up on Georgie's legs, sniffing feverishly.

"You know Georgie?" I'm spinning.

"Yeah, we visited him. Crispy went wild, cause George had all this greasy food. She started licking him all over. George thought it was the funniest thing."

Forget Marisol going to the Boyers', which is ludicrous. *My dad is visiting Georgie.* Holy hell.

"His name's Georgie."

"I call him George."

Why is everyone changing their names? I stare at her mouth. Her upper lip has two sweeping curves, indented like a book left open.

"Who's . . . ?" Anthony points a bewildered finger.

How do I introduce her? "This is, uh, my replacement." Cause that's it, right? That's why I feel like kicking her in the shins.

"Yeah, Crispy, get him, clean him good."

"Replacement what?" Anthony says.

"She's my dad's new daughter. Marisol."

"Hi," she says. "What's your name?"

"Anthony." He gives a real smile. He can act nice—be nice— even when things are crazy. "So your dad's here?"

"No," me and Marisol say at the same time.

Jesus.

"He's away for work," she says. "And he's not my dad. He's my mom's boyfriend."

"He's gonna marry her mom," I say. This is a full-on crisis; I need Anthony to understand.

She turns to Georgie. "Mis-ter George. Mis-ter George. Cris-py dog. Cris-py dog." She's poking his armpits, doing a rhythm like my harmonica song. "What are you guys doing?"

"We're on a . . . complicated journey," Anthony says.

"Coming here?"

"We didn't mean to come here," I say.

"Maybe someone did," Anthony says.

Holy crap. Right. Georgie's been dragging us here since the VFW. He knows stuff. Not always cerebrally, like he can't explain it to you. But Georgie has a goddamn compass in his brain. I forgot that.

"Georgie brought us here," I say, mostly to myself.

Goddammit. This is not the catapult I wanted. I want to fly through the air, a daredevil, a rocket girl. This catapult isn't a ride, it's a weapon aimed at my head.

"That's sweet. He wants to see his dad," Marisol says.

"Don't say that," I say.

"What?"

"His dad walked out on him, on all of us."

"George likes seeing his dad, I can tell you that," Marisol says. "I mean Georgie."

How do I not know Dad's been visiting Georgie? My mom must know. My mom knows all of this and isn't telling me.

"Well, Georgie's not trying to see him today," I say. "He's with his sister. His real sister."

"I'm sorry."

"Don't apologize. That makes it worse."

"Oh. Sorr—I mean, all right. I won't."

I sit on the curb.

Want to find out the truth? That was Anthony's question yesterday. God, no. I should have stayed home with the blinds down.

Someone's cooking on a grill, and the warm smell of garlic and hot peppers ought to make me hungry, but it makes me nauseous.

I'm crying. Where did this come from? My dad's a piece of crap. Who cares what he does? Who cares if he visits Georgie and not me?

Turns out I care. A lot. Turns out I do want my daddy.

Do your damn job, Dad. Walk out on us, go far away, and be an ass. Don't be a decent freaking stepdad to some other kid. Keep the story consistent: You're a selfish a-hole. You'll be alone forever. Don't quietly sneak back into Georgie's life. If you get back in touch with anyone, it's me. It has to be me.

That's it right there. He didn't run away from the relentless burden of a special needs kid. He ran away from me. And Mom. He ran toward another, better family. Toward this girl with her painstakingly combed hair and smiley questions. And when he wanted to reconnect with his old family, he didn't write me a letter or take me out for a difficult conversation over pizza. He went to Georgie.

God*damn* you, Dad. I'm the good kid! I'm the kid who doesn't make problems. I do my share, more than my share. The kid who tempers gets the visits? Gets a dad?

What's wrong with me? What's wrong with Alex?

I'm the good one, goddammit!

I tilt my head back. Two stories up, a toddler peers down, her chubby calves pinched through the balcony railing, her purple sneakers dangling. I wish I was up there. I wish I was three.

Today has been a good day. I've been on my feet. But this knocks me down. I'm back in my defensive crouch, cowering, awaiting the next blow. I need to stand the hell up.

The perfect response flashes through my mind. We call my dad—Marisol must have his number—and I get on the phone: *Hey, Dad, how are you? Yeah, I'm hanging out with your new daughter. Congratulations on the upgrade!*

For the first time since the blackout, I'm desperate for a phone. Please God, bring the power back right now. I want the upper hand. I want to shrug off this betrayal, and I want him to hear me do it.

I want to dish it out. I want to barely notice this.

Instead, I'm huffing and sobbing, tears I do not goddamn need tickling my chin while my ass cheeks numb out on the scratchy curb.

At least Marisol doesn't comfort me. She's not that graceful.

She steps back, like she's dodging a sick person's sneeze. *Don't let my misery infect you, sis.*

"I have to go," she says finally. "To a cookout."

I rub my eyes and look up. "What?"

Oh. She's talking to Georgie, holding his hand while he points toward the street.

"Yup. I'm going to a cookout."

"Aanh."

"I'm waiting to be picked up."

[Georgie lifts his face and looks directly into her eyes, something he only does with family and caregivers, and not often. No, Georgie, not with the imposter. He laughs, clucking on the inhale.]

Marisol giggles, sees me watching. "Your brother's really funny."

"No, he's not. He's a pain in the ass."

I never agree with people about Georgie. If someone is freaked out by him, I go: "Don't be ridiculous. He's awesome." And if someone says he's awesome, I go: "No, he's really god-damn hard." That's my position: Whatever you think about Georgie is wrong. This girl, this fake sister doesn't get to say Georgie's funny. She hasn't earned it.

Someone bumps a metal handcart up the concrete stairwell. *Bang. Bang. Bang.*

Now they're dancing around each other, a bouncy jig, Marisol bobbing her head in sync with Georgie's elbows.

172

You know what? It's time for us to go. "We're leaving, Georgie," I say. "Get in."

I open the pickup door and climb up. Georgie, who always loved Dad's truck, immediately comes over.

"Other side." I wave him around and open the passenger door.

"What are you doing?" Marisol says.

"Come on, Anthony, we're leaving."

Anthony hesitates. "Uh, Al, I don't think——"

"You can't drive the truck," Marisol says.

"Watch me."

"No, you don't understand, I'm——"

I slam the door. "Seat belts." I pull the center lap belt out for Georgie.

The setting sun glints off the windows of the building behind us, throwing a swirling golden light on the dashboard. We're lit up and ready.

Anthony waits to climb in. "You sure about this, Al?" he says.

"Yes. We'll go h-o-m-e. Georgie can see M-o-m. It's perfect."

"What about the truck?"

"My dad can come get it whenever he wants." That's the best part. Watching Mitchell—sorry, Mitch—shuffle up the front lawn, caught in his BS.

Marisol is shaking her head while the dog tries to jump in the back of the truck. I'm glad she's not throwing her body behind the wheels.

"Come on, in or out, Anthony."

"Move over, Georgie." Anthony climbs up.

Yes. This is the statement. This is the message my dad can come home to: Your old family took your new family's truck. How's that feel?

Key in the ignition. I never drove this truck. Dad disappeared before I got my license. Gas pedal, turn the key. This is great.

Wrum-wrum-wrum-wrum-wrum.

Hmm.

Parking brake. Okay, it's here on the dashboard. I yank the switch, and the hood pops open. Oops. I'll fix that in a sec.

Turn the key again.

Wrum-wrum-wrum-wrum.

What am I doing wrong?

Marisol taps the window.

I wave her off.

She taps again and shakes her head.

Wrum-wrum-wrum-wrum.

Jesus. You're kidding me.

Yellow light on the dashboard.

"No gas," I say.

I drop my forehead onto the steering wheel.

Oh god.

There's a big cry waiting here. There's a cloudburst surging in my head, a sloppy runny-nose deluge ready to fill this cab with tears and snot and moans and an agony so constant I didn't even know I was carrying it.

I hiccup a sob, which feels like I'm retching, a curling spasm in my gut.

"Aanh." *[Georgie points aimlessly at the windshield, urging the truck to move.]*

Here it comes. In front of goddamn Marisol.

Anthony giggles.

Nice.

He giggles again, then starts laughing. Hard.

And somehow, this pulls me out. It drags me from the swirling sea of grief and back onto the bench seat of this Ford F-150. "What?" I say.

Anthony is facing away, chuckling and trembling. We're both curled over by urges we don't want. In his side-view mirror, I see two teenagers walking their bikes and staring at our odd confrontation.

"What is so funny?" I say.

"It's not funny. I'm sorry." Anthony laughs harder, contracts into a ball.

"Apparently, I'm hilarious," I say.

"No, sorry. I'm not laughing at you. Seriously." He bangs the dashboard and laughs harder, his giggles turning silent as he runs out of breath. "Hoo . . . It's just . . . I saw it. I saw the badass gesture, us driving away. So glorious. And I saw it a week

from now, your dad gets back and is like: 'Where's the truck?'
And Marisol's like: 'Your other daughter took it.' It was magnificent. But now . . ." He laughs. "Now it's the opposite. Now
we're sitting in this damn truck we were about to steal, and we
have to—what? Get out and apologize? '*Here's your truck back.*'"
He starts giggling uncontrollably. "I mean, it's just too brutal,
right? It's agonizing, we're—" His voice goes high-pitched, like
he's sucking helium. "We're sitting here, look at us! I'm so with
you, Al, you know that. That's why I'm laughing. Like, how
perfectly goddamn excruciating is this moment, right?"

I bump a lever, and the wipers turn on hard, scraping the dry
windshield. I yank the key out.

"What am I doing wrong, Anthony?"

"Nothing. This was a genius idea. You just can't"—he
giggles—"start the truck."

"No, what am I doing wrong in my life?"

"Other than kidnapping your brother?"

"Why does this girl have my dad's truck? And my dad?"

"Oh. That."

"Why is everything being taken from me? It is because of
the . . . thing. The thing in the l-a-k-e?"

"Jesus, Al, no. None of this is stuff you did. There's nothing—"
Tapping on my window.

"One second," Anthony says holding up a finger.

"Come on, get out," Marisol says, her voice flat and tight
through the glass, the voice of an adult.

"One second!" Anthony yells. He leans over Georgie and me and tries to open my window, but the car is turned off. Georgie tilts into me, and I'm squeezed against the door, inches from Marisol's face.

"Hold on!" Anthony grabs the key, turns the car on, and leans in to put my window down. I grunt as both boys' weight crushes me against the hard plastic door. "We need one second," Anthony tells Marisol. "One second. We'll be right out." He is yelling as if the window is closed, and Marisol takes a step back.

"I have to go," she says.

"One goddamn second." He puts the window back up, yanks the key out, and slides back to his side. Georgie doesn't follow, and I have to shove him back up to sitting.

"Okay, wait," Anthony says. "What was I saying?"

Now I giggle.

"No, no, don't laugh. This is important. What was I saying?"

Hilarious. We're in a truck I just tried to steal, making Marisol wait while we figure out what the hell we're even talking about. How did we end up here? We're decent, reasonable people. Why is the world messing with us? Where did it all go wrong?

"Uh, I think you were gonna explain what's wrong with me," I say.

"Right. No, listen. You remember eighth grade when my dad pulled me and May out of school? He showed up and like basically took us."

"Like I took Georgie today."

"Yeah, but darker. Much darker. He was trying to take us back to South Carolina. So he drives us to Gram's to get all our stuff, but Gram heard what happened, so she has her boyfriend, Steve, and Steve's brother there, right? Big dudes, not having it. So it's this ridiculous confrontation, everybody yelling, everybody saying they're gonna call the cops. Gram won't let Dad take us cause she knows he can't handle us. I mean, at that point, we hadn't seen him in a year, right? He's full of crap, he's just trying to get back at my mom. Me and May are in the car, then we're out of the car, and finally I carry May into the bathroom and I'm holding her and she's screaming, and Gram comes in and she says this thing."

Damn. That all happened. I knew the facts, but not the scary realness of it.

"Gram grabs me." Anthony takes my shoulder and wags a finger in my face. "She goes: 'None of this is your fault, Anthony. None of it. Grown-ups are having problems, and part of what they're fighting about is you and May. But none of it is your fault. You are perfect kids. Us grown-ups are not perfect. That's us, not you. None of this is your fault.'"

Georgie leans his head on Anthony's forearm. He's ready for a nap.

"That's amazing."

"That's what I want to say to you. I want Gram to roll up here and be like: 'Alexandra . . .'" He says my name the way

Gram says it, rushed and squeezed together: *Azandra.* "'None of this is your fault.'"

"You believe that?"

"Definitely. You didn't do anything to cause this crap."

"No, I mean, about your family."

"Oh. I try to believe it. You know. I want to. It's hard." Someone laughs in the parking lot, and Anthony instinctively looks, as if they might be laughing at him. "Why do you think I wanted to be your friend?"

"No idea."

"You're a survivor, Al. You've always been a survivor. I could tell in that church parking lot. My family was a mess that summer. I needed someone like you who knows how to survive."

Georgie tries to pull my toy duck out of the dash, but it's permanent. Even my dad's thick, calloused hands couldn't wedge it out.

"I'm not sure I agree with you," I say. "But that's the best compliment I've ever gotten."

"Damn right. Best compliment I ever gave."

The dog whines and scratches at my door.

"Evil stepsister's getting restless," he says.

"God, I hate Marisol."

"She's the worst."

"I wanna punch her in the nuts."

"That'd be interesting."

"Why do I hate that she's good with G-e-o?" I say.

"She's not good with G-e-o."

"You saw them. They were laughing and singing."

"She doesn't have to deal with him, Al. Anybody can be nice to him for five minutes. You deal with him day in and day out. She doesn't know."

"She has no idea."

"Screw her."

"None of these people have any idea."

"Screw em all, isn't that right, G-man? Can I get a '*Hell yeah*'?" Anthony puts a palm up for a high five.

[Georgie pokes Anthony's hand distractedly with his wrist.]

Marisol pounds on the window, right next to my head. "I have to go," she barks.

"Okay, okay!" Anthony says, giving a thumbs-up. "Time to end this carjacking."

I step out and hand Marisol the key.

"Sorry I tried to take the truck."

"Don't apologize. Makes it worse." Ouch. Marisol is quick. "It's not me, okay? I didn't do this. I understand you're mad, but it's not my fault."

"That's what Anthony was just saying."

Marisol looks at him for backup.

"More or less," Anthony says.

"Lock the doors please. I have to go, they're here." She yanks the dog, opens her apartment door, and unhooks him. I get the briefest look at her dark home. Coatrack, dog toys, laundry basket. Are my dad's fuzzy work socks in that basket?

She starts toward the road, where there is now a clump of bicycles and—oh god—horses.

This is the moment to walk away from Marisol and end the humiliation, to regroup and process what the hell just happened, to figure out a way home before dark.

But now there are horses.

I grab Georgie's hand and pull him the other way. Maybe we can duck behind the building. Crispy is whimpering in the apartment and scratching at the door.

A horse sniffs and neighs. Georgie freezes.

"Come on, Georgie, we have to—"

"Aanh." *[He's pulling that way. He sees them.]*

"Marisol's leaving, and we—"

"Aanh."

Goddamn horses. Georgie's favorite thing since he was three. We got him piles of horse picture books and took him to watch people ride. Then the fixation got too intense, and we had to throw out all the posters and T-shirts and plastic horse figures.

"Okay, we can take a look, Georgie."

"Aanh." We follow Marisol. The parking-space lines, thick white paint like frosting, glow fluorescent in the twilight.

"Yes, cute horses." We'll just say hello, maybe pet the horses.

"Aanh."

And then we'll say goodbye to Marisol and just get the hell out of here.

"Mm-hmm. Four horses."

Oh crap, I forgot.

"Aanh."

There is no *just*, especially with Georgie.

CHAPTER NINE

Now I'm squished into a trailer, and not a comfy hayride trailer, a metal work trailer. I sit with Georgie at the front railing, as close as he can get to the team of horses pulling us.

Anthony is sprawled at the back of the trailer chatting—chatting!—with Marisol.

We're going to a community supper, hosted by a Christian group called Solar Village.

Georgie was not gonna miss this wagon ride. And the promise of free food helped. "Fresh hot pizza!" the twentysomething in the electric car bragged.

Anthony thinks we can get a ride home from someone at the Village.

"I'm great with the Christians," he promised.

"I recall you hiding in the parking lot with us heretics."

"When I want to be great with the Christians, I'm great. Give me five minutes, they'll be lining up to drive us home."

If there are any cars. This procession has one tiny electric car, a buggy really, but it's mostly engineless, a parade of bikes, horses, and this trailer with its creaking, straining axles. We clomp down the road as a kid on a mountain bike holds on to the railing next to me, not pedaling.

"You all going to the supper?" he says. "Where you from?"

"Near here."

"Can you believe how much we got?" He nods at the strange pile of merchandise in the trailer: a box of mason jars, three jigsaw puzzles, a power drill, a bag of yarn. Is someone moving?

"What is all this?" I say.

"We trade firewood for stuff in town. We give a lot away, too, at a nursing home and a school. But we also sell it, and most people don't have money, so I got that skateboard for like one armload of wood, something you could chop in five minutes. Isn't that awesome?"

Not for the kid who gave it up.

"Henry, no hitching. You gotta pedal." An older man on a bike waves him off.

Henry winks and lets go of the trailer. "See ya."

"Aanh."

"Those are the horses," I say for the fifth time. "They're pulling us."

Georgie leans into me, his ribs imprinting on my arm.

Anthony and Marisol are close to each other, but not quite touching, their legs parallel. There's energy and meaning in the space between them. I'm smooshed against Georgie, but it's a lifeless, heavy touch, with no spark or spirit.

Raising a kid like Georgie is intimate as hell. There's so much body and so much contact. Too much sometimes. Crushing hugs when he's willing to give you one. Helping him put his pants back on after a poop. Tick checks, baths, snot and drool wiping, wrestling down a temper.

I know Georgie's body the way most people know their partner's or their child's. I've spent so much time with this young man's arms, his rounded back muscles, the fuzz on his shins, his lopsided butt. I've seen more actual penis than any girl I know. Hours of penis.

Is this how doctors feel? Bodies are matter-of-fact and unmysterious. I look across at Marisol and Anthony, that simple tension and excitement, and I can't imagine it. I can't imagine heating up another kid's body. I can't imagine a crotch that didn't need to be washed or wiped or dressed. I think I'd just say: *Okay, that's enough. Now pull your pants up, and let's go have second snack.*

<hr/>

When did I become such a grandma? I used to dance, flirt, wonder about people. Where did that go?

I was adventurous as a kid, dirty even. I got two boys to show me their butts in first grade. We went far enough into the woods so the after-school counselors couldn't see, mosquitoes circling, my bare feet sinking into the moss.

The first one pulled his striped shorts down and bent over. His butt looked like mine.

The other kid's butt was flat, with little folds at the bottom, the promise of butt cheeks yet to come.

What do you say to a kid showing you his ass? *Thanks?* "Okay," I said.

"Now we get to see yours," the boy said. As I turned around and pulled my dress up, he added, "From the front."

"I wanna see your butt from the front" is a good line. I'll use it someday.

Before that, there was Elena. She threw a toy train at my forehead on my first day of preschool, then spent the rest of the day nursing me, bringing me cups of juice, putting ice cubes on my bruise. That became a ritual for us, caretaking each other's ailments. She'd "get sick," and I'd tuck her in. I'd "break my leg," and she'd carry me.

Hers was the first body I knew. In kindergarten, we'd have naked time in her room (unlike mine, her bedroom door locked). We'd leave our white socks on, telling ourselves we could get dressed quicker if someone knocked. To this day, there is nothing more naked to me than wearing only socks.

When she slept over, Elena would crawl into my bed and spoon me. We'd hold hands between my legs. It was the perfect balance of innocent and naughty: holding hands, but in the press of my thighs.

We moved away in third grade, because Georgie needed services our town didn't have. It was heartbreak. I saw Elena years later, on an eighth-grade field trip. She volunteered at this living history farm. Without her name tag, I wouldn't have recognized her. We hugged and talked, but I was frightened. Who was this woman in front of me with her huge hands and wire-rimmed glasses?

As the new girl in Little Falls, I was quickly pulled into the economy of crushes and gossip and rumors. And difference. Boys are this, girls are that.

I had "boyfriends" in fourth grade, short-lived dramas arranged and then wrecked by my friends. It was all for the breakup, the moment of crisis when the girls circle around, shake our heads, and protect our own.

I wasn't the most precocious—Dina Raveis was already tongue kissing—but I was in it. I dated Aaron Mosher in sixth grade. I initiated everything: hand-holding, kissing, rubbing. Michael Coombs, the summer after seventh grade, was the opposite. His tongue worming into my mouth, his hands clawing under my clothes.

Then I changed.

In ninth grade, Mom was back to work full-time cause my dad left, and I started watching Georgie. First, it was after school. Then I got good at it, so I did it other times, too: Saturday mornings when my mom slept till noon, a full six hours after Georgie would barge into my room. "Aanh!"

With kids like Georgie, when the seesaw starts leaning toward one caregiver, it only tilts more. Like a half-flooded boat, unbalance leads to more unbalance.

In stores, he followed me, not Mom. Tempers ended when I intervened. One Sunday, my mom gave him second snack, and he kept pushing it away. I diagnosed it from up in my room. "Bowl, mom, bowl," I yelled. She didn't hear, so I jogged down, dumped the plate of bananas and graham crackers into a blue bowl, slid it in front of him, and he started shoveling it into his mouth.

"How'd you know?" my mom said.

"*Because I spend more goddamn time with him than you do,*" I yelled.

No, I didn't. Should have, though. I just shrugged and went back upstairs.

That's how I switched from Sister of Disabled Kid to Caregiver of Disabled Kid.

I have to get home cause my brother's being dropped off.

I'd love to come to your party, but my mom needs me on Friday.

And I know, lots of kids have siblings, lots of kids babysit. It's different with Georgie. I'm always listening for him, thinking about him, checking. To be fully obnoxious, I'll say this: Other kids seemed immature to me, a little simple. All you do is go to school and take care of yourself? And you complain about *that*? I probably came off as aloof and judgy. I probably was.

I wasn't the only one withdrawing, of course. I saw the others who opted out: girls and boys skirting the center, choosing a line through the hallway and the day that kept them unseen. There are so many reasons to retreat. Your body develops too fast. Or, like mine, doesn't develop. Life at home gets too lonely. Life at home gets too intense. Grades aren't good enough. Grades are too good.

You live with your disabled brother.

You don't live with your disabled brother.

My goofy, curious, touchy body went to sleep. On some animal level, everyone knew. By the middle of ninth grade, I walked the halls like a lunch aide, an unnoticed body, nonexistent. Not disliked, not unpopular. Irrelevant.

I don't miss the drama.

But damn, I miss other bodies.

<hr />

We're on a dirt road now, cutting between two fields of early corn, the silklike doll hair, blond in the setting sun. With no gas, are they going to harvest the corn by hand? Seems like a lot of work.

Georgie taps me. "Aanh."

"That's Anthony."

"Aanh."

"Anthony."

"Aanh."

"I'm not gonna say it."

"Aanh."

"No, I'm not saying it."

"Aanh."

"You say it."

"Aanh."

"Fine. That's my evil stepsister."

Silence. We pass a tidy one-story house with four vehicles in various states of broken-down. I guess most vehicles are broken-down now. A little girl in a peach dress waves from the tiny front porch. Me and the trailer driver wave back.

"Aanh."

"I told you. Evil stepsister."

Georgie leans in front of my face, maybe threatening to temper.

"Yes, Alexandra is upset," I say. "Alexandra feels sad and angry, but not with you, Georgie." I rub the back of his head; like mine, his crew cut has a satisfying grain, silky on the way down and grabby on the way up.

"Aanh."

"I'm mad at Dad."

"Aanh."

"I'm mad that he's not around. And I'm mad that he sort of is around. I'm just mad."

My dad's an early riser. Morning was my time with him. It

was mostly functional: get dressed, eat, pack up, head to school and work. On the weekends, it expanded in time and color. We had two, three, sometimes four hours before my mom stumbled down. Georgie's meds made him a sleep monster, able to conk out where he fell, corpselike, until we shook him awake. Later, Georgie's meds would do the opposite, popping him fully awake at dawn. But in elementary school, our sleep schedules created two minifamilies. My dad and I, up early, greeted the crusted ice-cream bowls, the final hand of cards played but not reshuffled, the drawing abandoned midmarker. We ate last night's soft popcorn while we cleared the sink and poached the eggs.

My dad and I shuffled silently through these hours. We could sit in the quiet, in not-doing, because it was early. The obligation to perform, to provide dialogue and response—the assumption that talk is better than silence—came later, after food was eaten, hair was brushed, and the door to the day was shouldered open.

"Aanh." *[Georgie takes my hand and points at the back of the trailer.]*

"Jesus, Georgie, it's Anthony, and he's talking to Marisol. Like a traitor."

"Aanh."

"I don't know her."

"Aanh."

"You know her better than I do."

"Aanh."

"Why don't you tell me? Who is that, Georgie? Who is she?"

He exults quietly, pumping his forearms and squinting.

We're in a forest now, a great tunnel of green, the last rays of sun yellowing the branches that fork overhead like veins, like rivers. I lie down, sick of banging my neck on the trailer wall, sick of looking at those two.

"I wish you'd told me, Georgie."

[He stiffens, his breath pulsing out of his nose like a panting dog.]

"I mean, God, how long have you known all this?"

[He is clenched and waiting.]

I point to his lips, chapped and rosy. "I really wish you could talk. Be nice to get a little update once in a while."

We pass through a gap in the woods where locusts are trilling. It's a sound wash, a cicada shower that douses us and then recedes.

"Don't be afraid to say: 'Hey, Alex, Dad stopped by. Oh, and by the way, he has a new family.'"

"Aanh."

"Yeah, that'd be helpful."

I want to squeeze the truth out of him. I want to hold him by his ankles and shake his stories out. He's an information suck, constantly demanding to be told and retold every little fact and plan, but he doesn't give back. He knows crazy stuff about Dad and this new family, and he hoards it.

He makes the sign for *brother* again. He better not be saying he's Marisol's brother.

We bump over some ruts, and the mason jars clang. This is a long trip on some iffy roads. It might be hard to get back.

Georgie makes the sign again. When he moved in with the Boyers, he used the *brother* sign for Mason, the Boyers' son, and I refused to allow it. Mason is not his brother.

Hold on. No.

He does it again. *Father?*

Ohmygod, is that what he's been signing?

He made that sign obsessively when Dad left, so much that we stopped verbalizing it for him.

"You mean Daddy," I say quietly.

[Georgie's eyes tilt up, the green spotlight of his gaze on me.]

"Oh god, you did tell me, didn't you?" I hug his stiff torso. "You told me, and then you brought me to him. You sweet boy."

I think of all the confusion, all the excitement in him: *Alex, Dad came to see me!* What else does he have in there?

"You saw Dad. He visited you."

[Georgie looks down, hand frozen in midair, waiting for me to finish the story.]

"Aanh."

"You saw Dad. And that's when you met Marisol."

[Tiny head pump.]

"You met Marisol and her big dog."

[Stillness.]

"Thank you, Georgie. Thank you for telling me."

It's messed up. My dad's behavior is messed up. But Georgie is a goddamn gem. I put my forehead on his shoulder. He smells woolly, like an old carpet.

I love him so, so much. It's like a free fall.

It's like a catapult.

<hr/>

"I got the story on this Solar Village," Anthony says.

We're walking on a stone-lined path from the stables to the main barn at the Village. Georgie is peering into a greenhouse, clear plastic stretched over a pipe frame. Inside, rows of black flats sit on wood pallet tables. Tomatoes, peppers, cucumbers. I nudge him back onto the path.

"From who?" I want him to say it.

"Marisol."

"Seems like you two had a great time."

"She's being helpful. Which is nice, considering we tried to steal her truck."

"Yeah, she's wonderful. And so pretty."

"Not really."

"Bull. She's gorgeous."

We pass simple wood-frame buildings, some weathered, some half-built. Everywhere is the muddy, fresh look of new construction: stacks of freshly milled boards, piles of ochre earth next to newly dug foundations.

"It's not relevant," Anthony says.

"Ohmygod, you have a crush." I stop and let Georgie get ahead.

"Ohmygod, I don't."

"If you kiss her, I will literally end your life." I'm whispering, but Georgie can probably still hear.

"Good to know."

"I saw the looks she was giving you. Don't even think about it, not for a second."

"Hey, Al." He waves his hand in my face. "I'm on your side."

From inside the barn, I hear an old-timey hymn, sung in harmony with a fiddle and a guitar. *Wash all my sins away, wash all my sins away.*

"If you were on my side," I say, "you wouldn't buddy up to my nemesis."

"This isn't her fault, Al."

"Anthony, this is a ridiculously messed-up situation."

"Agreed."

"And part of how you get through a messed-up situation is by resenting the right person, and Marisol is the right person."

Georgie stops to stare at a goat behind a wire fence. Do I need to worry about electric fences here? Wouldn't that be hilarious: Georgie gets an electric shock in the middle of a blackout.

"She's not the enemy."

"She's on the enemy's side."

We smile at a neatly dressed couple walking the other way, overalls and a surprisingly hip print dress.

"She's not on a side. She's a kid," Anthony says.

"I can resent a kid."

"You're gonna hate what I say next."

Right. Here comes the straight-boy fake compliment, attraction disguised as respect. *Marisol's really wise.* Or: *She's so funny.*

"Then don't say it."

"I think she's gonna be part of your family."

I shut my eyes. "Oh my god, that's so much worse than what I imagined. And no, she won't."

"Come on, families change. My family's gone through changes, too," Anthony says.

"Totally different."

The mountain biker from earlier, Henry, is scaling a homemade climbing wall on the side of the barn, maybe showing off for us. "Don't go above the blue line without rope," someone yells at him.

"No, it isn't," Anthony says. "My dad was gone, completely. Then he popped back in our lives for a few months when I was seven, and, boom, later that year, I had a little sister."

Georgie stumbles down a hill toward a rolling chicken coop surrounded by a temporary fence.

"May's adorable. Marisol's creepy. And don't disagree with me. Your whole job as my friend here is to back me up. Could you please just shake your head and say: 'Yeah, Marisol's so lame. What a snotty little jerk.'"

"You could see her as an ally."

"And how about: 'Even though you shaved your head and

look like a pudgy twelve-year-old boy, you're way cuter than her, Al.'"

"I bet a year from now, you'll look back and go: 'Why was I so hard on Marisol?'"

"You do have a crush on her."

"No, this is how families work. We kids have to stick together, or else the grown-ups are gonna take us down cause they're all crazy. Which"—Anthony drops his voice—"brings me to this Village. Marisol says it's amazing and a little creepy."

"How nice of her to invite us then."

"It's off-the-grid Christians. Back-to-nature, like the Amish, but more hip and environmental. Marisol says there's gonna be a lot of bragging, a lot of I-told-you-so about the blackout. And her—*your*—dad did a lot of work for them, he set up that huge solar array." Anthony points past the barn to an acre of slate-gray rectangles angled toward the south. If they all tilted up flat, they could make a shimmering lake.

"My dad's part of this? Jesus, we gotta leave. I can't take it."

"We will leave. You get us some food, and I'll find us a ride. It's all gonna work out."

A bicyclist struggles to pull a trailer full of apples up to the barn.

"I want to go home, Anthony."

"Aw, look who's excited to get home now."

"I feel like you're not acknowledging the insanity of the past hour."

"No, it is insane. Completely. But we're good now. We're about to get fed and get home."

At the barn, you can see down through the cow pastures toward the last pink of the sunset. It's a country view, all nature, with the houses and gas stations tucked away in the valleys.

"And, for the record," he says, "you are."

"I'm what?"

"Way more gorgeous than Marisol."

Gorgeous.

I thought I said *cute.*

CHAPTER TEN

The food is ridiculously good, but there's a catch.

Outside the barn, two long tables are covered with soups and stews and foods you don't see much in the blackout: bread, yogurt, and pizza with cheese.

"Fresh and hot," says a bearded man handing me a plate. "Wood-fired, my friend."

Behind him, a woman with a flowered apron and a white headscarf slides a pizza into a fat outdoor oven, the red stucco blackened around the opening.

Pizza. Hell yeah. Sorry: Heck yeah.

I load half a pizza onto a plate, and thick slices of bread and butter and a hunk of quiche onto a second plate. At the end of the line sits a big glass cooler with lemonade and ice. Ice! Anthony's grandma puts two cans of Coke Zero in the stream every day, and they got coldish. But this lemonade is cold. Icy pre-blackout cold.

"Tastes good, right?" A woman with short gray hair, wearing boots and jeans, smiles at me. "Get a refill. It's all you can eat and all you can drink."

I open the spigot, itself cold, and fill my mug again.

"I'm Louise-Marie," she says. "Everyone calls me Lumi." Her cheeks are tanned, and her pores are large and shiny, like the dimples of a strawberry.

"Hi, I'm Alexandra."

"What brings you here today, Alexandra?"

"We . . . ran into someone who was coming, and she invited us." Don't say names, Don't leave a trail.

"Always nice to see new faces." She points over at Georgie, who's scampering away from Anthony. "And the boy you came with . . ."

"That's my brother, Georgie."

"Your brother? Wonderful. Seems like a great kid. Glad to have you here. I hope you both get to explore and see what we're up to."

She watches Georgie bounce on the balls of his feet, his teeth clenched. And she doesn't ask *what Georgie is*. That's rare. And refreshing.

<hr />

Georgie is many things. And he's been called many things. Autistic. Postencephalitic. Brain-damaged. Epileptic. And my favorite: pervasive developmental disorder not otherwise speci-fied. PDD-NOS, or, as I like to say, podnose. The less we under-stand a human, the more words we throw.

In those first years, my mom fought for a diagnosis, craved a label that could box in her grief. She wanted to tell herself and my dad: *He's X. Plenty of kids are X. And, look, here's a treatment for X.*

Mount him and label him like a butterfly. It's not hard to see how false that is, funneling Georgie's wild and unknowable consciousness into a diagnosis, an insurance company code. But diagnosis did do one incredible thing: It connected us to other kids, other families, other siblings in the Nation of Differ-ence. Hanging with other families who have nontypical kids was astonishing. Wait—this thing I spend every minute of my life managing and explaining and trying to get space for, it's okay here? It's beyond accepted, it's assumed?

I did get jealous, though. Those kids with Down syndrome, what a joy! They're all the beautiful parts of human beings—the love, the excitement, the curiosity, the desire to interact—and none of the bull.

Jesus, stop complaining, Alex. That's another way to be a crappy sibling of a disabled kid: wish he had a different disability.

Early on, some folks claimed they could cure Georgie, huck-sters with stories of kids "coming out" of autism, nonverbal kids who suddenly speak in full sentences. We spent a lot of time and all our money chasing that lie.

"We owned a house. We had savings," my mom still rants when money's especially tight. They spent everything, and guess what? Georgie's still Georgie. And the hucksters are off swindling the next family.

But the worst thing about those years chasing a cure was how I looked at Georgie. He was a problem to solve, a broken mind to fix. If we did the right therapy or diet or family process, we'd get the real Georgie, the good Georgie.

If I'm honest, I'm still recovering from that, still reminding myself this *is* the real Georgie.

It's crappy to wish your brother was different. I know.

It's also crappy to pretend you don't.

I walk into the barn, where the tables and benches are filling up. This is the catch: We have to listen to some speakers while we eat our free food. A reception this warm usually means you're about to be sold something.

When I was twelve, these smiley college kids set up goals on our local field and hosted a soccer game. They made teams with blue and yellow pinnies and refereed the games. All the bull that usually messes up a neighborhood game—the arguments, the shoves—went away. I scored twice. I remember thinking: See? When we play fair, I'm actually good. But there was a catch. You could play once for free, but the next time, you had to come to the prayer meeting afterward. Anthony went every week, said the prayer meeting was boring but harmless, totally worth it. I played once, begged out of the meeting, and never went back. I don't like catches.

I walk right through the barn and out the massive doors on the other side. Georgie and Anthony are down by the chickens, and I start toward them, but then I see Marisol. Grrr. I plop down in the grass and start devouring my dinner. Hot pizza and cold lemonade! One blackout revelation is how important temperature is. Without power, everything's the same middling temperature. Your food, your room, your drink: It's all 70-something degrees and mossy. No hot soup or ice cream or warm bath or air-conditioned car. It's like color was taken away and the world turned grayscale.

The crisp pizza crust steams when I bite it. The too-hot tomato sauce hiding under the melted cheese burns my tongue. God, I love this.

I'm almost full when I see Marisol following Georgie up the hill. Uh-oh. I instantly stand and pivot into the barn.

"Surprisingly, no. Health is not number one." Lumi is up front with a wireless microphone. They don't overuse electricity here—there are no big TV screens or air conditioners—but it still feels showy to have her voice amplified.

"What do you think, Alexandra?"

What. I'm shuffling toward a table in back, and I freeze when Lumi says my name.

"I was just asking everyone: What's the number one determinant of well-being? What's the number one factor that determines how long and how happily you live?"

Heads turn. I've been called on and called out, sneaking into class after the bell.

I swallow a shard of pizza crust. I say the first answer I think of.

"Fear?"

It's probably not correct, but it's not stupid. It makes it seem like I've been paying attention.

"Oo, I like that. Fear. And don't you love Alexandra's haircut? There's a kid ready to get to work." She winks. At me, but for the crowd. "No, the number one determinant of well-being isn't money, or health, or fear. It's connection. The thing most of us are missing. Connection to our neighborhoods, our friends, our families, our Creator. Human beings survive and thrive through connection. But now, for the first time in history, we go it alone, in our separate little houses and our separate little lives. Well, the collapse of the electrical grid is calling our bluff, isn't it?" That's an alarming description; *blackout* sounds temporary and accidental. "The dwindling fossil fuels, the end of mass agriculture, global trade at a standstill, it all comes down to one fear: How will I live without all of that? The answer is in the question. *I* won't live. *We* will."

Lumi takes a dramatic pause, which is filled by the unmistakable *thwok-thwok* of Ping-Pong somewhere.

I find a seat at the back and finish my food while Lumi preaches on. I look around, and I'm right under a rough human-sized wooden cross. This is the Village church, and I'm where the preacher stands. Yikes.

"I keep hearing people say: 'When are *they* going to get this straightened out?'" Lumi's walking through the crowd, relaxed and chummy. "When are *they* going to bring back my phone and my ice cream. Here's a little secret: *They* are not coming. Good news is: *We* are already here. Our Solar Village builds on what we already have, what cannot be taken from us: our community, our hard work, the earth and the sun, and the words of a crazy carpenter's son from Nazareth. By the way, we don't have ice cream, sorry, but we do have fresh whipped cream. Right, Alannah? Alannah, can you wave? See her for some whipped cream and apple cobbler, and if you are interested in joining our Solar Village, just stop by her table in back. We are excited you're here, and I hope this is the beginning of a deeper . . . and longer . . . connection."

Lumi waves off the tepid applause, and people get back to eating and chatting. It's an interesting mix: suburban families, a couple of loners, and hungry, tanned Villagers. Next to me is a guy who must be a farmer cause he's grilling a Villager about irrigation and beef cattle, and do you really plow with horses here. Mostly, no, apparently.

"How'd I do?" Lumi appears next to me.

"That was great."

"Liar. You were bored, I could tell." She sits.

"Compared to most things like this, you were great."

"Nice. I'm better than the truly awful." She picks up a half-eaten pizza slice from an abandoned plate. A tattoo on her arm reads 1 JOHN 3:18. "What can I say, it's part of the job. The dog-and-pony show. But the pizza's out of this world, right? That's what gets people's attention, a nice hot slice of pizza." She chews with her mouth open and looks over the mingling crowd. She has chunky silver rings on each hand; one is a circle of cut-out Christian fish. "I did like what you said, though. Fear. I'm gonna think more about that."

There's a pause. Should I say something?

"Hey, I saw your brother out there feeding the chickens. He's jumping right in."

"He loves animals."

"Look, I don't usually say this, especially to young people, but I think you and your brother could be a great fit here."

Huh.

Kids are lining up for whipped cream and cobbler, and their parents are reading Village pamphlets, scribbling contact information on Alannah's clipboard.

"I can tell when I meet people, and I get a good sense from you two," she says. "Are you surprised?"

"Well, Georgie's different. He's not like you and me," I say.

"Aw, don't say that. We all have more in common than we have differences."

"Yeah. I mean, *I* think that. But not everybody sees it."

"I'm gonna be honest with you, Alexandra, cause you seem like a straight-up person. We are strongly committed to building an inclusive Village, one that welcomes everyone. Please tell your brother that, and your whole family."

Not sure Georgie will care, but my mom will be happy to hear it. "That's great to know."

"Again, you sound surprised."

"Georgie's not always welcomed. People get uncomfortable. People make assumptions."

Villagers are resetting the barn to its church arrangement, dragging wooden benches across the wide plank floors. One show's over, and they're loading in the next.

"Ridiculous. I can only imagine the nonsense he puts up with. And you, as his sister." Her voice gets louder over the echoing scrape of heavy wooden tables. "The great thing about building something is: We get to decide. We're building our Village on our values. All assumptions and discrimination end at the front gate."

"That's great." I'm almost yelling. It's loud as a construction site in here.

"Now, I know you look around here today, and you don't see a lot of people like your brother. I get that. It's a challenge we're working on, getting a more inclusive community. That's part of why I'm saying this to you. People like your brother are essential to our ministry. Essential. I want everyone to see him and know how inclusive we are. And I want anybody who's biased—who, as you say, makes assumptions—to see him and stay the hell away."

Wow. Lumi's a Christian who says "hell." And she said it in defense of Georgie. You don't hear that kind of talk much in the Nation of Difference. The Nation can be careful, insular, sometimes apologetic. Nobody tells ignorant Normies to "stay the hell away." And we should. Georgie should live in a world where he doesn't have to face that crap every day. Where my mom doesn't have to face it.

Lumi continues. "And I'm not saying you need a Bible to learn how to be tolerant, but it is in the Bible, right? Jesus can't open his mouth without talking about it."

It's silent suddenly, the room restored, the rows of benches—pews, now—facing me and Lumi. We are the pulpit.

"Sometimes, I hear so-called Christians say things, and I go: Are we reading the same book? Cause tolerance means everybody." She points as she splits the word. "Every. Body."

Who is this Lumi? How does she know what to say?

Look, I'm not moving to this Village, can't imagine it. But being invited by the boss, being told me and Georgie should be a part of it, feels tremendous. The Village is a bright spot on a dark map.

It's grand to sit here in the pulpit and whisper to an empty congregation about embracing Georgie. And every body.

"Sorry," I say. My smile melts into a sob. "It's been a crazy day." A heck, no, a *hell* of a day.

"If it ain't worth crying over, it ain't worth doing." Lumi places a hand on the back of my buzz cut, the warm and practiced touch of someone who's used to people crying in front of her. "Now, it's almost bonfire time. They're gonna say they're making s'mores, but it's total bull. We have apples you can roast with a little cinnamon and honey. It's not bad, but it's no s'more. You and your brother should get one."

Another wink, and Lumi saunters over to the recruitment table, puts a hand on the back of a mom, and meets the two-year-old in her arms, big eyes and whipped cream–smeared cheeks.

Even though I'm supposed to like Lumi, I do.

I don't like catches, but this one caught me.

<hr />

It's true, a roasted apple is no s'more. But it is a sugary mouth-scalding treat when you dip it in honey and cinnamon and, if you're Georgie, smear it on your cheeks, chin, and nose. He devours his and circles the fire, shadowing the other apple roasters. He won't let me wipe his sticky hands, which are collecting dirt and pine needles. He's urgent and a bit reckless, maybe exhausted. I wonder what time the Boyers put him to bed.

I relieve Anthony, who goes to wait in line for the composting toilet. I stand uphill from the bonfire, away from the throbbing heat but close enough to grab Georgie if needed.

People are smiley and chatty, mostly non-Villagers enjoying the novelty of this food and this place. Like this lady, big smiley teeth and broad shoulders under her poofy lime-green blouse.

"Hi."

"Hello."

I face the fire. She faces me.

"I'm Marisol's mom."

Holy hell.

"You're Alex."

No, no, no.

I nod. Her black hair is streaked with silver, and bracelets dangle on her wrists: gold, gems, a watch.

Of course she's here. Who's next, my dad? Arleen from Child Protective Services?

"Marisol said you came by our place." That's a hilarious description. Yeah, we just stopped by to say hi and steal your truck. "It's nice to see you."

I nod, like: *Yes, that is how you feel.*

"I've heard a lot about you," she says. Her skin is warm-toned like Marisol's but darker, and her eyebrows are stark, two black arches that suggest alarm, though her smile is kind. Her forehead is rippled, not the deep worry lines my mother has, but gentle furrows like corduroy.

Deep breath. "Wish I could say the same," I say.

"Yes, well, I know this is all a bit awkward. But I understand you need a ride."

"Oh. No, we're okay," I lie.

"We charged the electric car, so we can take you wherever you need to go." Her tone is businesslike: There's a problem; she will solve it.

"We're fine, thanks."

"It's no trouble. Please, let us help you."

"I don't need help." One lie, an overly long pause, and then another. "It was nice to meet you."

I walk toward Georgie and the fire. Conversation over. Please, God, let it be over.

[Georgie pumps his arms slowly down by his waist. Not celebratory elbow flexing—this is tense, his hands bent into claws.]

"I almost didn't recognize you with your haircut." She's next to me again, her hoop earrings glinting in the firelight. "You look different than the photos."

"I didn't recognize you because I didn't know you existed until an hour ago."

[Georgie comes close, sensing the two of us, more with his body than his eyes. He swerves away, bouncing on his toes. He's hyper, unsteady.]

"That wasn't my decision," she says. "I'm sure you understand."

I'm sure I don't.

[Georgie does a throaty inhale-yell and jabs both arms out to the side, almost smacking a Villager.]

Be nice, Alexandra. She's trying to help.

"Do you see this?" I point at Georgie. "Now, correct me if I'm wrong: Whenever Georgie sees you, he probably sees his dad, right? I mean our dad."

"Yes."

"Who isn't here."

Her mouth puckers, cracking her lipstick. "Mitch is away at the moment."

"Right. And, as you can tell, Georgie's starting to temper, and I think it's cause he expects to see his dad."

"Hey." Anthony's back. Horrible timing. I am not introducing him.

"So if you can't give Georgie what he's fixating on," I say, "if you can't magically produce my dad or Mitch or whatever you call him, could you please just leave us alone?"

"I'm offering to drive all of you—"

"Leave us alone. Please. And I'll calm Georgie down." I've said enough. I should stop there. I don't. "Which I've been doing since long before you met him, and I will continue doing long after you're gone from his life."

Anthony straightens up, alert, a slight smile on his face. There's a truth about people that's revealed only in moments of conflict, when emotions are raw and inflamed. My mom flutters and waves her arms, shoos it away. My dad rages and stews. I run away, or I used to. Anthony gets still and leans closer. He's interested in fights and hot-blooded drama. He rises to it, relishes it.

"You don't have to do it alone," she says. "We can help."

"I don't need help!" I yell, which sends her alarmed eyebrows higher. "I know how to take care of my brother. I know what's best for him."

"Do you?" Her chin stiffens. "Are you sure?" She gives a little laugh.

Time slows down. What is that laugh about?

[Georgie, jogging on his tiptoes, bumps into a little girl. The father yanks her out of the way and puts his body between Georgie and the kid.]

"What?" I say.

"Well, it's not entirely true that you're great at taking care of your brother, is it?"

"What are you talking about?"

"I mean, that's why he's not living at home. That's why—"

Two things happen so quickly they are one thing, a choreographed trio. I lunge at Marisol's mom and shove her. Not much, I mostly push her shoulder. And Anthony catches my arm and pulls me back.

"What was that?!" She looks around for support, corroboration.

"It's fine," Anthony says to her and the entire bonfire crowd. He's so goddamn reasonable. "It's been a long day."

"You have a special needs child here." She points an angry finger at Georgie, who's pumping his elbows, seemingly ecstatic, actually upset. "And no way to get him home. Oh, but you know what's best, do you? I highly doubt that. It's no wonder he's in foster care when you won't even——"

"Whoa." Anthony—levelheaded, calm Anthony—releases me and spins on her, gets in her face. "That's enough, lady." He's taller than her, and he glares down. "You need to stop talking about stuff you don't understand."

She huffs out her nose, but she's shook.

"You can go. We'll take care of Georgie," Anthony says.

She stamps away, then turns back, wagging her finger, bracelets trembling. "You better. You better take good care of that boy."

She straightens her blouse and marches to a sleek black electric car in front of the barn. Marisol is in the passenger seat, window up, staring at us.

"I think that went really well," Anthony says.

"I can't believe you told her off. You called her 'lady.'"

Marisol's mom slams the driver's-side door, and the car blinks noiselessly to life, its bluish headlights x-raying the trees.

"I'm not gonna stand there and let her talk smack about you," Anthony says.

"I thought she was part of my family now."

"There's limits."

Marisol is listening to her mom rant. The interior of the car is garishly bright, like a movie set.

"Feels good to resent someone, doesn't it?" I say.

"If they deserve it, yeah. Plus, who wants a ride home in a comfy car when we can be stranded here?"

We'll be fine. Lumi was so welcoming, I'm sure she'll take care of us.

Marisol's fingers touch the car window, a Georgie-sized wave in our direction. Her mom puts the car in gear, and the interior goes dark. The headlights sweep across the bonfire, strobe-light blue washing over orange flames.

"You're the best," I say.

"Thanks for noticing," he says.

"Sorry if I messed up your chances with Georgie's hot sister."

"You"—Anthony watches the electric car glide silently away, the red taillights stuttering over bumps—"are Georgie's hot sister." Joke or compliment? If it's a compliment, it doesn't last long. "Marisol is his sophisticated sister."

"Bite me."

"See?"

<hr />

Anthony goes off in search of another ride. He's determined to get us home, but the few people with cars keep telling him they can't afford to drive that far.

With Marisol and her mother gone, I catch my breath and take in this crazy village.

Industrious Villagers of all ages scurry around, focused but unhurried, feeding the bonfire, cleaning dishes, carrying slop to the pigs. Maybe we'll spend the night here. That could be lovely. They're smiling. We're all smiling.

Except Georgie. He's surfing the edge of a temper. He's manic, heedless. He's looking around—for Marisol and her mom? for our dad?—and getting way too close to the fire. He gobbles down another honey-soaked apple. Maybe it's too much sugar, cause he ramps up. When he sees me toss my apple core into the bonfire—lots of people are doing it—he starts throwing all kinds of things in: a stick, an uncooked apple, rocks.

We get yelled at by a self-important teenager who says we aren't allowed near the bonfire with a "behavioral issue."

I tell him it's not behavioral, it's developmental.

We argue. It's the typical Normie misread of Georgie.

Finally, I say: "You know what—go tell Lumi. She'll explain."

So often, I have to swallow people's BS. I know they're wrong, but I suck it up and walk away. It's a luxury to say: *Go get the boss. She'll tell you to embrace Georgie or stay the hell away.* I never get to be smug like this. Thanks, Lumi.

I ease Georgie back from the fire.

"Aanh." *[He immediately does the sign for "father," thumb to forehead.]*

"He's not here, Georgie."

[Thumb to forehead. He is sweaty from the fire and from his agitated state.]

"Daddy's not here. Alex is here, and Anthony is here. Daddy's not." *Daddy.* I never use that word anymore.

[Georgie's on his toes, straining upward.]

I put out an arm to keep a little kid out of his range.

"Alexandra, is he with you?" Lumi's here, pointing at Georgie.

"Yeah, of course." I step next to him, claiming him.

"I'm sorry, but we can't have people with behavioral issues. It's a Village rule. No behavioral issues, no drugs."

"He doesn't have behavioral issues, he's disabled. Remember?"

In the barn, someone drops something fragile and substantial—a platter or a bottle—and it smashes, turning heads. But not mine and not Lumi's.

"The result of his disability is a behavioral issue." Lumi gives a brittle smile. "Which means he poses a risk to himself and others and requires a higher level of supervision. We simply aren't set up for that, I'm sorry."

"But we talked about this. You said it's your goal, you want to be inclusive."

"I was referring to your brother, Georgie."

"This is Georgie."

"Oh. Gosh. So sorry. No, I meant the other one, the . . . the Black boy. Is he also your brother?"

My god.

No goddamn way.

She wants Anthony, not Georgie.

"I'm sorry, Alexandra, it's not personal. We simply don't have the resources. And we have had issues in the past, serious issues, which is why we—"

"God*damn* you!"

People back away. Maybe not all Villagers curse.

"I'm sorry if it was unclear. I was referring to your other brother."

Including everyone doesn't include my family.

"That's not my brother! This is my brother." I touch Georgie's shoulder, and he flinches.

"You need to get him away from the fire," the bossy teenager says.

"Shut up."

"Yes, Alex," Lumi says. "He's about to—"

"Both of you shut up!"

Everyone stares, even Georgie, even the people in line for the composting toilet. Firelight flickers over their frozen, wide-eyed faces. It's a diorama of the last decade of my life: Alarmed Normies recoil from my brother and, when I stand with him, from me.

"You." I say it loud so everyone can hear, and also so I don't start bawling. *Send this sorrow outward, Alex. Don't break.* "Are a fraud."

The fire pops, and a log falls, shooting a flare of sparks skyward, my own goddamn solar storm.

"We're looking out for everyone's safety, Alexandra," Lumi says. "And our focus must always . . ." *Blahblahblah.* She drones on, another snoozy promotional talk.

I tune her out, put a hand on Georgie's back, and whisper, "We have to go find Mom. She's waiting for you."

"Aanh." *[His hands are clenched, frozen in midtemper.]*

"Mom's waiting." A hot tear falls on Georgie's shoulder. I'm breaking. "And she has your movie." I am lying, saying anything to get out, get away, and the lies make my tears come faster. "We can watch your movie."

Lumi's still yammering: ". . . and personal responsibility, which is at the heart of our values and, to be honest . . ."

"Mom's over here, Georgie." I'm whimpering in his ear.

[He looks me in the eye, searching for the reason for my emotion. Then he turns and, blessedly, lumbers off down the dirt road.]

The mountain bike kid—did he see this whole thing?—gives a tiny wave as I pass and mouths, *Bye.*

"Alexandra!" Lumi calls. "Where are you going?"

I should keep walking, let her question bounce off my back, unanswered.

Nah.

I spin around and put up both middle fingers. I'm walking backward, leaving the saloon with guns drawn.

Pow. Pow.

CHAPTER ELEVEN

"Wait up!" Anthony's running.

"Aanh." *[Georgie's middle finger points back toward the Village. I agree. Screw that place.]*

"We're leaving. They're evil," I say.

A wood-fired furnace, a beige metal shed in front of long stacks of aging firewood, puffs sweet smoke, the smell of November in May.

"I thought they liked you," Anthony says.

"I was wrong. She said she was inclusive, and my brother would be welcome because he's different."

"That's awesome."

"She didn't mean Georgie, she meant you. Cause you're not white."

"Whaaat? Oh dang."

"She wants you cause you make it look diverse, but not G-e-o, cause he's a freaking behavioral issue."

"Oh, no. Uh-uh."

"She called you '*the Black boy*.'"

"Oh. Oh. Nope, son." He turns around and gives double middle fingers. "Take that, racist-ass Village."

"Aanh."

Georgie understands some of this, maybe a lot. Ugh. I can't explain it now.

"We're going home," I tell him. "You, me, and Anthony."

A broken trampoline sits near a heap of discarded blue barrels. Away from the cleaned-up Village, you see the pragmatic sense of nature most people around here have. Any piece of ground can be your junkyard.

"Aanh." *[Georgie grabs Anthony's arm, clamping, on the verge of a temper. Too many unanticipated changes, no structure.]*

"It's okay, Georgie. You're okay. We're walking."

I'm not scared for Anthony; he's been through many tempers. But I'm scared for us if Georgie falls apart. As hard as this moment is, Georgie tipping over the edge would be much, much worse.

"It's pretty dark," Anthony says.

"The moon's bright. We can see fine." Maybe not fine, but we can see. The moon was full a week ago. How do I know? Moon cycles have become a big conversation topic in the blackout. A rhythm that had no meaning in my life is now vital and present. The first nights, the new moon, were surreally dark. This waning moon (learned that) makes nighttime reasonably navigable.

"Al, we maybe shouldn't walk off into the darkness."

"Do not mention going back. We don't want a t-e-m-p-e-r." I'm superstitious about discussing tempers in front of Georgie. I don't want him to know the power they hold over us.

"We're just gonna walk into the woods?"

"You can stay if you want. Me and Georgie have to go."

"No, I'm coming. Just wait here a sec." Anthony jogs back toward the brightness.

"Aanh."

"Anthony's coming back. Then we can walk."

A breeze fills my nose and mouth with the ammonia stink of compost.

"Aanh."

Anthony returns carrying a sparking, overflowing ball of fire on the end of a stick. Georgie is mesmerized.

"It's a two-hour torch," Anthony says. "According to the racists." He rotates it in the air, a ring of yellow light.

"That thing is smelly."

"But it's bright."

"Like us."

"Aanh."

"Yes, Anthony has a torch."

We stare into it. It crackles and swells, the cloth ball like a liquid, teeming with sparks.

"Aanh."

"Anthony has to hold it. It's only safe if he holds it."

"Aanh."

"Yup, you can look at it. But don't touch."

Georgie watches an ember drop to the ground.

"Tiny fire," Anthony says. "We have to put it out." He squashes it.

Georgie stares.

"Someone likes this," Anthony says.

"Yeah. Good job."

"Good job, you, getting us out of there."

"Shut up."

Georgie pulls my hand. "Aanh."

"Yup, we're walking. You lead the way."

The torch blots out the moonlight, a warm circle of light pushing back the wall of darkness. Before, we walked in a vast gray landscape, trees throwing long moon shadows across our path. Now, we are an island, a golden raft in a black sea.

[Georgie walks ahead, stops, and turns to watch the flame, pumping his elbows. When we get close, he walks ahead again and starts it all over.]

I sing. "I got a girl in Baltimore, Little Liza Jane."

[Georgie reaches the edge of the light, spins around.]

"Street car runnin by her door, Little Liza Jane."

[Elbows pumping. Barking laugh.]

"Oh, Little Liza, Little Liza Jane."

[Awestruck as the fire gets close.]

"Oh, Little Liza, Little Liza Jane."

[Turning, stomp-walking into the dark.]

When you find the right loop, the right circuit of sensory excitement, Georgie soars. He is at home in the world, more than we Normies will ever be.

I keep singing. "I got a girl in Chicago, Little Liza Jane."

So many of Georgie's moments are strained, overloaded, defensive. The friction of the world rubs him raw. But when he finds flow, he is air, he is music.

"Walk and feel the cold winds blow, little Liza Jane."

He loves a loop that returns with variations, like this song. Like moving down this road, torchlight trembling, shadows twisting around the trees as we walk. He cycles through, savors the deep nourishment of perceptions that change while staying knowable.

"Oh little Liza, little Liza Jane."

This is an exquisite loop. It has familiar things (me, Anthony, Liza Jane) and new things (this road and the spectacular torch). It's physical (walking, turning, pumping arms), spatial (moving toward and away from the light, which also moves), visual (the ever-changing fire), and musical ("Little Liza Jane"). Put those four elements together right, and Georgie is born.

As always, we've stumbled upon it. You can't contrive

it or force it. Those turn to fixations. Loops have movement and change. They're too layered and complex to harden into obsession.

I take Anthony's free hand. "Not bad, huh?"

"It beats a sharp stick in the eye," Anthony says, one of his mom's signature compliments.

An orange newt scampers across our path and into the brush.

Get home, little guy. It's late.

And now, it's later.

The road forked twice and, though I think we guessed correctly, we were guessing. Away from the bonfire, the night deepens and the dew drops, spreading a chill over my bare legs. And this road is looking small, a two-track with tall grass in the middle, not something that gets driven on every day. We're slowing down. Anthony has been silent for ten minutes.

[Georgie finds a branch shaped like dog bone. For a moment, his step picks up.]

"Hey, someone found a treasure," I say.

"Glad he's having a good time."

"Come on, Tony. It's not so bad."

"Yeah, it's fantastic. It's the middle of the night—"

"Not the middle."

"And we're in the middle of nowhere."

"I know."

"And everyone connected to you, me, and Georgie is currently panicking. But Georgie found a stick. Things are looking up."

We step over a fallen tree limb. Hmm. Either that fell in the last couple hours, or this is not the road we came in on.

"Well. I'm sorry. I know it's been a long day," I say. The nudists, stealing Georgie, the VFW, Marisol, the Village. So damn long.

Anthony's shaking his head, tiny tremors that are part of some internal conversation, a fight with himself. "We're just wandering in the dark. What are we supposed to do?"

"What do you mean?"

"I don't know what the right thing to do is," he blurts, the words running together in a half yell. "Should I run back and beg for a ride?" He's looking at the ground, dictating the debate in his head. "Should I drag you back to that barn and make us sleep there? Can we even find our way back? Should I yell for help? There's gotta be something."

On our right is a crumbling stone wall, and our torch scribbles jittery shadows on the rocks.

"You always do the right thing, don't you?" I say.

"Certainly not. But I like to know what the right thing is."

The stop-motion flutter of a bat circles the torch, then stutters away.

"Can we keep going and trust the right thing will show up?" I like this question. I'll paint it on a sign in our yard.

Anthony stops. "No. It's too late for that," he whispers. He looks straight up and huffs out a breath, then whines, "What are we gonna do?"

Wow, Anthony's giving up. You don't see that much. Ever, really.

"Well . . ." What do we do? My jazzed-up brother wants to hike. My dear boy Anthony is shivering and despondent. Our two-hour torch is growing faint.

Anthony is whining up to the trees. "What are we gonna do?"

Frogs and peepers croak far off. I breathe the rich oxygen of deep forest, the pine sap, the leaf rot, the cold of night falling.

"We're gonna make a fire," I say.

It's perfect. It's *what we've been waiting for*.

"Right in here where it's flat." I stomp into the woods, toward what I hope is a clearing.

It will warm Anthony, ground Georgie, and turn this middle-of-the-night wandering into an event. Sitting around a fire will make our whole fiasco look intentional, even magical.

"You guys make a pile of pine needles, just the dry top ones," I say. "Crisp leaves, too. I'll gather some big stuff."

"Aanh."

"Yup, help Anthony find pine needles. We're building a campfire."

I know how to build a goddamn fire. I learned at the campgrounds we went to before Georgie got too restless for camping.

227

And I rediscovered it three weeks ago, when we started cooking outside. This'll be easy; we have a whole untouched forest to pillage.

I stumble out of the torchlit clearing into the black woods. My eyes adjust to the silver moonlight fingering through the pines, slanting lines like windblown rain. The stars, impossibly bright, flow like a river between the treetops. The night sky is primal and vivid in the blackout, because our billions of bulbs, our endless light pollution is gone.

Night is massive. The blackout showed me that nights are shockingly, disconcertingly long, a good ten or eleven hours. What did people do all night before electricity? Think?

Away from Georgie and Anthony, away from their strain and worry, the forest is calm, unhurried. And indifferent. I could wander off and be lost in minutes. I like that about nature. It's there for you, but it's not interested in you. It doesn't wonder how you're doing or put you in the center. It is the center. I'm a tolerated guest, climbing over root-clenched boulders and the damp, crumbling trunks of fallen trees.

I find a hardwood branch twice my height, with limbs as thick as my arm down to twigs like spaghetti. The perfect fire starter. A fire is a tree in reverse, from needles to twigs to branches to trunks.

I stand holding my giant, twisting staff. Anthony's torch twinkles in the distance.

I am alone. Unaccompanied and unaccounted.

This spot would be dark and silent any night. But knowing our whole state is in a blackout makes these woods feel ancient and majestic. Civilization is reduced to darkened settlements, and the forest is reclaiming its quiet, eternal power.

Maybe nature is the key. Maybe I should get out of the house, not to socialize but to come here, lay my body on this spongy bed of pine needles.

I have the urge to take my clothes off. Thanks, Joanne and— what was his name?

I wasn't comfortable for a minute till I was comfortable in my own skin.

I put down the branch.

I wish I'd known earlier. That's what the naked guy said.

I'm sixteen, early enough?

I pull my shirt off. The cold, wet air washes goose bumps over my shoulders. I pull my shorts down, leave them around my ankles. Chill seeps up from the forest floor and submerges my legs, fingers of cold air slide up my butt. Shiver.

I'm in first grade again, showing my butt in the woods. But I'm not showing, I'm not displaying. I'm standing. I rub my hand from my fuzzy scalp, down my neck and shoulder and belly to my cool thighs.

I want to be unified, like those nudists, one continuous body, no parts.

I want to be comfortable in this skin. *As* this skin.

How do I start?

"You okay?" Anthony calls out.

I giggle. I should waddle over with my shorts around my ankles. He'd really think I'm losing it.

"Yeah, I'm coming back!"

I like that Anthony's there, wondering where I am.

I also like being here, ass out, unseen. A body of the forest.

I get dressed and head back to the clearing, where my crew is hurting. Anthony's shivering, fists tucked in his armpits, torch smoldering dimly on the ground. Georgie is sprawled over an evergreen shrub, his face smudged with dirt, making a half-hearted *food* sign.

"My guys, my guys. How we doin?"

They've made a tiny pile of pine needles, three handfuls.

"Aanh."

"Yes, we're building a fire. How are you, Anthony?"

"Well, the torch is almost out, which seems like a bad thing."

"Come on, buck up, boys. Let's get this going."

I'm the one who bucks up. They watch me scrape armfuls of pine needles into a mound, sprinkle birch leaves over it, and stack the tiniest twigs on top.

I give Anthony the big limb to break. Having a task drags him out of his cold stupor. He jumps on it, snapping it into usable chunks. Two thick branches become the frame. I lay medium sticks across it. It's a fairy bed, a funeral pyre for a squirrel.

I pull out my day kit. Thanks, survivalists. You're helping us survive.

I scratch the wooden match across the box. It bursts into a fat, golden flame. These are good matches. I open a space in the pine needles and slide it in.

And I blow gently.

Nothing.

I blow.

Maybe we need drier needles. Maybe I shouldn't have wasted time showing my privates to the woods.

I blow.

The sizzle as the pine needles ignite.

I cough. And blow.

The crackle as the fire spreads.

I break off more branches and lay them perpendicular.

And I blow.

The freight-train rumble as it all combusts.

Sparks trail up into the black sky. Smoke in my face, the syrupy sting of burning pine.

"Sit, Anthony."

I bring them both close to the blaze on the windward side.

"No touching the fire, Georgie."

I root around for more wood. This fire's gonna burn hot. I drag a long log across the fire. Once it burns through the middle, I'll break it in two and slide both pieces on. I shove wrist-thick branches into the bottom of the blaze. I'm cranking the flames so high they sear away our stress and fear. The embers shine orange, then red.

"That's prolly enough," Anthony says, backing away. "I'm sweating."

I scavenge more branches, a ridiculous supply, enough to last all night and more. I'm stockpiling, putting up wood for our little tribe. I can't get Georgie home, and I can't stop Anthony from stressing. But I can warm the crap out of em.

"Snack time, my mens," I say.

"What you got?"

"I double-dipped at the buffet."

We devour smooshed apple tart and a folded half pizza.

"Damn, I was hungry," Anthony says.

"Feel better?"

"Yeah, cept now . . ."

"What?"

"So tired."

"That's good."

"No, we gotta get moving."

"Just rest. We'll all be better with a little rest. Oh my god, look."

Georgie is passed out, hand by his open mouth, legs tucked in.

"That was quick," Anthony says.

"He's exhausted. Think of how far he walked today."

"What about how far I walked?" Anthony says, stretching out.

"Very proud of you, Ant-nee. Now close your eyes. I'll watch the fire. Here."

I scooch over and get his head in my lap. He tucks his knees up. Like a little guy. We're all little guys. The nudist in his armchair. My mom in Georgie's bed. We snuggle in, puppies squirming for warmth and softness.

Somehow, I'm not tired. And I love this. I push the coals into piles with my fire stick. I poke the flames while Georgie snores softly and Anthony twitches in my lap, stumbling into sleep.

In the trees, two tiny eyes shine in the firelight, crystalline, like the clear tone of a spoon tapping a glass. Then the hedgehog or porcupine or skunk ducks away.

There'll be a lot to pay for tomorrow, anxieties to calm and transgressions to answer to. I'll have to tell Mom something, tell Georgie's fosters something, and tell Anthony's grandma something.

Anthony Golden. You sweet, sweet human. His lips purse and tremble, dream talk.

I drop a fat branch on top of the fire; sparks gush into the sky. Anthony grumbles, resettles.

Georgie's breath slows, the gentle, back of the throat *haaaaaa* that signals he is asleep. It will go silent, then reemerge as a soft snore when he enters the deep sleep from which nothing will wake him.

I should stay still. Wait for Georgie's snores.

I can't.

This day. This body.

I am with my two constant boys, these men I know and trust. These are the boy bodies I notice: This one got taller; that one cut his hair. The two men I am most comfortable with in the world. A family campfire.

Except . . . one isn't family.

I slide Anthony's head out of my lap and lie down in front, scooching back into him. He doesn't move.

I reach back and pull his arm around me. He allows it but doesn't move close, doesn't spoon.

On any other day, I would stop. It's ridiculous to follow whatever this urge is. This is Anthony, for god's sake, my steadfast, my dear, dear friend, my hilarious companion through the nonsense.

Today, it's ridiculous not to follow it. It's what we've been waiting for. I think.

I put his hand on my belly.

It's also this strange forest, the rejections of Marisol's mom and Lumi, the flirting of Kimmy. And our outsider camp here, heretics declaring our freedom. It's independence and permission. Bets are off.

I poke his middle finger into my belly button. It goes pretty deep.

The flight of a bird through the trees, the sudden thrash of leaves, the whip of wings, then silence.

It's not enough.

Anthony's awake now, sharply and entirely.

Some people say: "I don't know if I'm attracted to this

person. I can't tell." I know. It's in the breath, the smell, the folds of the fingers. I want it, or I don't.

This, I want. I reach back and pull his other arm under my neck. It's better, almost an embrace. But.

He's tensed, waiting.

"Anthony," I whisper.

"Yes, sir."

"There's something I want from you."

"I'm guessing it's not more pine needles."

I move both his hands to my bare belly, press his handprints into my soft flesh.

I turn my head around, close to his ear. "Can I?"

"Yeah."

I slide his hands across my belly, down my thighs, over my chest. One pops out of my T-shirt collar and wraps around my neck.

This is it. This is what I want. Our hands everywhere, wrapping, pressing, grabbing.

Everywhere. That's important.

I slide one of his hands down between my thighs. I arc my head back to his. "Yeah?" I whisper.

"Uh-huh," he says. The tremble in that word and the sugary smell of his breath.

I slide his other hand down the back of my shorts.

Our four hands meet down between my legs. There's no

front or back to me. I am continuous, a circle, endless and whole. My butt is not behind me, it is me. My body is inflamed, insistent. All four of our hands grab, pull, and slide. It's a swing, a saddle, and it's lifting me up off the hard ground. We are soaring, spinning through the air.

I toss my head back and—ow!—bang the back of my skull into Anthony's cheek.

He yells.

"Sorry," I say.

He'll have a shiner over his left eye, and I'll have a bump where my head slammed his. But all of that later. I'm still flying.

I have a body that can get what it needs. And Anthony—the boy human who does more than anyone on the planet to convince me that all the BS is worth it—Anthony's body is giving my body what it needs.

I flip over, panting, dizzy. He is grimacing from the headbutt.

"Sorry," I say, "I just have to . . ." I pull up his shirt and mine, pushing our bellies together. It's a warm, soft embrace, but then his hand grabs my shoulder and squeezes hard. "What are you—"

"Aanh."

Oh crap. It's Georgie's hand. He's awake, on all fours, tugging my shoulder.

"It's okay, Georgie."

I don't want to pull my shirt down. I want my sweaty flesh and Anthony's armpit hair and our soft bellies. I want the

236

Möbius strip of us. No front or back, no Anthony or Alex, no boy or girl, no mine or yours. I want you, Anthony, without a plan, without a story.

And definitely without Georgie prying me away.

"Georgie, gentle."

"Aannnnh."

"Go back to sleep. It's bedtime."

"Aanh."

"We'll talk about it in the morning." I'm talking to Georgie, but I'm looking at Anthony, the outline of his fuzzy hair. His fingers, so recently all over me, rest politely on my lower back.

No more polite. Please God, no more polite and no more careful.

I aim my mouth for Anthony's. I want to chew on his lips, his cheeks, his—

Whoa. Georgie pulls, and I slide backward, Anthony's mouth receding.

"Aanh!" Georgie says, loud now and a little frantic, reaching above his head.

I grab Georgie's leg as I stand. He reaches for me, but I'm not stable, and we both stumble. I catch him in a hug and feel his rigid muscles and straining breath. Poor guy. He woke up in the woods in the middle of the night.

I talk him back down, retelling our day twice, especially the long list of treats he ate. At last, he plunges back into sleep, and I creep away.

I lie behind Anthony, spooning him. Not enough. I need more.

I pull his sweatshirt and T-shirt up.

"Hmm?" he mumbles.

"Shh."

I pull my shirt up, and place my bare belly and chest against his smooth, wide back.

I don't know what all this means, but I know this: I am meant to be here, warming this dear boy with a fire I built by hand and with the heat of my body. Maybe this is what people did before electricity.

Anthony is alert, edgy, maybe on the verge of talking. He adjusts to my embrace but doesn't quite relax. Until suddenly, he does, the warm sighing breaths of sleep, my hand on his ribs counting his heartbeats.

What are these bodies even for?

This.

CHAPTER TWELVE

The night is endless but abrupt.

I can't sleep much, and when I do, I'm awakened by animals or the fire or my stiff neck or Anthony rolling over. Or Georgie needing to be told where the hell we are and what's happening, understandably.

"Aanh."

I ignore it.

"Aanh."

"We're sleeping, Georgie."

"Aanh."

"That's right, your bed is here tonight."

"Aanh."

"We're sleeping."

"Aanh."

"That means no talking."

"Aanh."

"No talking."

"Aanh."

Anthony twitches in his sleep.

"Aanh."

Two dreams later, Georgie is standing, the sky a tiny bit light behind him.

"Aanh." He holds his groin.

"You can pee on the trees, Georgie."

"Aanh."

"Pee on the trees. Like Bald Mountain." That's Mom's favorite place to hike. Georgie has a spot near the top where he pees. Every time, he pulls down his pants there and tries to urinate. If the pee won't come, he'll stand there, and we have to bribe him to keep going.

"Aanh."

"Anywhere in the trees. I'm sleeping. You can pee by yourself."

He stumbles over a tree root into the woods.

I'll stoke the fire when he comes back. Maybe I should get up and start the day. There's enough light to move around. But I like curling around Anthony, his sleep tremors, the growl of his belly.

And I don't want this day to begin. I can't imagine it's gonna be as fun as yesterday. I want to linger in our freedom. Just a few more minutes of yesterday.

Wait, what?

I sit up.

Oh crap. It's full-on bright now. Morning's here, Georgie's not.

"Georgie."

I fell back asleep.

"Georgie, where are you?"

I listen for footsteps.

"Jesus, Georgie!"

I'm on my feet.

"What?" Anthony sits up, his cheek wrinkled with dirt, twigs in his hair.

"Georgie's gone." The sun scatters through the mist, giving the woods a bright, even glow.

"Where?"

"He went to pee a while ago and didn't come back."

"How long?"

"I don't know, I dozed off. It was barely light. Georgie!"

"I'll check the road." Anthony jogs off.

I race into the woods where Georgie went.

I yell his name as I stomp over tree roots and hop over boulders. I stop, listen for a reply, for anything. A startled chipmunk, confused, runs toward me, and I almost step on it.

These are the woods where I was naked last night, the primal forest that accepted me. Now, it is bright, warm, and endless. Trees that embraced me last night act like they don't know me. *A boy? You're looking for a boy? No idea, sorry.*

"Georgie!"

I remind myself that a disabled kid is like any other kid, he can get lost, but he's not more likely to get injured. There are no cars here to run him over, no cliffs to fall off. He's wandering, that's all.

I slam through a spiderweb, which collapses into a sticky gel on my face and arms.

"Georgie!"

Then I see the lake.

No.

No!

"Anthony!" I am tearing through the forest. "Anthony!" The trees go right to the water's edge. I weave through them. Saplings, tipped with pale new growth, whip my legs. "Anthony! Help!"

The brush is too thick. I jump down into the water and run along the shore, boots sloshing through cold ankle-deep water, sand and rocks glittering in the dawn sunshine.

"Georgie!" I should stop and listen. "Georrrrrgieee!" I am shrieking, I am wailing. I freeze and listen, my panting breath loud in my ears.

A voice up the hill—maybe Anthony's, definitely not Georgie's.

I splash ahead. A spit of land juts into the lake, a sunny point of rocks and tall pines. I am out of the water, on a path now. It leads onto the point, faded beer cans half buried in campfire ash. For an optimistic second, I think: Maybe there are people here, campers or hunters who found Georgie wandering. Old men frying bacon and feeding him donuts.

Then I see his shoes.

Georgie's filthy gray sneakers are strewn across the trail. Then his socks. All leading down, down toward the water.

God, no. That polite boy knew to take off his shoes.

"Georgieeeeeeee!"

I'm in the water, yelling, swirling my hands and feet.

"Georgie!" I dive down, windmilling my arms along the bottom.

Too shallow here—he could stand. Look where he can't touch.

"Georgie!"

I dive again and plow my body over the rocky, mucky bottom. I grab at seaweed and stir up plumes of algae.

Up for a breath.

"Alex!" Anthony is nearby.

"In the water! Georgie went in the water!" On those words, I choke and heave. I am going to throw up.

"Where are you?" Anthony yells.

"In the water," I shout back, enraged at him and me and all of it. My fury burns away the nausea. I dive back under.

I grab a slimy branch, slam my ankle on a rock. I can see near the surface, but the bottom is murky, weedy.

How long have I been in? How long has Georgie been under?

"Al!" Anthony is on the shore. "What are you doing?"

"I think he went in here. He left his shoes, I think he went in."

"He wouldn't go over his head."

"What?! Of course he would."

"Which way did you check?"

"I came from there." I point back to where I ran along the shore.

"I'll look this way. I'm sure he's not underwater, Alex."

What? I can't listen to this. I dive back under. If Anthony's not gonna help, I'll swim twice as hard.

More rocks and sand. I'm kicking up the muck, making it harder to see.

I keep my eyes wide open, trying to catch a flicker, a gesture, a movement in the green water. I surface. Everything's blurry. My eyes burn.

This cannot be how it ends. I cannot brush against Georgie's hovering leg, his bloated face staring at nothing.

No.

I scan the polished surface for bubbles or ripples. It reflects back the upturned trees, pines pointing down into the lake, down to the bottom.

No, not there.

This is not how it ends.

"Alex!" Anthony shouts.

"What," I whisper.

"Alex!"

"What?!" I shout.

"He's here! He's okay! I got him!"

I am weeping. Instantly. Sobs rippling the glassy surface, tears mixing with the lake water and bottom mud on my cheeks.

"He's fine, Alex. Are you okay?"

This makes me cry harder, a flood, an open hydrant. My throat closes, and I can't answer.

"Al! Are you okay?"

I'm shivering. The water is, it turns out, painfully cold.

"Yes. Yes. I'm coming."

I am coming for you, Georgie.

<hr>

Georgie lies on one hip on the silt and sand of the shore, feet crossed, chewing a piece of grass. He often drops into relaxed, careless positions, sometimes landing on a recognizable posture. This one is a middle-aged dandy by the lake. He should be smoking a pipe. I stagger over and lie on top of him, pressing lake water onto his dry clothes.

"Aanh." *[He pushes me with his forearm.]*

"He's good. He's okay." Anthony rubs my scalp, my stubble throwing mist into the air. "He's good."

I'm laughing.

"Georgie, you rat!" I kiss his cheek.

I wrap around him, swallowing him up in my arms, and I don't care if he doesn't like it. I am heaving with laughter and sobs, dripping cold water and hot tears on his head, his shirt. I am a barnacle on his still, warm body.

I will never let you go, Georgie. I held you when you were minutes old, a wiggly seahorse yawning and whimpering, my flesh and kin, my dearest playmate, my brother.

"Aanh." *[Georgie pushes my face gently with the back of his hand, unhappy with how wet I am. He's not shoving me off, just asking how long this is going to last.]*

I take his face with both hands, something I never do. We're nose to nose, a position that, despite our constant proximity, we rarely get in. Staring into his eyes, something bubbles up, and I say it: "I miss you so much, Georgie."

A sob spits out of my mouth. And Georgie barks out a loud, throaty laugh, thrusting his head and squinting with glee.

He's right: It is funny.

"I can't believe you ran away, you little rat!" I'm tickling his armpit, which gets him laughing louder.

He rolls to the side. I shiver in my wet clothes.

I need a body, I need touch.

I reach out to Anthony. "Help me up."

Something was scraped off of me on the lake bottom. I molted.

I pull Anthony down on top of me.

"You're soaked."

"Get down here." I pull his dry lips to mine. "What?"

"You're all muddy."

"Come on, kiss me. Pretty please."

He leans in. Our lips brush back and forth. I stare at his shiny face.

"I'm the luckiest girl."

"Muckiest girl."

"You like me anyway."

"You smell."

"Do I?"

"Like a farty swamp."

"Say that again, it's sexy."

He lowers his voice. "Farty swamp."

"Aanh." *[Georgie brushes his fingernails along the ground, drawing grooves in the sandy soil.]*

"Yes, Anthony's talking about farty swamps."

"Aanh."

"I think it's funny, too."

"Aanh."

"Guess I better rinse off if I want more kisses from this boy."

I stand and pull off my soaked shirt and bra. "Come on, Ant-nee. It's a beautiful day. Let's swim."

"It's cold."

I take off my waterlogged boots and step in. "Oo. Yeah. My god." It is damn cold. I didn't feel the temperature before. I didn't feel anything. The scrapes and bruises of my underwater flailing start to throb. I pull off my shorts, then my underwear, and wade in. I'm a full-on nudist now. *Don't ever let em shame you.* I'm naked and whole, like last night. But now I'm in the glimmering, crisp light of morning. And Anthony's here. It's different, riskier. Better.

"My god," he says.

"What?"

"You're naked."

"Is that a problem?"

"Well, now I can't take my shorts off."

"Anthony Golden! Not in front of G-e-o."

"I blame your butt."

I stare out at the rippling water, a trail of liquid gold leading from me to the sun.

"You should see it from the front." I dive under.

The frigid water washes the muck from my arms and the seaweed from my legs. I am cleansed, anointed.

"Come on, AG!" I float on my back. I'm a bare-chested island of goose bumps.

"Too cold." He stands in his boxers, shivering like last night.

"I'll warm you up."

With no hesitation, he stomps into the water, high-stepping till he falls forward. He swims hard, in a big arc, splashing the silver water white. "Ohmygod, ohmygod, so cold."

A mama duck leads three fuzzy teenage ducks away from our commotion.

"Come here, chilly boy." I wrap my legs around Anthony's

waist and clamp myself onto his torso. I'm a water koala. "Better?"

"Way better. I mean, I'm freezing, but I don't care."

Two crows caw and rattle, their call-and-response falling in and out of unison.

"I never did this before," I say.

"Swim in the Arctic?"

"Been naked with a boy."

"Too bad for every other boy."

A fish jumps, its silvery body flashing in the air and sending long concentric circles toward every shoreline, a liquid broadcast signal.

"Lotta firsts," Anthony says.

"*Lotta* firsts."

"Aanh."

"We're swimming," I say.

"Aanh."

"You can come in, Georgie."

"Aanh."

"It's cold, but it's worth it," Anthony says.

My god, yes.

<hr />

This day won't be easy. The bill for our adventures has to be paid.

But after scraping my body along the bottom of that lake, dredging for my drowned brother, all of this is gift and godsend. Even the crappiest day will be bright and weightless.

On top of that, Anthony's shoulders and neck are a delightful place to rest my hand. Which I'm allowed to do, right? We're walking around the lake toward the paved road on the other side, where, hopefully, we'll find a ride.

"You're grinning," Anthony says.

"Nobody drowned. So, yeah, I'm giddy."

"I can't believe you thought that. Georgie wouldn't go over his head."

"Oh my god, Anthony, of course he would. He did."

"Long Lake was different. The dock got him in trouble."

"Being in eight feet of water got him in trouble."

"No, when Georgie goes in from shore, he doesn't go over his head. He's smart. But on the dock, there's that illusion. You look down, and the water looks three feet deep, but really it's eight. Long Lake is clear, it fools you. I blame the dock. If I were you, the story I'd tell about that whole day is: 'That damn dock tricked Georgie.'"

It's a good thought. And maybe if I had more control over my mind and heart, I could rewrite that day. It's not that simple. Something is loosening, though.

I'm not blameless. I can't pin it all on the dock. Sorry, Anthony. But I am—what? Still here. Stacking new days on top of that one awful day that defined me, or tried to.

Almost redrowning my brother—or thinking I did—is no moment for a victory lap, I know. I should have gotten up with Georgie, helped him pee, and laid him back by the fire. Hell, I shouldn't have brought him into the woods in the first place and made him sleep on the ground. I'll face consequences for that. I'll nod through lectures. I'll come clean about stealing Georgie. Mom and the fosters and the vice principal will be *outraged*, *concerned*, and *most of all, disappointed*.

Hey, Georgie's not at the bottom of the lake, and I'm not to blame. Doesn't that count for something?

Probably not.

Ugh. I'm not ready.

I'm not ready for how nicely yesterday confirms my carelessness, my irresponsibility. *No wonder Georgie is in foster care.* That's what Marisol's mom said.

I feel that story constrict around me, a scratchy shirt that's tighter every time I put it on.

Maybe that's why this next conversation doesn't go well.

"I have some questions," Anthony says.

Or maybe this conversation never goes well.

"Bout what?"

"That thing we did last night. It was pretty unexpected."

Behind us, Georgie hums tunelessly. He's docile this morning, not driven and excitable like yesterday. Maybe we all are.

"Yeah, it kind of came to me," I say.

"You never thought about it before?"

Such a good question. "Not specifically. But doing it felt like: Ah, finally."

We step over a tiny stream, the water startlingly clear before it's swallowed into the green-brown lake.

"I thought about it," he says.

"A lot?"

"Um, whatever would feel weird to you, like way too much, it was slightly less than that."

"Just below creepy."

"Maybe." A woodpecker knocks insistently: *Let me in, dang it!* "I can't tell how honest I should be."

"How about completely?"

"God. That's . . . No."

"You're scaring me, Anthony."

"It's mutual."

"Say what you're trying to say."

"Oh my god, I am saying it. You're dodging it."

"There's nothing to dodge."

"You're ridiculous."

"You're ridiculous."

Facing the adults is gonna be hard enough. I need Anthony on my side. I need easy, can-do Anthony.

The sun is up and hot. I put a hand on my sweaty skull. My scalp feels sunburned.

"Look," Anthony says finally. "Do you want to kiss more?"

"Definitely, yes," I say. "Oh, you mean kiss *you*? I don't know. Have to think about that. I'm kidding, I'm kidding."

He grins, happy with the joke and happier with the answer. "Okay. So, right now, we're still kissing."

"No, if we were kissing *right* now, we couldn't talk."

I lean over and put my lips on his. "Arrwanewsohdewna-mayee." I pull away.

He's smiling, eyes closed.

"See? What did I say?"

"I want something with gravy?"

"No, but that is true," I say. "I'm famished."

Georgie bends to pick a bright-pink wildflower, yanking it out by the root. Picking flowers for the table was one of his jobs, and he was wonderfully uncareful about it, grabbing fistfuls of dandelions, leaves and all.

"But would you say—"

"You have too many questions, Anthony."

"Yes, I do. Was yesterday, like: You shaved your head, kidnapped your brother, kissed some guy?"

"I did those things, yes. In that order."

"So it's a blackout fling."

"A what?"

"Would you say . . . ?" He trails off. "Okay, right now—"

Enough. "Right now, Anthony, I'm hungry. Right now, I'm

scared to go home. Right now, I'm floating in a way I've never felt before."

He doesn't nod or agree, or even acknowledge he's heard.

We help Georgie over a fallen tree that disappears into the lake. Dead leaves cling to the underwater branches, waterlogged and pale.

Anthony and I come face-to-face. We don't kiss.

"You can't be a dick," he says finally.

"What?"

"You can't put my hands between your legs and then go: 'I don't know, I'm floating.' You're a big deal to me, and what happened last night was a big deal so don't be a dick."

"Wow, sorry."

"Don't apologize. Just say what you want."

Georgie picks a stick out of the water, bleached gray, both ends whittled to points by beaver teeth. It's an iconic stick, a cartoon drawing of Stick.

"Everything," I say.

"From me, though. Do you want a friend? Do you want a boyfriend?"

"Can I say: Yes?"

"Uh-uh."

"Why not?"

"Cause . . ." Anthony's staring down, contracted like yesterday after the VFW. "When you have strong feelings for a long time, it's . . . a lot."

God. *Strong feelings for a long time.* For me. I'm a messy, sad, selfish little shut-in. I've been hiding in the dark for a year. Who wants to be with that? Who wants to be with a girl who let her autistic brother almost drown? *Twice.*

Anthony Golden, turns out.

A glossy green pine needle is tangled deep in his hair, a souvenir from our night. I pluck it out, and he flinches at the unexpected touch.

"That is a lot, Anthony, and it's lovely. Can we think about it? We're exhausted, and it's early, and—"

"I get it."

"What?"

"'Let's think about it' means 'I don't have feelings for you.'"

"No, it means 'Let's think about it.'"

"I've thought about it, Al. I don't need to think about it. And, to be honest, if you do, that tells me a lot."

"Jeez, Anthony, slow down."

A duck lands loudly on the water, flapping and graceless, then paddles away, dignified.

"I feel like I wandered into something I don't understand," I say. "You have this big story built up about me."

Anthony is silent. Morning mist rises off the lake, pent-up energy swirling upward.

"What I love about the blackout and our crazy day yesterday is there's no story," I say. "Nobody knows what the hell's happening. We're making it up as we go. The nudists are making it up. And I'm making it up. I've been stuck for a long time in that stupid story about me and Georgie and our family. I don't wanna fall back into that."

"Don't blame that story on me. I always said that whole thing was bull."

"I know. I'm saying I'm shifting, I'm changing. And that's what I did last night. With you. I did something I wanted, and I wasn't trying to fit it into a story."

We climb over a tangle of tree limbs. My hips ache from sleeping on the rigid ground.

"No." Anthony shakes his head.

"No what?"

"You can't say that."

"All right. I did, though."

"Two people caring about each other and touching each other is not a goddamn story, Al. Don't call it a story. It's more real and alive than any of this crap." He flaps his hand, dismissing us all, that hand that was on me, all over me hours ago.

"Wow," I say. "That makes me want to kiss you."

"Oh my god."

"That was such an honest thing to say."

"I get upset and it turns you on."

"Kind of."

"You're impossible."

"Apparently, you like that, though."

"*Rrrrr*," he growls. "I do. *Dam*mit."

He jumps off a lichen-covered rock and lands on the silty shore.

"Here." I draw a line in the mud between us. "Do you realize where you're standing?"

"By a lake?"

"In the supply room."

"The what?"

"Anthony, would you walk through a wall in the physical school?"

"Oh, you're talking about Harrison High."

"Would you?"

"I don't know. Sure."

"Then do it."

He steps across the line to me.

"See?" I lean in to his neck, that warm burrow I nestled in last night. I draw a slow circle with my tongue, from his collarbone up toward his ear, an invisible tattoo.

He gasps.

I remember my lips on his shoulder in the firelight. I remember yearning to whisper him awake, yearning to have his hands all over me again.

"That's what I want, Anthony." I turn and follow Georgie.

And heady what-does-this-all-mean Anthony is speechless.

CHAPTER THIRTEEN

It's morning rush hour on Route 107. Not a traffic jam, exactly, but cars do pass every couple minutes. A police officer pulls over and says she can't give "nonemergency" rides. "Otherwise, that's all I'd do."

A doctor stops—they must get gas—and offers to drive us a mile, but it's not worth the headache of coaxing Georgie into an SUV. A crowded van pulls up, some kind of informal bus service, and the driver says she can fit three more, but "it's a buck a mile each."

Hunger is kicking in, and the sun is getting hot.

And then, our ride comes over the hill. I step into the road to wave it down. We cram into the back of—yes!—a minivan, stuffed with suitcases and boxes. I sit on Anthony's lap, and we stretch the seat belt across both of us.

"Where in Little Falls?" the driver asks, her bright-blue

glasses peering at us in the rearview mirror. She's accelerating slowly—experimentally slowly—taking a good minute to go from zero to forty, probably to conserve gas.

"Lost Brook Road, the right-hand side of the Loop."

"Hold on," Anthony says. "We should drop off Georgie first."

"Mom's gotta see him," I say.

We are wedged into a jumble of supplies. Some are obviously useful: toilet paper, cases of water, two-by-fours sawed to log lengths. Others are puzzling: hockey goals, cans of paint, and a half-inflated rubber boat.

"Alex, I'm sure his fosters are freaking out."

"We'll get him there, just not right now."

"We can't be reckless about this."

"I'm not being reckless."

"They probably told the cops about us," he whispers.

Damn, that's true. I assumed I'd be the one to get in any trouble, but Anthony was there when I took Georgie from school. And the idea of cops—even the word *cops*—has a different edge in Anthony's world.

"Everything all right?" the driver asks. She has three phones plugged into the dashboard, the optimism of the addict. Until the cell towers work, a charged phone is basically a camera.

"Yeah, we're fine," I say.

"We're not fine."

"Yes, we are. Lost Brook Road, please."

We pass Reedman's Ford, where the new trucks—LOADED! $0 DOWN!—are coated with dust.

"Al, if we go home, we have to get Georgie all the—"

"You don't have to be involved, Anthony."

"I am involved. My gram's gonna be furious. Georgie's people are gonna be furious."

"You're off duty. You're done."

"From your point of view."

Jesus, we're literally strapped together. I can't get away from him.

"Can you drop it?" I say.

"Oh, I get it. You're scared of the Boyers," he says. "You don't wanna see them. You're gonna make your mom take the hit."

"Please drop it." I unhook from Anthony. "Here, Georgie. You can sit on my lap."

I undo Georgie's seat belt and slide under him. "God, you're enormous."

I stretch the belt around the giant lump of Georgie and me.

"I'm not dropping it," Anthony says.

Georgie twists and elbows my gut. When I push back, his skull bonks my forehead.

"Ow!"

Anthony smirks.

The minivan stops at a crossroads. A young girl dangles her

legs from a table of milk jugs and five-gallon water cooler tanks. CLEAN SAFE WELL WATER, $4 GALLON, $3 BYOB.

My crushed leg is falling asleep. "This is horrible," I say. "He's so heavy."

"You deserve it," Anthony says.

"What a terrible decision."

"Like so many of yours."

"I'm dying over here."

"If Georgie crushes you, I can get him home sooner."

"You're the worst." I hug Georgie, mostly to pin his arms down. "And that's not his home."

We pass by Kimmy's place. It's early, 9:17, according to the dashboard clock, and no one's digging the hide. I crane my head, hoping for a glimpse of Kimmy or Gabe. Was that only yesterday?

Oh, and wait. Up here.

Yes.

"Miss! Could you stop for a second?"

"Is this where you live?"

"No, I just have to talk to this woman."

I dump Georgie on the seat, and slide open the back door.

"My gosh, is she . . . ?" The driver peers through the windshield, shielding her eyes from the sun.

"Nekkid," I say, and jump out onto the hard, cracked soil. "Hey there! Joanne, right?"

It's just her. The other recliner is empty.

"Morning." She sits up, her breasts slosh down. She has a bite on her forehead from a mosquito, or maybe something meaner, and scratch marks radiating out.

"I met you yesterday."

"Of course, yes."

Branches and cardboard smolder in a charcoal grill by the front door. So many people have fires always burning, and never burning well.

"I wanted to tell you I, uh, tried out the lifestyle."

"Did you now?" Her reddened cheeks wrinkle up.

"It was great."

"That's wonderful. I'll tell John. He'll be so tickled."

"Is he here?"

She nods. A chain saw growls to life next door.

"Is he coming out?"

She smiles, squinting, and shakes her head.

The chain saw snarls into a piece of wood, idles, then snarls.

"Maybe tomorrow," she says. "He's having a hard day." She nods. "Mm-hmm." She nods again and lies back.

The chain saw cuts out. Silence. Someone yanks at the pull cord five times, then gives up.

"Liver disease," she says. "It's a hell of a thing. He doesn't have many good days. Yesterday was special, we were out here for hours. Not a lot of those left, I'm afraid."

God.

She's nodding, her grin turning to a grimace. Glassy slivers line her eyes.

All these bodies. What will become of them?

I bend down and hug her. Her sweaty back has lines mapping the folds of her recliner.

She trembles and grunts out a sob.

All this flesh.

"Poor man," I say.

"Such a good man," she whispers. "All heart."

I stand back up. She nods many times, wipes her eyes. "You're very kind, son. God bless you."

"You too." I want to strip off my clothes and lie in John's recliner. I bet she'd stop calling me "son."

"Good luck with the lifestyle," she says. "Wherever it takes you."

I jog back, the coconut smell of her sunblock on my cheeks and hands.

"She has dog food," Anthony says as I climb in.

"Always happy to trade," the driver says, beginning her long, slow acceleration. "I got a little of everything, as you can see. Got a box of comic books under your seat."

"Everything all right?" Anthony says.

I shake my head. "The husband's sick," I whisper, leaning my head on Anthony. "Liver disease."

God bless that man for putting his cancer-soaked body out on that lawn. Rip off the hospital gown and the shame. Stop hiding.

Anthony squeezes me close.

He should stay out there till he dies, let us witness that body, that decline, that truth.

"He doesn't have many good days left," I say, tucking my arm around Anthony's warm hip.

We do, though. Don't we?

We pull into the Loop.

"Almost there." The woman looks at Anthony in the rearview. "Still interested in a trade?" This is a rolling store, and she's eager for a deal.

"Yeah. Um." Anthony looks at me.

I unzip my bag: granola bar wrappers, harmonica, notebook, and the day kit, all smeared with apple pie from the Village.

"How about water purification tablets?" I read the handwritten slip of paper the gun-toting grandma put in. "One tablet makes a quart of safe drinking water. There's eight."

"Aanh." Georgie recognizes the bridge over the creek. We are close.

"Sure you don't need them?" she says.

"Not as much as we need dog food," I say.

"All right. A bag of kibbles for the tablets."

Anthony mouths, *Nice.* Dog food will help, right?

Yesterday, we set out to contact Anthony's mom. A day later, here we are in front of my house with my AWOL brother and a plastic smiley-face bag of Kibbles 'n Bits Original Savory. I wave for an awkwardly long time as the minivan inches away at two miles an hour.

Georgie's tired and maybe feeling the tension of this moment. He sits in the gravelly grass next to the road.

"I should go see my grandma," Anthony says.

No. Please stay. "Definitely," I say.

"You gonna be okay?"

"I'll use Georgie to distract my mom from everything else."

"That's what I'm gonna do with these kibbles."

"Wow." I squeeze his hand. He smells ripe from the lake and the sweat and the sleeping out. "It was like you said: 'Walk a few miles, walk home. Simple.'"

He's trying to go, already gone. "Don't ever listen to me," he says.

"Sorry, what?"

"See you, G-man."

"Come on, Georgie. We're home." I drag him to his feet. There's a smoky haze stinging my eyes. Everyone cooks and boils water in the morning.

"Aanh."

"Anthony's going to his house."

"Aanh."

"He has to see his grandma and May. We'll see them later."

The sun gleams off my bedroom window, still open from last night, the ripped screen fluttering.

"Aanh."

"After we talk to Mom." I pick leaves and dirt off Georgie's shirt. "And get you cleaned up."

Georgie pulls away and jogs after Anthony. "Come on, Georgie, you can't—"

The front door bangs open.

"Oh my god!" Mom is running out, flip-flops slapping, arms jiggling as she reaches for me. "Thank god you're all right!" She hugs me tight. "Is that Georgie? Oh my god, what happened?" She holds me at arm's length, and her face is gray, from worry or lack of sleep, or both. "What happened to your hair?"

Right, she hasn't seen it. More firsts.

"I cut it this morning. Yesterday morning."

"Where have you been?"

"Anthony and I ended up visiting Georgie. I took him out of school."

"God*dam*mit, Alex. I specifically told you not to go with Anthony."

"I know, I—"

"And you took Georgie out of school? Without permission? Where did you go?"

"We took a walk. We ended up . . . camping." Sounds better than: *We got lost and slept on the ground.*

266

"Camping? Oh my god, Alex. What were you thinking? I was so scared." We're holding hands, speed-walking after Georgie. She wobbles, slowed by the hip trouble that flares up regularly. "And we're gonna be in big trouble now."

I know.

Anthony stops to wait with Georgie. Georgie is pointing, and Anthony is explaining. Two sweet men.

"Oh, my baby, look at you!" Mom swallows Georgie up in her arms. Mom always hugs the hell out of him, whether or not he returns it.

"Aanh."

"Yes, you're back in our neighborhood."

"Aanh."

"Yes, Anthony lives over there. He's going home." She gives Anthony a hug and a frown. "I am very upset with you, Anthony, both of you. And your grandma is, too."

"Sorry, Ms. Waters. I, uh, thought it was gonna be an easier trip."

"Any luck?" She pauses. We stare. "Your mom, did you talk to her?"

Right. Remember why we set out? I barely do.

"Oh. No, that didn't work out."

"That's a shame." Mom fusses over Georgie, flustered and bewildered. "And now we have this to deal with. Anthony, you go home and tell your grandma why you've been gone for"— she looks at her digital watch—"twenty-seven hours."

I want to say: *Your watch is wrong. It was twenty-six hours and forty-five minutes.* I want to make Anthony laugh. I want to remember our magical night, our hands and hips. But he's trudging away with the sagging plastic bag, the only thing we brought back that won't cause trouble.

Walking to our house, the neighborhood is lovely. Bright sun, chirping birds, azaleas blooming. It's a gorgeous spring day, no electricity needed. And the three of us are walking home. My shadow, next to Mom's, is taller than me, and bald like a soldier.

"I'm sorry, Mom, I know this must have been scary."

"You don't know, Alexandra. You have no idea what it's like to be a parent and have your child go missing. And then Georgie was involved. I mean"—she shudders—"thank god he's okay."

"He is okay, Mom. He's amazing." I haven't spent this much time with him since the Long Lake nightmare. "I wish we could keep him."

"Sweetie. Please."

In a neighbor's yard, sheets and towels are spread out to dry, a grid of colorful squares like a giant game board.

"The lights are out. Everything's a mess. Maybe that means we get another chance."

Why go back to the old setup? Start here, start over. *You lost Georgie. You gave him away.* I got him back now.

"That's not how this works."

Georgie, my dear brother who led me for miles yesterday

down dirt roads and through forests, is sluggish, his steps lazy and slurred. He needs a nap. I want him to curl up in my bed while I read.

"I miss him so much, Mom."

"I do too, Alex, but you can't do things like this."

"I can't go see my brother?"

"Unannounced. Without permission. No."

"I'm family. I shouldn't need permission."

"But you do. We all do, for now. And this foolishness is not going to help. You're making everything harder."

Someone's dribbling a basketball and missing shots, the ball bricking off the backboard. *Thup-thup-thup-clang.*

"At least I'm trying," I say.

"What does that mean?"

"You gave up, Mom. You don't even try anymore."

"That's not true. And don't say that in front of . . ." She nods toward Georgie.

"Why not? He understands. Georgie understands everything. He knows about Dad's other family. I met them."

Her eyes dart, her lips miming words that don't come out. This is her compliant, shriveling body, the body that sinks into her chair for days, mouth-breathing and resigned.

"Sweetie, your father doesn't have another family."

"He does. There's a mom and a daughter named Marisol. How could you not tell me?"

"Well, I don't . . ." She put her hands up, palms out, an

athlete saying, *I didn't foul anyone.* "I don't know everything your father's up to. I'm aware he's sometimes back in the area, but he's unpredictable."

"So you kept it a secret."

"Honey, after he left, he kept reaching out and then disappearing on you, on all of us, and I didn't want you to go through that again. I'm sorry."

"When did he meet this girlfriend? When did it start?" My questions are rapid-fire, automatic. This is the big story: I don't know what the hell is happening in my family.

"I'm not sure exactly," my mom says.

"Was it before he moved out?" This is important. I don't know why.

"That's . . . not something I feel comfortable addressing with you at this moment."

"I'm not a child. I'm grown-up. I have the right to know."

"You are not a grown-up, Alex. You're sixteen."

"I'm grown-up enough to check Georgie's meds and change his goddamn underpants. I think I'm grown-up enough to know if my dad's getting married again."

Our awkward neighbor, Donny, a thirty-year-old who lives with his parents, is pulling a squeaky cart full of construction scraps, two-by-fours, and chunks of plywood. He's bent over with his hoodie up, like a peasant in an old painting.

"Did they say that?"

"Yes. His new daughter said, *'My mom's gonna marry Mitch.'*

They call him Mitch." I'm crying. Dammit. "What's going on, Mom?"

"What else are you not telling me?"

"Honey, I'm sorry. I'm doing my best."

Well.

Long-haired Alex would nod and agree.

Someone bounces on a trampoline. *Sheak-sheak, sheak-sheak.*

"No, you're not," I say.

"I am trying."

Bald Alex isn't having it. Bald Alex goes off.

"No, you're not. You're stuck, Mom. You're stuck in the house and stuck in yourself. You gave up."

"I did not give up."

"Georgie, Mom gave up!" I'm yelling and pointing at my passive mother.

"Please—"

"She sleeps in your bed and she plays solitaire and she cries in the bathroom because she gave up!"

"Alex, please! I am not giving up. I want Georgie in our house again, but it isn't time yet." She's dragging her fingers through her matted hair, tidying up, talking herself into something. "And you know what doesn't help? Taking your brother from school in the middle of the day."

"I'm done, Mom. I'm done apologizing. You should have seen us, we ran through that field, me and Georgie, we ran so fast and so far no one could stop us."

"That is not something to be proud of."

I step in front of her. "Yes it is. Cause you do *nothing*, Mom." I poke her chest. "You sit in your moldy old chair and do *nothing*."

She curls over like she's been punched. Little choking sounds are muffled by the hand covering her mouth.

I should apologize, tell her she's a good mom. But that's exactly what we've been doing. *Poor Mom, poor us.* Screw that. Go ahead and cry, Mom. Let's feel what we're feeling. Right now, I feel rage.

"*Do* something, Mom," I say. "Stand up and *do* something."

"Everything okay?" Another neighbor, breaking sticks into kindling, has been watching.

"Hi, Lily!" My mom wipes her eyes and waves brightly. "We're fine. Alex is home safe, everyone's good." She makes the saddest possible gesture, a thumbs-up that's glistening with tears.

We are squared off in the road, face-to-face, standing on two tire skid marks, a double J burned into the pavement by a car desperate to stop.

"Look at you." She runs her hand over my scalp.

I am ready for more, ready to yell, ready to be furious and unfair.

"You look tough," she says.

I giggle-sob, and a drop of spit tumbles onto the pavement.

"I am tough, Mom."

"I know." She smooths my stubble. "I can't imagine how you got Georgie out of school. They won't even let me pick him up."

"Yeah, I got into it with the vice principal. I might have shoved her."

"You shoved her?"

"Mom, she said some things—"

"Oh, I know that woman. I've had meetings with her." She tucks her hair behind both ears, straightens her necklace. "I'm glad you shoved her." She strides into our dark house, her limp gone. "Next time, smack her in the mouth."

Well.

All right, then.

Now this crappy ride to the one place I do not want to go.

At home, Mom fed us room-temperature chili. Georgie kept getting up and walking around the house, and Mom kept going to the window, worried the Boyers might pull up.

Mom begged a couple gallons of gas yesterday and drove around looking for us. Imagine if she'd found us. Mom beeping at us outside the VFW. Mom rolling up as Marisol and I argued about the pickup. Would have been a very different day.

The tank's now close to empty, but mom says it'll get us there and back. We coast down hills and roll through stop signs.

She's going to pin it all on me, the reckless daughter who wanted to see her brother and screwed everything up. The girl who stood in line for cake while Georgie almost drowned. That one.

"I can't be blamed for this, Alex, or we'll never get Georgie back." She leans over the steering wheel and doesn't slow for a darkened stoplight. "Now, it's the blackout, so maybe it won't get reported. Maybe Protective Services never needs to know. We have to play this right, though, and that means taking the blame." Me taking the blame. "Hopefully, they'll be relieved Georgie's back."

Driving, even slow, gas-saving driving, is so damn fast. The landscape we hiked for hours yesterday blurs by.

"I'm sorry, Alex."

"It's okay. It's my fault, I'll take responsibility."

"No, I'm sorry I've been stuck." She wipes her eyes. "It's been a lot to handle. Too much." She grabs my hand. "I want to stand back up. I'm *gonna* stand up." She nods and nods. "But right now, we just have to . . . try to make this right."

We turn onto the Boyers' road. She glances over at me once, then twice. "I can't get over your hair," she says.

I pull down the visor, and the smudged mirror reflects my shaved and sunburned head, my puffy eyes. This is the girl Anthony made out with.

Mom whispers, "Oh god."

I flip the visor up and see a police car parked by the Boyers' manicured flower beds.

Seriously? The whole state is in crisis, and the cops come here? Maybe I'm in real trouble. Maybe this is beyond apologies and Protective Services.

"*Dam*mit!" Mom straightens her blouse. "Okay, why don't you wait in the car, Al. Come on, Georgie."

Screw that. I shoulder open the stuck passenger door.

"The main thing is: We brought him home." Mom is talking to me but mostly to herself. "We solved the problem. Don't answer questions if you can help it, especially questions from the police. They don't need the whole crazy story." She clears her throat. "Hello, Officer. I'm Georgie's mother, bringing him back safe and sound."

"Hello, ma'am." His hands are on his belt. Has he been waiting for us? "I guess you heard what happened."

"Well, yes. My daughter explained it all to me." She nods gravely.

The Boyers' ranch house has two-toned brick walls and a huge garage. Through the picture window, I see the table where we ate our first excruciating dinner with them, my mom sobbing as I picked at fish sticks and a dry baked potato.

The cop's radio squawks. He puts a finger up, listens, then turns it down. He is in touch with people, in communication. It feels miraculous. "It's been a rough night," he says.

"Well, yes, from the Boyers' point of view," my mom says. "But I just want to say, as Georgie's mom, I wasn't scared at all. I actually think it was a good thing."

"I'm sorry?"

"A little adventure and experience can be great for children with developmental challenges."

"Oh my god. Georgie!" Sara, a part-timer from the community college who helps at the Boyers', runs out, arms wide for a hug Georgie doesn't return. "You won't believe what happened."

Inside, the Boyers' son, Mason, also autistic, is playing his electronic keyboard. Same four tones. *Do-fa-mi-fa.* The Boyers had to stay home with Mason, so they figured: Why not take in another one? Georgie helps offset the cost of caring for their own kid. Nothing wrong with that, it just seems a little opportunistic.

"Everyone was so worried about you, Georgie."

I start to answer. "Yeah, I went to see him at school—"

"Something scary happened." Sara grabs my hand. "Know what, let's step away from the door. Mason doesn't need to hear this again." She herds us off the concrete walkway and into the tall grass. The Boyers' shrubs are trimmed, but their lawn is unmowed. "Georgie, are you listening? Yesterday, Mr. Boyer got very sick." She whispers to me and Mom, "Diabetic seizure."

For the record, if a kid understands language, whispering

won't keep it a secret. It's like yelling when someone doesn't speak English. Volume is not relevant.

"His insulin monitor wasn't working, I guess, and he did the wrong thing and it got really bad. Anyway, they went to the hospital, and he's still there. It was serious, but he's getting better."

What.

"Anyway, this wonderful officer came and got me, and we picked up Mason from the hospital." She pulls her hair back and ties it into a ponytail. On her wrist is a wrinkled pink hospital bracelet. "And he didn't know which way was up. The hospital was packed, as you can imagine, and all lit up, cause they have generators. They were playing a movie on the waiting room TV, and Mason was just mesmerized. You know the Boyers don't allow TV." Another sign of our weakness, that we let Georgie watch his Disney movie. "Dragging him out of there was almost impossible, but he is going to be so happy to see you, Georgie. Come on inside."

Wild.

I see immediately that this pushes my offense to the bottom of the list. I won't get yelled at till the Boyers come home, if at all. Hey, maybe it was even helpful they didn't have Georgie last night.

"Hold on." My mom grabs Georgie's shoulder. "Where are the Boyers exactly?"

"They're at Harford Hospital. They're keeping him for observation," Sara says.

My mom, bless her, sees the real opening.

"Officer, are you aware of this?" Mom opens the circle to include the cop.

"Sorry?"

"Are you aware that the people responsible for caring for my special needs son are hospitalized?"

"One of them is hospitalized," Sara says.

"Has Developmental Services been contacted, Officer?"

"Ma'am, it's difficult to contact anyone, as you know."

"When exactly was I going to be informed?" Mom's on a roll.

His radio beeps, and someone asks about an ETA. He reports in: "Copy, I'll be there in ten." He puts it back in his belt. "We're doing the best we can here, ma'am. This all just happened last night."

"Don't worry, I can take care of the kids until the Boyers come back," Sara says, wrong-footed but trying.

"I'm sorry, are you certified by the state to care for two disabled children? In a house that isn't yours? In a blackout?"

"Georgie knows me. He trusts me."

Sara takes Georgie's hand. Georgie's staring at Mason, who's now rocking on the porch swing Georgie isn't allowed on, supposedly because it's dangerous but really because Mason is territorial. He's a good kid, Mason, but he turns mean at unpredictable moments, an only child who suddenly acquired a complicated brother.

"I don't care that my son knows you. I care that he is in a safe environment with state-approved caregivers."

"Well, you took Georgie out of school yesterday without permission," Sara says. "They were all frantically—"

"Yesterday was my mother's birthday," my mom says. "We arranged with Developmental Services months ago that Georgie would spend the day with us and with his grandmother. I have ten emails at home from his caseworker about it. Now, you may have forgotten, but we didn't forget. So, yes, my daughter picked Georgie up, as agreed, from a high school that is currently functioning without a building. Did you know this, Officer?"

Time out to applaud this little brilliance: *ten emails*. Totally convincing, totally a lie, and totally unverifiable with the power out. My mom is good.

"Ma'am, I am not—"

"Out of doors. My special needs son is being kept all day in the sun and the rain and the who knows what. Luckily, my daughter retrieved him from there, and he spent the day with us as agreed to. In writing. Months ago."

"Ma'am, you and the Boyers can discuss all this when they get home," the officer says, taking a step toward his car.

"We certainly will. And in the meantime, as it would be inappropriate and possibly unlawful to leave my son in this precarious situation, we'll bring Georgie back to our home. If and when Mr. Boyer recovers, and if and when the lights come back on, we will discuss all of these issues. With our caseworker present, of course."

"You can't take Georgie," Sara says.

"Take Georgie? No, no, no. There's no one here to provide adequate care for him. It would be negligent to leave him. I mean, were you ever going to inform us of this crisis? Or inform his caseworker?"

Sara stammers, "I didn't have any——"

"Officer, is it possible to make a formal complaint?"

"Ma'am, I don't have jurisdiction here."

"Write this down. Please. George Waters will be in the care of his family until such time as the Boyers demonstrate their household is safe and adequately staffed. That's all. Questions or concerns should be addressed to caseworker Andrea Denis at Developmental Services. D-e-n-i-s. I can give you Ms. Denis's email, Officer."

"Email isn't working, ma'am."

"I am not making any accusations. I will, of course, presume the best until we know all the facts. But I am keeping my options open. Does that make sense?"

"Ma'am, I really can't help you with this. The Boyers are in a tough situation here. I know they were greatly concerned about the whereabouts of your son."

"Greatly concerned. Would that be enough for you, Officer? If it was your disabled child, would concern be enough?"

Mason is swinging. *Squeak-squeak. Squeak-squeak.*

"It's not my place to comment or speculate on that."

"Of course not. And thank you, Officer. I can only imagine what a challenging time this is for law enforcement. And, Sara, thank you for stepping in when the Boyers are incapacitated. Please give them our love. And if they don't come home or you get overwhelmed, feel free to bring Mason to our house. We'll take care of him as long as necessary."

So genius. She flips it, makes us the caregivers offering help to a chaotic household.

Sara doesn't stand a chance. She's flattened. "Okay. And I know the Boyers will be glad to hear Georgie is all right."

"He sure is. Back home where he belongs. Come on, guys."

I get in back with Georgie and rush to get his seat belt on, my mom saying, "Let's go, let's go!"

We round the corner, Mom gunning it as she pounds the dashboard, receipts and cough-drop wrappers bouncing with every slam.

"We got you! We got you, Georgie!"

[Georgie holds my arm and leans in. He has so many questions he can't decide where to point.]

"Oh, we dodged a bullet back there, didn't we? Whew! I don't know how long this'll last, but what a gift! Georgie, you're coming home with us." Mom puts her hand on the sunroof. "Lord, you know I would never wish harm on any of God's children, but thank you, Lord. Thank you for this opportunity to spend time with my son. And may Mr. Boyer recover his full health." She winks at me in the rearview mirror. "Not too quickly, though, Lord. Let's wish him a long and healthy recovery." She smacks the dashboard again. "Ha!"

"Aanh." *[Georgie points at the windshield, looking up at me.]*

I look into those gemstone eyes, the ones I stared at on the shore of the lake this morning.

"Yeah, Georgie," I whisper. "We're going home."

CHAPTER FOURTEEN

It doesn't last.

And maybe that's good because, boy, are we not prepared to have Georgie back. There's no boiled drinking water, barely any food, and three sticks of kindling. Sleeping outside was rough, but at least the forest has firewood.

Georgie doesn't mind. He bobs through the house, a little frantic, a lot underslept. He stamps into the kitchen to scavenge for food. He's not allowed in the cabinets, but he's darn good at spotting crackers on top of the fridge or bananas in the fruit bowl, none of which are here now.

"Give me a minute, sweetie," Mom says, giddy and flustered. "I'll find you something."

He heads upstairs.

I follow, and turn in to his bedroom, which is empty and darn messy. "Georgie?"

He's in my room, in my bed, the sheet half pulled over him. "You sneak."

My stuffy, dim room. Yesterday, I crept out of here at dawn with a full head of hair and no Georgie. Remember that girl? I do.

"Aanh." *[He's requesting a song. He gets one before afternoon rest and two at night.]*

I push him over and sit down. I sing slowly, "I got a friend in Bal-ti-more." His bedtime song can be anything, as long as you pace it like a lullaby. "Lit-tle Li-za Jane."

I need to air my room out, change it up, but I'm also appreciating it. This was my refuge, my cocoon. The stripy wallpaper that looks like brushstrokes. The overflowing plastic bin that's my hamper and dresser. The wood tray for carrying up nachos and noodles. Maybe it turned into a cell, but it held me safe when I wasn't safe.

"Aanh." *[Georgie points downstairs, or maybe toward the Boyers'.]*

"We'll talk about that after your rest."

I put my hand on his warm forehead, this brain that has so many questions, so many twitches and stutters, so much light that ricochets around the peculiar prisms and mirrors of his mind before it slips out through his shining eyes.

A nap is the right idea. We should all start with a lie-down, let our dreams absorb these changes.

A breeze fills the room with the smell of sun-warmed grass.

Makes me think of swimming. I curl in next to Georgie and slide the pillow over so I get half.

[He raises his hand slightly, a murmured sign before conking out.]

He smells like woodsmoke, and I smell like pond. Together, we're a terrarium.

"Sweetie?" My mom opens the door. "Oo, sorry. Is he sleeping?"

I nod and close my eyes. Time to snooze.

A minute later, Mom's still there, watching, cheeks red with tears.

"We got him, Mom," I whisper.

"For now." She rubs her finger where she used to spin her wedding ring.

"I like it."

She coughs out a sob, but her eyes smile. "Me too."

Georgie's lips ripple into a snarl. He's tasting or smelling something in his mind.

Sweet dreams, Georgie.

We are working.

All day, every day.

Mom's convinced CPS is going to pull up any minute and take Georgie back to the Boyers'. "Let's make it real nice for when they show up," she says. "Let's show em how wrong they were."

She puts a checklist on the fridge: everything that must be cleaned, fixed, childproofed, thrown out, prettied up, rearranged, and answered to. Most of it comes from Arleen's evil letter, the evidence of our neglect and instability. Some of it's ambitious. Apparently, we're all going to learn CPR from Diane, a nurse at our church. How's that going to work?

It's exhilarating and exhausting.

We're clearing out our year of collapse, the remnants of giving up. Anthony bags up heaps of recycling on the back steps and rolls old magazines into logs for our cooking fire. Mom rehangs the curtains in Georgie's room ("essential for effective sleep hygiene," wrote Arleen) while Georgie half naps on his mattress. May and I sort the bathroom shelves: nail polish remover, razors, the broken hair dryer, all the "potential hazards in plain sight and within reach." Now, we'll each have a bathroom caddy by our beds. Bring it with us to the shower, pack it and stow it when we're done.

I donate my reread stack to the library book sale. *Bye, old friends with reliable endings.* The library is open and overrun, flashlights flickering through the stacks, a hand-lettered sign complaining and bragging: VOLUNTEERS NEEDED! URGENT! HELP US SERVE OUR MANY NEW PATRONS!

I stack my five new library books, the "blackout maximum," on my windowsill. I think I'm ready for new stories. I look out the window at Anthony, who's piling our old dishes and toys by the street. Mrs. Cleary, our neighbor, is picking through our FREE PLEASE TAKE pile and chatting with Anthony. Chatting *at* him. Anthony leans his head back, the silent laugh he gives people out of courtesy, the opposite direction of his genuine laughs, which double him over. His face scrunches up, encouraging Mrs. Cleary to keep telling her story. Anthony Golden.

"Forgot we had this." My mom stomps in and hands me a folding window screen. She's sweaty, glowing, a baseball cap backward on her head. "It'll do until we can get this fixed." She pulls the torn screen out of my window, frame and all. Didn't know you could do that. "I took that front door screen out, and it looks so much better. Walking in from the street, you can see the . . ." She's back down the stairs, still talking.

Mom's definitely out of her chair, on her feet, barking orders and making lists. She's impressive and a bit overwhelming. I worry she might crash at some point.

I slide the new screen in and pull the window down to meet it. Solid. I can hear the outside world, but I'm not gonna fall through.

Later, we'll take apart the crumbling patio furniture ("appears likely to collapse under the weight of an average adult") and put childproof latches on the cupboards and a lock on Georgie's bedroom window. The hollow-headed stagger of our shame is cleansed room by room, replaced by the reassuring strain of work.

"Let em try to take Georgie now," my mom says, painting over the scribbles and scratches in his bedroom. "Let Arleen bring her goddamn checklist now."

Sky blue paint fills a scar in the drywall that Georgie gouged with a pen or a spoon. For a moment, the wall is seamless and solid. Then the paint stretches and pops, and the cut, glossy and blue, opens again.

⊶————————⊷

Seven days after Georgie came home, I'm digging up dead bushes in our side yard. "*Like the inside of the home, the yard is neglected and chaotic,*" Arleen wrote.

I hear it. A window air conditioner shuddering to life. Music from across the street. An alarm far off. Yelling and cheering.

The lights are back.

I'm not ready.

I'm not prepared for regular life. I'm still wide open.

I picture the nudists, dragging their chairs back inside, pulling on trousers and bras and one-size-too-small shirts. Bets are no longer off.

I run.

I'm not ready for questions about my hair or my brother or Anthony.

I sprint down the street, across Mrs. Cleary's lawn, down the hill.

When will they come for Georgie? How much trouble will I be in?

My reflection is doubled in the cracked storm door. For a second, my face slides into Anthony's, my mouth shimmers over his round cheeks.

"Hey, the power's back," he says, opening the door.

"Come here." I pull him onto the porch, bring his mouth to mine, and slowly, thoroughly kiss him.

"What's this?"

"It wasn't just a blackout fling." May is in the living room, clicking the lamp on and off and cackling. "It's also a lights-on fling."

"Oh, good. Guess I won't have to blow up the electrical grid then."

Twenty minutes later, the lights go off, maybe because we all turned everything on at once. But it's back.

We're going to start having rolling blackouts. They'll tell us in advance so we can plan. They're restoring all the systems damaged by, yes, a massive solar storm. The sun got mad and knocked our lights out. Can't blame her. She gets a lot more respect now.

It seems so brief, looking back. During the blackout, we looked out toward an endless emergency. But it ended instantly, too soon.

We're like Georgie. *The lights are never coming back!*

No, wait—they were never gone!

Everything's starting up again, and everyone's swapping stories and photos from the blackout. *The New York skyline with no lights on.*

And all I want to do is take Anthony away. I want to lay him down in the woods. Or in my room. Maybe even white socks, butts from the front.

Dang it, Anthony Golden, where are your hands?

On the second day with lights, I wait on his porch. He went to borrow tools, because their toilet has water—hurrah!—but now it won't flush.

Across the street, a guy in a black bandanna is power-washing his driveway, a surprising priority for day two. Steam rises from the blade of water. Next door, a woman and her kids are taking apart their campfire circle, dragging dining room chairs into the house, and filling the fire pit with dirt. The neighborhood bonfires were great. It's a shame we're all going back inside.

Finally, Anthony returns, carrying a long stick with a twisty spring on the end.

"What's that?"

"A nasty tool to uncrap the crapper. I am not looking forward to what this pulls out."

"Aw, you're the man of the house."

"Nah, Gram's the man. I'm the lackey."

"Hey, does your grandma know?"

"About what?"

"Us," I half yell over the metallic roar of Bandanna now power-washing his pickup.

"Oh. Yeah."

"What did she think?"

"She wasn't surprised," he says. The black eye from our collision at the campfire has faded. I remember that collision. "She likes you a lot, obviously." I remember his gasp when our chests met. "She gave me a big talk, though." I remember his armpit flexing and the goose bumps when my hand nestled into it.

"About what?"

"Responsibility. Rules. Condoms."

"Condoms? Yikes."

"And the interracial thing."

"She knows I'm white?"

He grins. "Somebody must have told her."

The power washer turns off, and I hear the far-off rumble of . . . wait—the first postblackout airplane? No, just a truck, its air brakes thumping.

"What did she say?" I say.

"She's talked about it before. You know, her son, my dad, is a white guy who married a Black woman, and it was complicated. They got a lot of crap."

"We might get crap."

"Yup." He leans the toilet tool against the railing and sits.

"It's worth it, though, yeah?"

"Goddamn right. Gram said: 'Gotta love who you love.'"

The late morning sun throws his silhouette into my lap. I wish his actual head was resting there.

"I'm not saying it's love," he says. "I mean—"

"Yeah, yeah. But, in terms of your grandma, if you and me wanted to go up to your room, close the door, and—"

"Mm, no," he says.

"Such a bummer."

"Glad you think so."

Inside, May yells that there are no clean spoons. Her grandma tells her to wash one. Washing's so easy with running water.

"My mom doesn't know about you yet," I say.

"Are you hiding it?"

"I'm keeping my options open."

"To kiss other people?"

"No, to kiss you. In my room. Before my mom makes rules. Anyway, she's not home right now. You'll never guess what she's doing."

"Hanging out with your dad."

"How'd you know?"

"Twins."

"Yeah, he's back in town and they're talking about what happened, why Georgie's staying with us. But that's not the point." I put a hand on his bony kneecap. "The point is, she and Georgie are out. Which means my house is empty. Which means we could go . . . celebrate. In my room."

"Why the hell are we still sitting here?"

We're walking to my house, holding hands. I'm going to roll around with Anthony in my own damn bed. No hard dirt ground, no brother poking us.

I smell laundry tumbling, the humid, chemical fog of a dryer sheet. People blast music, windows open, thrilled to be back in our loud, powered-up lives.

I'm also thrilled.

You know when you're anticipating something delightful, and you're not there yet, but it's coming and nothing can stop it? That's the most delicious moment. The wanting. The mutual wanting. Anthony's fingers, threaded through mine, will soon be all over me.

Almost there.

Oh no.

There's classical music coming from my house.

Mom's back already? Aargh.

"Sweetie, oh my gosh." Mom pauses the music on her phone. "I was looking for you. Hi, Anthony."

"Hi, Ms. Waters."

"I have something for you, Al." She looks back and forth at us. "Your father wrote you a letter."

Oh god. Bad enough that she's home. Now this. She hands

me a plain white envelope with *For Alexandra* scrawled in blue ballpoint.

Georgie, swaying in his rocking chair, points at the phone, his groove interrupted. "Aanh."

I should open it. I should want to open it. I just want Anthony.

"A lot's been happening, Anthony, as you know," Mom says.

"Yeah, you prolly need a minute, Al," he says.

No! Don't go.

"If you want to just go up and read it in your room . . . ," Anthony says.

Stay. Please.

". . . I'm happy to sit with you."

Brilliant.

"Oh. Yeah. I need a minute, Mom." I start up the stairs. "Come on, Anthony."

I have an excuse for locking my door: I'm processing my dad's letter. Except I'm not ready for that.

"Come here," I say.

Before I read the letter, before CPS comes back around, before my mom knows about me and Anthony, I deserve this one moment.

I pull him to the bed. I should have changed the sheets. I'm clean, but my bed smells like recluse. I nuzzle his neck. He sits stiffly next to me, formal like a blind date. I put my hand on his thigh, and he pats it. This is not what I pictured.

"You're not interested?" I say.

"Maybe this isn't the time," he says.

Christ, what's a girl gotta do to get a kiss around here? "Why?"

He laughs. "Uh, you just got a letter from your dad."

"Terrible timing."

"Hard to imagine there's a good moment."

Mom's music drifts up, the Christmas chorus she plays for Georgie.

"I don't want to read it," I say.

"Of course not."

"But I have to."

"Yup." He gives me an unromantic shoulder nudge. "Come on, what's the worst thing that can happen?"

"Complete catastrophe."

"Didn't that already happen?"

"Good point. Why are you on his side?"

"Al, if my dad wrote me a note, I would have read it five times by now."

Right. Anthony spends so much time missing his mom, I forget his father took off. *Not in the picture* was his phrase at the VFW.

"Okay, here's the deal," I say. "You spoon me. And I'll read any especially messed-up parts out loud, and you go: 'Damn, that's ridiculous.'"

"Damn, that's ri*dic*ulous!" He swats the air.

I lie down, and he curls behind me. Our shoes clunk against each other. I place his hand on my belly.

My dearest daughter, Alexandra,

The tears are instant. I'm not crying in response to my dad's words. I'm simply crying. Gushing.

I think of you every morning, especially when I'm the only one awake.

Even with Anthony wrapped around me—my shield, my guy—I am shoved, knocked back. The jolt isn't from the scribbly handwritten words; it's from deep in my gut.

Of everything I've lost these last couple years, I feel sorriest and stupidest about losing you.

He makes some cheap excuses and defenses. *Parents aren't perfect.* Really? *I found someone new.* No, actually, you abandoned your wife and kids.

I put Anthony's hand under my shirt, up on my chest. That helps, especially when I read this:

Our household was complicated, and you were easy. Maybe that meant you got less from me. I wish I gave you the attention you deserved, not the attention you demanded.

God.

The attention you deserved. Those words make my face hot.

The letter ends with a sentence so crappy I read it aloud, sputtering and indignant. "'*I hope you'll give Sofia and Marisol another chance.*' Are you kidding me?" He wants me to work it out with his new family before he's gotten straight with the old fam.

"Ridiculous," Anthony whispers. He's been reading over my shoulder.

I push the paper away and pull Anthony's arms around me for a good long cry. I do want my daddy. God*damm*it.

Everything I've lost these last couple years. God, yeah. My father. My spiky, beautiful brother. Friends, money, sympathy. And this goddamn fountain of my body, which craves and gasps. This body that used to glow warm in the twilight, and then the only sign of life was a cold flashlight beam in the upstairs bedroom. I lost my hunger.

I cry for it, my tears saturating the musty sheet, the smell of my cowering.

Downstairs, the blender screams to life, Mom crushing ice and sugar and whatever else she can find into a slushie for Georgie.

And then.

I wipe my face on the damp pillow. I'm done crying.

I turn to face Anthony. "He's right."

"Your dad?"

"Mr. Gonsalves. I felt what I was feeling." I kiss the hollow at the base of Anthony's throat, the soft egg cup. "Feel what you're feeling, and then kiss Anthony. That's the second part."

The bumps on his shoulder blade, the tufts of dark hair in his armpit, his mouth chapped and eager. My arms scraped red from the lake bottom. The dimples at the base of his spine, like rippled clay where his top and bottom were put together.

Touching Anthony is nourishment, a healing beam, sunlight on my withered crops. From now on, when crappy things happen, I'm gonna say: "Let me touch Anthony about that. Let's figure this out with Anthony's leg between my thighs, his lips on my neck."

I'm hungry and I'm bald and my mouth is right where it belongs, sharing Anthony Golden's warm breath.

CHAPTER FIFTEEN

Sadly for us, the Child Protective Services and Developmental Services get up and running quickly. Can't get a loaf of bread anywhere, but the bureaucracy bounces right back. And they do not agree with my mom that this is a reset. They show up the next day, day three of lights on, and put Georgie back with the Boyers, even though we fixed almost everything on Arleen's list.

But. They promise a full reevaluation and a home visit from Derek, the new Arleen.

Derek wears a dapper orange tie and wire-rimmed glasses, and narrates his note-taking in the plural. "We're seeing locks on the cabinets below the sink." "We're seeing an organized, well-lit bedroom."

I don't want to like Derek. I want to resent him. I want to blame him and Arleen for everything. But he's lovely, cracking little jokes, complimenting our paint colors. When he says, "My number one goal is getting your brother back home," I believe him.

And now I love Derek, because he gave us an A. It's a qualified A, stipulating that "daily in-home support is urgently needed."

Thank you, Derek.

And I don't disagree. Support sounds great.

⚹

Things are coming back, fitfully and strangely.

The digital world is a delightful mess. The stuff on computers and phones is all there. Stuff online is chaotic and, at first, thrillingly retro: simple graphics, slow speeds, and no ads.

The economy's more screwed-up than I would have guessed. Turns out a lot of people and businesses were a month away from being broke as hell. So now they are. Everybody's arguing about bailouts and debt forgiveness. Money is once again the top story.

And there's far too much talk about grades and interrupted sports leagues, the many asterisks that will attach to this year.

My asterisk, on the other hand, is fabulous.*

The preppers and end-of-the-worlders, confounded by the sudden return of civilization, grumpily describe the blackout as our "final warning." There should be a word for that feeling of

---

* During the blackout, Alexandra Waters was a hairless badass. She isn't sorry.

disappointment when a disaster isn't the apocalypse. I get it. I don't want a collapse, and I don't have a Reckoning binder, but when I'm riding the school bus or walking into the drugstore now, I do picture it. What if it all turned off again? The shiver I get is not fear, and it is not unpleasant.

But everything that is coming back pales in comparison with one return. Two months after the lights came back, fourteen months after he was taken away, a week after the last of four (loooong) meetings with CPS, Georgie Waters officially, legally, moves back into his room.

My god.

He rushes through the house, heavy feet on the carpet, past the organized bookshelves and the clean kitchen counters and the new stairway handrail. He stands in his bedroom.

"Aanh." *[He points at his bedroom ceiling, his face angled down.]*

"It's your new bed." It's used, technically. *New to you,* my mom says about things from the church thrift.

"Aanh." *[He turns his face slightly toward me.]*

"Uh, we painted your room?"

No.

We go back and forth until I finally land on it.

"Oh. We played hide-and-seek, and May hid under your bed." A moment imprinted in Georgie's mind. For weeks, he looked under his bed daily, in case this unimaginable, hilarious, and slightly scary event recurred.

[Arm wiggle, celebration.]

He's not ignoring all our cleaning and repairing and renewing. He's acknowledging it by turning away. He's marking it with a memory from before his walls and furniture changed. *[This is still my room, and I'm still me.]*

⋯⋯⋯⋯⋯⋯

We get regular visits from CPS now.

"COPS are coming Tuesday." Mom calls them that. "Wash all your dishes."

The visits are stressful, but I'm not worried. We are on our feet.

And CPS's "permanency plan" includes our secret weapon: Louisa, who does specialized home care. Louisa comes for three hours every day, which doesn't sound like much, but it's transformative. Mom can do her errands and tasks at a predictable time, and Georgie has something to look forward to, a structure, a rhythm to the day. We go to Anthony's two nights a week for dinner, and Anthony and May come to our house for two nights.

Louisa's a goddamn treasure. She talks to my mom, reflects about Georgie, checks in. How was his morning? His weekend? She points out little solutions to problems that have dogged us for years. Keep his shoes on the porch so leaving and getting shoes on are the same thing. Whaaat? How many times did I physically drag Georgie back into the house, risking a meltdown, forcing shoes on those feet so eager to stomp out the door.

And Louisa knows people: a dentist who's amazing with disabled kids, a speech therapist who does signing and speaking. That's all theoretical in the mess of postblackout. But even thinking about it feels productive. The "caring circle" around Georgie—a Louisa term—is already twice as big as it was before, and it can keep growing.

Louisa can be a know-it-all. She thinks we don't pray enough. She has unsolicited opinions about our diet. *Too much cheese will kill you. Tomato soup is not a vegetable.* But I still grin when she lugs her huge bag through the front door and says, "Where's that boy?"

Georgie turns away. He raises a hand like he's blocking his view of Louisa.

That's how you know Georgie Waters is excited to see her.

And guess who's paying Louisa to come for *six hours* every Saturday? Mitchell, the dad who flew the coop. I mean Mitch, the soon-to-be stepdad living with Marisol and her mom. My mom, making up for her earlier silence, gives me lots of updates, maybe more than necessary.

She says Dad's making good money, cause everybody wants solar now. I don't know all her feelings about him—there are still things I'm not grown-up enough to be told, according to her— but she's thrilled about the money. And she's gently, steadily, encouraging me to connect with him. We all go for Chinese food. Dad drives us to Georgie's doctor's appointment. It's agonizing. And agonizingly normal.

And none of it's going away. My dad, his girlfriend, Marisol. I bet Anthony's right: They're all gonna be part of my family now. Lordy.

A collapsed home can make a new home.

If the materials are strong.

Our materials might actually be strong. Or strong enough. We'll see. Of everything that showed up in the blackout, that's the most surprising.

Georgie bangs through my door every morning at five thirty. The Boyers got him waking up even earlier. Why, oh why? It's like a smack in the face to start the day. I hate it and I love it.

I tell him today's structure.

"It's Friday, August twenty-ninth. We'll have breakfast and clean up."

"Aanh." *[He sits on my bed, the snowmen on his pajamas glowing.]*

"Then we'll wake up Mom."

The horizon shines with first light, a narrow rainbow of color through my now-repaired window screen and new safety bars. Did I mention the time at our old house when the neighbors called my mom and said: "Your son is on your roof?" Never again.

"Aanh."

His cheek is wrinkled with folds from his pillow. He's sprouting whiskers. My god. Man Georgie is coming. I can't wait.

"You and Mom will do stories and music."

"Aanh."

"Louisa will come and take you out for a walk."

"Aanh." *[He taps my arm. He's wound-up, as always, but more eager than anxious.]*

One morning, he climbed into bed with me and snuggled. It was so unprecedented, so shocking and delicious. I lay there, frozen and thrilled, thinking: How long will this last? Less than a minute.

"And you'll have first snack and then second snack."

"Aanh."

"You and Louisa will eat lunch."

"Aanh."

"Then you'll have rest."

Headlights throw a trapezoid across my ceiling. Engines and airplanes and machines are back. I still remember them gone, though, still carry those weeks of silence in my body.

"Aanh."

"Then we'll have home time. Games and drawing."

"Aanh."

"And then we'll go to Anthony and May's for dinner." Anthony's mom is back safely and cooking glorious dinners. Turns out, ships don't have blackouts. She says all they did on board was worry about us back home. When she heard about me and Anthony, she said, "I thought you two were already dating."

[Georgie points vaguely toward Anthony's house.]

"Yes, they always have dessert, you little piggy. Big dessert in

Georgie's stomach." I dig my fingers into his abdomen and feel the teenager muscles under his soft belly flesh.

It still gets exhausting, honestly. Georgie's needs and energy are still relentless. He wakes up in the night sometimes and can't get back to sleep, and my mom is bleary and surly the next day. He tempers on a walk or grabs food from May's plate for the hundredth time. He isn't the best houseguest. But even May knows what to say now, standing on her chair and announcing, "No dessert for Georgie if he eats my food!" Georgie pushes her plate back, caught again.

Anthony jokes that I've been demoted "from savior to sister." I still do more than most teenagers, for sure. I'm Georgie's official barber, and I gave him a respectable fade this week, nearly bald at his ears, gradually transitioning to a fuzzy crew cut up top. I'd like to clean up the back, but my client's not interested in sitting still.

Mom stays home the nights we go to Anthony's. She eats by herself in front of the TV, something she finds so astonishingly restorative that she's always bubbly and chatty when we traipse back at eight o'clock for Georgie's bedtime. She stretches it to the last second, shouting, "Hold on!" I keep Georgie on the porch while she turns off and covers the television.

"Go ahead, Georgie. Mom's ready." The screen door bangs as he lumbers in.

The cicadas buzz in the hot night. Summer's over but you wouldn't know it.

"I like the new rug." Anthony looks in the window.

"It covers the water stains." I hug him from behind.

We watch Georgie dawdle in the kitchen while Mom shoos him toward the bathroom. I slide my hands into the front pockets of Anthony's jeans and press his butt back into my belly.

"You picking my pockets?"

I get on my tiptoes and take his earlobe in my mouth. It's bread dough, chewing gum. I'm hungry for it.

"This is getting inappropriate," he says.

"You like?"

"No, this." Anthony points. Georgie's in the hall by the bathroom, stripping. He tries to step out of his jeans and gets stuck, leaning against the wall in his white underpants.

"Quick, kiss me while Mom's distracted," I say. She knows about Anthony now. It's harder to get alone time.

"We can't neck in public."

"Yes, we can. And don't call it 'necking.'" I pull his face down and push my lips onto his. The poke of his crooked tooth, the taste of peanut butter cookie in his mouth.

Me and Anthony get to keep figuring things out, too. We get to mess things up and try again, these warm, scratchy bodies that long for each other, these skittish hearts that trembled when the sun came up on our intertwined legs, bark in his curly brown hair, splotches like bee-stings on my chest.

You left a mark, Anthony Golden. I wear it proudly.

Maybe I do belong with you, Anthony. I don't belong *to* you, though.

I belong to me.

First thing I plugged in when the lights came back? Those clippers.

This girl needs a trim.

ACKNOWLEDGMENTS

Gratitude to:

My hero, my mother, Kathleen Conway, who (still) raises her sons with unimaginable care, persistence, and patience.

Every glowing human, gentle caregiver, badass radster, and exhausted parent in the Nation of Difference. This world is lucky to have you.

Morten Anker. I don't know what we did to deserve your generous, selfless spirit.

Camphill communities, coworkers, and friends, for living truthfully and showing what is possible when you do.

My agent, Faye Bender, for insights and candor, and for asking the right questions.

Rebecca Stead, for walking with me as an agent and, even more, as a writer.

My editor, Joy Peskin, who nourished this story from seed to flower.

Melissa Backes, devoted reader and leader in the Nation of Difference.

Christina Zani, who knows about tender hearts and bodies.

Michaela Pommells, dear reader and truth teller.

Ucross, The Studios of Key West, and the Grand Marais Art Colony, for space to write and artists to talk with.

Andrew Solomon, for *Far from the Tree*, a truly radical and loving account of difference. Read it.

Jesse, who takes people as they are, and teaches me how.

Nico, for long walks with me and your uncle, and for sharp answers to all my novelistic questions.

Elizabeth, for singing harmony with my off-key voice. *We both dove and rose to the riverside.*